BLACK SHADOW
DETECTIVE AGENCY

DEMON FOR HIRE

COUNT S. A. OLSON

Copyright © 2024 Count S. A. Olson.

All rights reserved. No part of this book may be reproduced, stored, or transmitted by any means—whether auditory, graphic, mechanical, or electronic—without written permission of both publisher and author, except in the case of brief excerpts used in critical articles and reviews. Unauthorized reproduction of any part of this work is illegal and is punishable by law.

ISBN: 979-8-89419-503-2 (sc)
ISBN: 979-8-89419-504-9 (hc)
ISBN: 979-8-89419-505-6 (e)

Because of the dynamic nature of the Internet, any web addresses or links contained in this book may have changed since publication and may no longer be valid. The views expressed in this work are solely those of the author and do not necessarily reflect the views of the publisher, and the publisher hereby disclaims any responsibility for them.

One Galleria Blvd., Suite 1900, Metairie, LA 70001
(504) 702-6708

THE SHADOWS UP CAPER

CHAPTER

I glanced at the clock on my wall. I had been on the line for nearly 10 minutes listening to a woman ranting on about her cheating husband. She wanted someone tracking down her husband to get juicy pictures for her divorce case. I don't do divorce cases—they make me feel sleazy—but she hadn't given me a second to speak.

I jumped in as soon as she took her next breath. "I'm sorry ma'am but I don't work divorce cases."

"But you're a private detective. I thought all you guys do are divorce cases."

"I'm sorry that you were under that impression. I don't handle such cases. If you want I can recommend you to someone who does, and she's very good at it." I gave the ranting woman the name of a detective who specialized in tracking cheating husbands.

There are days I wished I had a secretary and this was one of them. So far today I had gotten three other calls to work divorce cases. I used to do the occasional divorce but stopped a very long time ago. I think my last was back in the forties. I hadn't had any case in the last few weeks, but I wasn't hurting for money.

When it comes to getting a secretary, the problem is finding one who won't be scared off by the kind of people I deal with on a regular basis. It's hard to find someone who is qualified to answer a question like, "Have you ever dealt with Witches, Vampires, or Daemons of any kind?" That would scare off the average person coming into apply for the position.

I also want a beautiful, female secretary who'd sit on my lap while I dictate letters. Okay. To be honest, that last part isn't a requirement, but I can always dream. I know I could have hired a Succubus for the beautiful lap sitting part, but from my understanding, they are horrid typists. Apparently typewriters never made it big in any of the Infernal realms where they can be found so it takes them forever to learn to use a 'QWERTY' keyboard with any real proficiency. For the time being I was stuck answering the phone myself.

The office was designed for a secretary. I was currently using the front room where normally a secretary would be answering calls and greeting clients. In the back room is an old leather couch that is beat to hell but very comfortable for napping. It also has my gun safe, which was home to the weapons that I acquired back when the twenties roared and before. Back then St. Paul was run by the mob. They made payoffs to the Chief of Police and funded the policemen's ball. It was different back then, a romantic time, and my office still pays homage to that lost period of history. It may be the twenty-first century now, but the office still looks as if not much has changed since I first dawned fedora and trench-coat, looking like a hardboiled detective out of some dime store pulp novel by Dashiell Hammet. Almost a hundred years after my start as a private investigator even my furniture is the same, though it's been reupholstered a few times.

I was getting ready to call it a night when there was a loud, fast knock on the frosted glass window of my office door. A silhouette turned its head to look up and down the hallway outside. During those turns I noticed that the silhouette belonged to a woman. I was glad; women have always brought me my most interesting cases.

"Come in," I called out loudly.

This better be good master, my crow familiar, read magical helper that annoys the piss out of me, Shadow, said directly into my mind. *I want to go home and watch television.* I ignored him. I didn't want to freak out a client by talking to my familiar if she wasn't from the magickal scene.

The woman—just a girl I realized now that I could see more than her silhouette—threw open the door and slammed it shut as soon as she was inside. She was panting, pressing her back against the door as if to barricade it from someone or something that was after her. I had seen that look of terror on a face before, and it always meant trouble, the kind of trouble I'm well accustomed to ending.

"Help me," she whimpered. "I was told that you may be the only one who can help me and I really need help."

I got up from my desk and calmly walked over to her. "Don't worry, miss," I said in my most soothing voice. "I'll lock the door, and I assure you that no one will hurt you here." I reached past her to lock the door.

"Now why don't you have a seat and we'll discuss your problem." I took her gently by the arm and guided her over to the recently reupholstered, deep leather armchair across from my side of the desk. I could still see the office window. Having her back to the outer door may have made her uncomfortable but there was no helping it. I sat behind my desk, reached into the bottom left drawer and pulled out a bottle nerve medicine, actually just cheap bourbon, and two lowball glasses. I poured two fingers of the liquor into each glass and pushed one over to her. "Here, this will help you relax a little, but just sip at it. It's got a bit of a boomerang effect to it."

She took her first sip without gagging. Remarkable. Most of my friends can't stand the stuff. She really must be scared. With her second sip I got over my surprise at her lack of reaction to the cheap booze and took the time to study her.

She was a stunning redhead, in her early twenties I guessed, looking like a modern Ingrid Bergman. Bright green eyes were burning with fatigue. Her long, wavy hair was disheveled and wet from the cold, April rain falling outside. Her tasteful clothing was grimy, as if she hadn't had a chance to change in several days. Add everything up and the conclusion was simple. She was, or at least thought she was, being followed by someone or something and was too scared to go home.

She was shivering a little as the adrenaline coursing through her system went stale. "So tell me, what brings you to my office?"

"I'm being followed by two men. I think. And I think ... no, I *know* that they want to kill me," she said staring into her glass, which was shaking in both her hands. It gave her the appearance of a child holding onto a mug of hot chocolate after coming in from the cold. But in this case the little child was a young woman and the hot chocolate was a few shots of bourbon.

"You seem to be pretty scared if you only think you're being followed, Miss ...?"

"Cross," she said filling in the blank. "Jamie Cross. I don't mean that I only think that I'm being followed. What I mean is that I'm not sure if the people that are following me are really 'people'. I not sure they're human."

I nodded with a vague understanding. This sounded just like my kind of case. Once again the Gods had pushed a good case my way in the form of a female client. "What makes you think these men after you aren't human?"

She took another sip of the bourbon before she answered. "I can only see them out of the corners of my eyes and in reflections from mirrors and window glass, but when I turn to look at them, they're not there. It's like they're ghosts or something. I feel like I'm losing my mind."

Shadow squawked, hopped from his perch on the back of my chair to the top of the desk, cocked his head and stared at her. He blinked a few times and squawked again.

"Well let's first clear out a few possibilities so that I have a better idea of what we are dealing with. Now, these questions are not meant to sound insulting, but I have to ask them." I took a deep breath, before I started since I knew she was going to feel that I didn't believe her about her current situation.

I knew from experience that my prospective customers often have a hard time believing themselves what is happening to them. "First, are you on any medication for psychiatric problems, or do you have a history of using recreational drugs?" I didn't want to waste my time, and her money, chasing hallucinations when it would be better for her to go to a hospital where she could either be put on the right medication or get off the recreational drugs.

There are far too many things that can cause a person to hallucinate. However, sometimes the hallucinations aren't actually hallucinations. They may be rooted in stuff that causes us to see a separate reality. It is that reality which hides things that can torment a person with false promises of delight, or show them a true evil. Either way, anything that causes one to see a distorted reality should never be consumed. It leads to some of the worst of evils. I've seen people tear their skin off trying to rid themselves of things that exist only in their mind.

"What!!!" She screamed as if I had just slapped her across the face. She stood up and leaned across the desk to grab me by my tie, pulling me closer to look into her eyes. "I'm not crazy! I'm not a junkie! What I am is in danger!"

I gently took her by the wrist and used just enough force to remove her hand from my tie, which had gotten uncomfortably tight. "I am sorry if I offended you, but I just had to ask. Now, since you're telling me the answer is 'no' to both questions, we can get to the real heart of the matter."

I took a notebook out of another desk drawer along with a pen and got ready to take notes. I really didn't need to write anything down, but I find it helps people realize that I am indeed taking their situation seriously. "Well first I'm going to ask some questions about you. I need to get a clear picture of who you are so I can understand what is going on, and why it's happening."

I took a sip of bourbon and got comfortable. "Where did you grow up?"

"The bay area, just outside of San Francisco. Why?"

I jotted it down on my notepad. "I'm just trying to get a feel for you. Do you have any relatives back there? When was the last time you were there?"

The confusion was still evident on her face as to why I was asking these questions and not about the two individuals who were following her. "Most of my family still lives there, except for my sister. She moved to New York three years ago, hoping to make it on Broadway. Why are you asking?"

"And you were last in San Francisco when?" I prompted. I knew from all my past experience that this type of information could often prove to be invaluable when looking for clues as to who might be behind something like this. I also knew that it sometimes tended to aggravate my clients.

She sighed, probably realizing that it was going to be easier if she just answered without asking 'why' at every question. "I was home last Christmas."

"What brought you out here? Can't be the weather."

"I came out here for college. I was studying international business. Now I have a new job with a multinational trying to get my foot in the door so to speak." Her voice had the tone of frustration. Not at me but more likely the situation she found herself in.

"How old are you?"

"Twenty-two. I turn twenty-three next month." She really was just a kid.

"What kind of work do you do? I know that you said you are working for a multinational. So what do you do there?"

She looked at the floor and sighed. "I translate manuals. It pays okay, but I keep putting in bids for better positions. The problem is that all the upper management types keep saying that I'm too young and inexperienced. On top of that, my direct supervisor has the hots for me and doesn't want to lose me."

I nodded. I could easily understand her boss could be attracted to her. She was very easy on the eyes. With her looks she could have been a model rather than a corporate drone. She was the kind of looker that almost made me wish she wasn't my client. Stupid scruples.

"Now let's discuss the two people who have been following you for the last few days. Can you describe them?"

Miss Cross cocked her head to one side and closed her eyes in concentration. "One of them is a tall, thin, white man, almost painfully thin. The other is a short Asian man. They've been dressed in black suits that look well-tailored, but since I can only catch glimpses it's hard to say for certain."

"You say you only catch glimpses of them out of the corner of your eyes or in reflections?" I needed to confirm her answer because what she had described often meant serious trouble.

She nodded again. "They're never there when I turn to get a better look at them."

If my guess was the right, men following her were almost definitely Shadow Men she really was in serious trouble. The question was, who had called them?. They rarely traveled to the Human world of their own accord, so someone must have brought them here. "Why come to me and not go to the police?"

"I did go to the police," she said. "With the exception of one, they all told me to check myself into a hospital."

"I take it that the exception was the one that gave you my business card?" It was a rhetorical question. I had worked with the police in most of the cities and towns that make up the Twin Cities metro area. Occasionally when they were desperate for a lead on a kidnapping or murder, a detective would come to me. Those who had used my services would usually keep a couple of my business cards with them in case they met someone who could use my help. Those business cards are my main source of advertising. Still they hated having to give those out, since it was an admission of defeat.

"Yes. She said that if there was anyone who could help me, it was you." If it was a 'she' it was probably Helena McKarren. Tough broad, that one; once saw her jerk a guy's arm out of its socket when he gave her too much trouble. Helps that she's a Werewolf. The two of us had known each other for a while now, mostly through her real boss. She may be a cop, but when it really counted, she reported to the Court of Night.

"Well I'm sure I'll be able to help you. Now back to the questions." Another sip of bourbon. "Since you haven't corrected me yet Miss Cross, I take it that you're not married?"

She shook her head again. "No. I haven't found the right guy yet." When she did I hoped it would be someone interested in her for more than just her looks, to be more than just a trophy wife. She deserved better than some loser who would always want her to grab him a beer while he watched football. And if the guy was the type that would use her as a punching bag I hoped she would come to me so I could put the guy in his place. No woman deserves to be hit, especially a girl who looked like my soon-to-be client.

"Do you have any life insurance?" Just because you're not married doesn't mean someone's not after you for your insurance.

"Just the fifty-thousand I get from work."

Not a lot of money to kill for, but you could never tell these days. "Who's the beneficiary?"

"The Defenders of Wildlife," she said proudly, and I liked her for it; it showed she had real character.

"Well, I seriously doubt a charity is going to have you killed," I said with only a slight smile, not trying to make light of her predicament. "Do you have any money other than your insurance?"

"I have a few thousand in savings for emergencies and I'll be happy to give all of it to you if you can help me," she said desperately.

"Don't worry. I'll try to solve your problems without bankrupting you." I wasn't about to rob her blind, she was too pretty for that. "Now for the big question. Did anything unusual happen to you before these people started following you? I don't care how unimportant it may have seemed at the time. I need to know everything."

There were any number of magick users, cults, covens, and the like that could summon Shadow Men. This was going to be a process of elimination to get an idea of who had summoned these Daemons. Anyone who would summon those things were the kind of people who would sink pretty low to get their way.

"Let's see…" She closed her eyes and tilted her head in concentration. "There was a group of protestors at my office building. They were protesting one of the other companies that has offices there."

Shadow jumped onto my shoulder and pecked my ear lobe. *Doubt it boss,* he said. *Anyone who could call Shadow Men into our world wouldn't make that kind of rookie mistake to get an innocent involved.* I merely nodded in reply; he was correct on that account.

"Next..." I prompted her.

"I got into a bit of a road rage incident when I forgot to use my blinker. The woman I cut off pulled alongside me rolled down her window and screamed her head off at me."

Anyone who had the kind of power needed for the ritual would have needed to have been having a really, really bad day not to have calmed down before finishing drawing the summoning circle. Again, it was Shadow putting in his two bits, which he had been doing since I inherited him from mother. She had been murdered centuries ago and he has been my constant companion since then. I found it's not a good idea to let him watch political talk shows unless I want to listen to him screaming in my head.

I shook my head. "Next..."

She still hadn't opened her eyes. "My boss made a rather heavy-handed pass at me. I probably shot him down harder then I needed to."

"How so?"

"This was the third time he made a pass at me, and the third time I told him no. I told him that next time I'd go to H.R. and file a harassment complaint."

I felt Shadow giving the idea some weight. "What do you think Shadow?"

Doesn't sound very good boss. I doubt a magick user that powerful would be working in a corporate setting.

"What about the Silicon Slaves? Many of them are the corporate types."

"Why are you talking to your bird?" Jamie asked, obviously confused.

"He's a familiar, basically a servant of sorts. He's smarter than most people and makes for a good second opinion."

Ask her what kind of company it is that she works for.

I nodded. It was a fair question. "What kind of business is your company in?"

"High end medical equipment." She answered.

"Silicon Slaves are still a possibility," I said.

I still don't like them for it. Not their style.

I nodded again thinking about it. "You're right. They'd be more inclined to erase her digital footprint."

"What do you mean erase my digital footprint?" Jamie asked me.

"They'd cancel your credit cards, erase all bank records, pull the record of you having a driver's license," I told her. "You'd effectively not have any history as far as computer records were concerned."

"They can do that?" she asked bewildered.

"Any good hacker can do it if they're willing to really work at it, but they'd probably miss a couple of things. Silicon Slaves can just do it a hell of a lot faster and they don't miss anything, but Shadow's right. Summoning Shadow Men, while easily within their power, is not their style.

"Now anything else? We are dealing with some really nasty pieces of work; there must have been something."

"No. I can't think of anything," Jamie said shaking her head. Then her face lit up with a eureka moment. "Wait! Yes, there was something else. There was this filthy homeless woman who ran into me. She scratched me and said something bizarre to me. I had no idea what she said, it was just gibberish."

The words 'oh crap' quickly ran through my mind, this could be bad. "Can you give me a better description of her?"

My client closed her eyes again. "She was wearing a filthy, ragged dress, and she stunk as if she had been bathing in polluted water." The 'oh crap' thought ran through my mind again far more intensely. "Her eyes were yellow and she was missing teeth, and part of an ear."

I looked over at Shadow. "You thinking what I am?"

Shadow's answer consisted of two dread filled words. *The Ladies.*

I nodded agreement. Turning back to Jamie I noticed that her glass was empty and poured another two fingers of medicine for her. "I hate to tell you this Miss Cross but you are in very serious trouble."

Jamie swallowed hard and started to shake again. "You can you still help me can't you?"

"I'm probably the only person within a thousand miles who would be willing to do so," I said simply. "I'm going to be honest with you, the people who have summoned these Shadow Men are a very dangerous group of women. To make it worse, they aren't the ones who want you dead. They're just contractors."

An understandable look of sheer terror took hold of Jamie's face. "Who are they?"

"They are known as the Ladies of the River." I decided that I needed to make things as clear to Jamie as possible. "They are what people think of when they think of witches that sell their souls. The Ladies of the River sell their souls to the Daemon of the Mississippi River. For that they receive powerful magicks, though it causes them to burn out quickly. The Human body isn't meant to run magick through it in that way. A person can learn magicks that are just as powerful as those used by the Ladies of the River, but it takes a long time of serious study. By selling their souls, the Ladies cheat the system but it catches up with them quickly and in about ten or twelve years their bodies simply burn out, leaving a mere shriveled, husk of a body."

"Why would anyone do that to themself?" Jamie asked in disbelief.

"For the most part the Ladies are made up of runaways and the homeless. By selling their souls they gain a power that no one can buy for any amount of money. For that short time, they can do things that even Arabian oil princes could never do despite all the money they have."

Jamie's next question showed her understandable confusion. "If they have all this power then why do they hire themselves out as contract killers? I mean it doesn't sound as if they have much need for money."

I nodded in agreement. "It does sound silly I know but it's safe to assume that they'll send the money to an environmental group that will work to help clean up the river, thereby increasing their own powers. The cleaner the river, the more powerful the Daemon of the river is, and thus the more powerful the magick they receive from it."

"You can stop them, right?" she asked hopefully. "I mean they have sold their souls for magick, what can you do?"

"I have studied magick for a very long time, plus I come from a deep family line that has provided me with more than a little natural talent. I have taken them on before, and as you can see, I'm still very much alive. So yes, I can help you, but not only will I have to take on the Ladies, but I will also have to find out who hired them before they can hire someone else to hurt you. The question is, who would wish you harm?"

Jamie shook her head in frustration, which was a clear sign to me that I was going to end up just as frustrated. "I can't think of anyone. I don't know of anyone who would want to kill me. I mean, I have disagreements with people, but nothing major. The only real person I could think of would be my boss, but I can't see him going that far even though I turned him down."

I hate it when people think they have no enemies, just shows that they are blind to the world around them. Or, they want you to think that they are a really nice person whom no one would dislike.

I once tracked down a rapist for the brother of the victim. I talked to the bastard for a while and I turned the conversation around to the subject of enemies; he claimed to not have an enemy in the world. He was certainly surprised when I showed up on his door step the next night with his victim's brother. After the brother beat him to death I spent a couple hours cleaning up all the evidence. I made damn sure the body was never found and that no one would think he had been murdered. After child molesters, I hate rapists more than just about anyone else in the way of normal Humans.

The real problem in my line of work, is that if a client tells you they have no enemies you have to start the investigation from scratch. Now don't get me wrong, I love a challenge, but it make things more difficult. The thing is, it could be that she didn't have a real enemy. She may have gotten on the wrong side of someone who really knew how to nurse a grudge. Either way it didn't matter in the end, the results were the same. She was in trouble and I was the only one who could help her.

She sighed, obviously she had hoped that this would have been a simple matter of dealing with a couple weird men whom she thought wanted to kill her. But now she realized that she was hiring me to track down someone truly bent on hurting her.

"How much is it going to cost me to have you keep me alive until then? I'll give you everything I have for you to keep me safe."

She meant it too. She probably would have even offered up her body if she thought it would keep her alive. Had I been almost any other private eye I may have asked for just that, but I'm not like that. Mixing business with pleasure was something I've never done. That sort of thing always screws you up if the client back stabs you, which has happened to me before. I'm not saying that the thought of spending time with her in my bedroom wasn't appealing, she was incredibly attractive, but I'm a professional. I'm not like Dashell Hammett's detective Sam Spade. I may look and sound much like the Humphrey Bogart image of the character, save for the bright white streak running through my black hair, but I keep things purely business. I'm not about to mix romance with business.

I opened up the file drawer in my desk and took out one of my knight in shining armor contracts. Even though I wear a trench coat now, and haven't worn armor since my last stint in a Hell-bound army during the Knights' War, I still call it my knight in shining armor contract. I wasn't about to rob her blind, but I needed some payment. I placed the contract on the top of the desk facing me. "The fee for my service is $250 a day with a five-day retainer to be paid upfront," I told her pushing the contract and a pen towards her.

Jamie quickly read over the contract and nodded. She wrote her signature next to the 'X' and pushed it back to me. Reaching into her purse she pulled out a checkbook and cut me a check for the retainer. "There, twelve-fifty. Now what is the first thing that we need to do?"

It was time for me to start earning that money. "Well, first we have to figure out where to keep you until I can track down the person who is after you. I can't leave you exposed to danger from another assassin."

"I can't go back to my apartment," Jamie said simply.

"Of course not. That would be the first place they would go. No, I have two options for you. First, you can stay here. I've got a comfortable couch in the back room you can sleep on, and there are a lot of places in the area that deliver so food won't be a problem. There are also many magickal protections here that will block most supernatural beings from coming here. The downside is that there's no shower where you can really wash up, though there is a small bathroom down the hall."

Jamie nodded and looked around, not knowing if she'd feel comfortable sleeping in the office. "What's my second option?"

"You can stay at my place. I have a spare bedroom and you are more than welcome to use it. You'll have to cook since not as many places deliver there, but it is probably the safest place you can possibly stay."

Jamie gave me an appraising look. "How do I know that you're not going to try anything funny?"

"You're my client," I said with only the trace of a smile. "And while you are incredibly beautiful, I never mix business with pleasure."

Jamie raised one eyebrow when she looked at me with a questioning gaze. "Are you sure you'd never do that?" she asked.

"Scout's honor," I said as I held up my hand in the Boy Scouts' sign.

"You were never a Scout," she said humorously.

"You're right. I was too old," I agreed, referring to the fact that I had been far too old to join the scouts when they had first formed.

She smiled slightly, probably thinking I was making a joke. "Then I'll stay at your place."

"Now that that is settled, let's go to your apartment so you can pick up a few changes of clothes and anything else you might want."

I stood up out of my chair and headed over to my gun safe. I pulled out my shoulder holster and Colt 1911, which I had nicknamed 'The Ace of Spades' for the image of the playing card in the mother of pearl grip. I wouldn't need the other guns in the safe, at least not until I met with The Ladies. I traded out the magazine with everyday .45 rounds and swapped it with one loaded with enchanted silver rounds designed for use against many different magickal beings. Normal silver is too light to tumble properly so the enchantment allows it to fly straight. In my line of work, it pays to be prepared for such things as shooting Daemons. The silver bullets were more for Werewolves, but in a pinch they would work well enough against Infernals. At home I have banishing bullets, which are nasty pieces of work. I so rarely need them that I don't keep them at the office, but now I was definitely going to need them.

I wasn't expecting an ambush at her apartment. It isn't a Shadow Man's style to ambush someone at home. They prefer to chase a person around and maddeningly stay just on the edge of sight, to the point of their victim having nervous breakdown. Once the target was on the verge of madness they'd strike and it would be a messy death. That said I wasn't going to risk them changing their m/o even once.

CHAPTER

As we headed to her apartment in my heavily modified '41 Buick Special, I kept an eye out for any sign of a tail. I wasn't the only one watching; Shadow was following us from about sixty feet up and a couple hundred feet back. If he saw anything, he'd contact me immediately. Thankfully nothing other than the usual characters showed. Due to the latent mystic energies flowing through the Twin Cities, the area is chock full of various magickal entities, but no one of interest showed up to take notice.

Once at Jamie's apartment building, Shadow flew down to land on my shoulder. *Nothing to report master,* he said.

"I want you to fly around the apartment building a full block out and keep your eyes open for any signs of trouble."

Sure thing boss, Shadow replied before he took off.

I took a good look at the apartment building and the neighborhood it was in. The building looked to have gone up in the late seventies or early eighties and aesthetics hadn't been much of a concern when it had been built. The neighborhood was nice enough, at least for Minneapolis. It was definitely not the kind that had earned the city its ominous nickname of Murderapolis. This part of the city was mostly bland apartment buildings with a few corner stores of all kinds. As I said, not great, but not so bad as to see an armed dealer on every corner.

Jamie pulled a key ring out of her purse, quickly found the key she was looking for and opened the outer door. I followed her in and kept looking up and down the hall. The problem in dealing with Shadow Men is that they can show up just about anywhere they want. Thankfully they didn't show up because it would have been hard to explain to the police why I had been involved in a shootout in the middle of an apartment building.

When we got to her apartment I had her give me her keys. I pulled 'Ace of Spades' out of her holster before I opened the door. I jerked the door open and quickly stepped through the door with my gun in my hand. I took a quick look around to survey the front hall of the apartment and saw nothing right away. I motioned Jamie to follow me through and close the door, but not to come in any further. I made my way through the rest of the apartment, gun in hand. I wasn't about to let my guard down and risk my client's life because of a careless mistake.

I motioned for her to come into her bedroom, which was a mess. I could easily tell that she only used the place to sleep and keep her stuff while she was out around town either working or just having fun.

"Okay. Pack up what you need. You may also want to get some stuff ready for a shower, because it looks like you haven't had one in a couple of days," I told her, motioning her into the room.

"What's the shower thing supposed to mean?" she asked in a rather irritated voice.

"Only that your hair seems a little oily, like it's been a couple days since your last shower," I said, trying to placate her. "I figured you might feel better taking a shower now rather than waiting until we got back to my house."

"You're right, I could probably stand a shower, I feel pretty gross." She grabbed a change of clothes and quickly ran into the bathroom.

I stood in the hallway where I could keep an eye on the door, but close enough to the bathroom in case she called out for help. I didn't think she'd need help since I had already checked the place for the

Shadow Men but I wasn't going to take any chances. Thankfully she was quick; I heard the water turn off. A few minutes longer and she was out of the shower.

"Thank God, that feels better," she said when I turned to look at her. She hadn't taken any time to put on makeup, but as far as I was concerned she didn't need any. "I needed that shower. I didn't realize how gross I felt."

"Okay go to your room and pack up anything you feel you might need for a few nights. But please try not to pack your whole wardrobe." I had once had a girlfriend a few decades back who always seemed insistent on bringing almost everything in her closet for a two-night stay on the lakeside.

Jamie grabbed a decent sized duffel bag and efficiently packed it with a practiced style that I had seen mostly used by military people. Within ten minutes she seemed to have enough changes of clothes for four nights. "Where did you learn to pack like that?" I asked her.

"Dad was a Marine," she answered, confirming my suspicions. "He taught me how to pack for trips so that I didn't need several suitcases for a trip that would last for only a few days."

"Okay let's get out of here," I said as I motioned her out into the hallway and out of the apartment.

"You seeing anything, Shadow?" I asked the thin air, knowing full well that the crow would hear me.

Nothing yet, I heard his answer.

"Let me see," I said. My vision of the immediate surroundings faded and I was seeing the area around the building through Shadow's eyes. I was glad to see that my familiar was right—there was nothing supernatural in the area.

"Okay Jamie, let's be on our way. The sooner we get to my house the better off you'll be."

CHAPTER

As we headed toward my house, Shadow tailed as before. The drive wasn't long. We passed more than a few supernatural entities on the way, but no one I had to worry about. The typical Fey doing shady business with Humans, and some nonHumans, who were in the know. If you knew who and what to ask, you could find just about anything. There are easier places to do business as long as it's on the up and up. Here the rules were faster and looser and none of the major players would get involved.

Jamie was impressed with my old Victorian. "I thought all you detectives lived in run down apartments near their offices, because you don't have much money between cases."

"I don't really need to do detective work for a living," I told her. "It's more of a hobby for me."

"Odd hobby."

I shrugged. It really wasn't odd as far as I was concerned. "Well, with the things that I've seen in my life, it's about the only thing that can keep my interest."

"What sort of stuff have you done?" Jamie asked as she stepped out of the car.

"I fought in several wars, one of which still isn't public knowledge," I said. Only conspiracy nuts would believe that it had ever actually happened. Anyone else would have said it was an interesting 'alternate universe' look at World War II.

"What sort of wars?" Jamie asked.

"Let me put it this way. World War II wasn't the only war being fought back in the forties," I said seriously. "And it was a lot less scary than where I was."

"Riiight," Jamie said drawing out the word. "Am I supposed to believe you're old enough to have been fighting during World War II, when you look no older than late thirties, early forties?"

"You can believe it or not; that's your choice. Truth is, I'm even older than that."

"Whatever you say."

"Well, you're the one being chased by Shadow Men. Is it so hard to believe that I'm a lot older than I look?" I asked as we walked passed the fence gate that marked the barrier blocking all magickal entities that weren't on the guest list.

"I guess not," She finally admitted. "So how old are you?"

"Let me put it this way. I killed more than my fair share of Tories and Loyalists while fighting alongside Colonel Marion," I said with a shrug.

"I assume that means you fought in the Revolutionary war. But who was Colonel Marion?" Jamie asked.

"None other than the old Swamp Fox himself," I said with a grin. "Now he was a truly scary strategist."

"I thought he was a general?"

"When I started fighting under him he was still a colonel."

"That means..." Her voice trailed off as she realized how old I was.

"Yep. Because of my blood lines, I'm pretty damn hard to kill. Even Old Man Time tends to leave me alone," I said smiling.

Jamie gave an impressed whistle when she entered the kitchen from the back door. I was fairly sure that seeing my kitchen would help her ground herself in the "un-realness" of the situation. Though the fact that a private dick lived in an old Victorian mansion probably made little sense. "Very nice. You really must have a fair bit of cash in order to afford a place like this. How much did it set you back?"

"About $10,000," I answered.

"What?! All this for $10,000?"

"Well $10,000 went a long way in the mid-eighteen hundreds when I had it built. Remember I'm pretty old."

"Okay, I have to ask. How is it that you can be so old?"

I shrugged slightly. "I'm a half-Daemon. Thankfully my dad, who was from an Infernal realm, was bit of a romantic and stuck around for a while so I actually got to know him. He even sends me birthday cards from time to time. We also get together for a nice dinner on the anniversary of my mother's death."

"You're a half-Daemon?!" Jamie yelped taking a half-step back from me.

"Yes and I am also a pretty nice guy. I have always fought to protect the land where I was born and raised. I try my hardest to protect the innocent. I just need to charge people for my services or I'd be flooded with too many people to help."

Jamie nodded slightly, obviously trying to figure out how much she was going to believe me. "If you're a Daemon, then why are you going to help me by fighting other Daemons?" It was obvious that she wanted to believe me but wasn't sure if she should.

"I'm only a half-Daemon. My allegiance is firmly set with my Human side. There are also Daemons like my father who will, to some extent, side with Humanity." I hoped she'd believe me. I didn't want her to run off and die because she was too scared of me to let me help her. "Look, you are my client, which means I am here to help you."

"I guess I'll just have to trust you then. I really have nowhere else to turn. Do I?" She still sounded nervous of me and I really couldn't blame her.

"As I said, I'm probably the only one who can help you that you can actually trust."

"You mean there are other people who can help me?" I could tell from the tone in her voice that she was hopeful.

"Yes there are others who could help, but trust me, you wouldn't like what they would want in exchange," I said ominously.

"More expensive than you?"

"If you define 'expensive' as giving up your mortal soul to become something completely different than you are now then yes, they are insanely expensive." The Court of Night could help her, if they were so inclined, but she wouldn't remain Human for long if they did help. I have been on very good terms with their leader since the early forties when I had rescued her from a Nazi experimentation facility. If she went to them, she'd end up as either a Werewolf or a Vampire, and she wouldn't get a choice as to which.

"Okay I think I'll stick with you then."

"That's probably a good idea," I said with a humorless smile. "Now let's get you set up in the guest room."

She followed me upstairs and I told her to make herself at home while I got ready for my meeting with the Shadow Men. I went down to my basement workroom and searched for the small box of banishing rounds. I found it after 10 minutes of searching and realized that I'd probably have to engrave the spells on a few more bullets since the box was uncomfortably light. I opened it and saw that only three bullets remained. I was pretty sure I wouldn't need more than one clip's worth, but I didn't want to risk it. Setting up everything necessary to make more of the bullets, I prepared myself for the hours-long ceremony to create a couple dozen banishing bullets. I needed silver, salt, exotic oils, and about two hours chanting in Sumerian. Most people think Latin is a better language for banishing, because people are used to exorcisms in movies. Sumerian is actually a better choice as almost no one speaks it and it catches Daemons completely off guard.

Coming up from the basement, I could smell an omelet being cooked. I knew my pantry and fridge were almost empty but I was glad she had felt comfortable enough to make a meal with the few provisions I had.

When I made my presence, known Jamie turned to look at me. "I hope you're hungry," she said in a non-question.

"I'm starving," I lied.

"Good. From what my friends tell me, I'm a lousy cook and only a truly starving man could stand eating my food," Jamie said with a slight smile.

"Lady, I ate my share of K rations during the Knights' War. I'm sure you can't possibly make anything worse tasting than that," I said. "And when you're hungry enough, even that crap tastes like a feast prepared by one of the greatest chefs to ever grace the world with their presence. Of course, when I wasn't starving, I wouldn't have subjected even a Nazi dog to eat that stuff as it could be considered cruelty to animals. Besides, you were able to use real eggs, unlike that toxic sludge known as powdered eggs. I had to choke that crap down more than a few times."

"Then I hope you still have that cast iron stomach," Jamie said. "So you know, there is no milk in the omelet."

"Why on earth not?" I asked. "I know that I have milk in the fridge."

"Well, judging by the smell of it, the milk died a month or so ago."

"Note to self, go grocery shopping," I said, trying to make a joke. It failed badly.

"By the way, I hope you don't mind, but I gave the last of the bacon to your crow. What's his name again? Shadow?"

Tell her not to cook this stuff next time, Shadow said to me.

"Yes, his name is Shadow," I confirmed. "Don't worry about giving the last of the bacon to him, that's what it's there for. As far as cooking it, he would ask that you not cook it next time. He likes it raw. He just doesn't like it cold. So all you have to do is throw it in the microwave for ten seconds to warm it up for him."

Jamie pulled a sour face. "Raw? Yuck."

"He's a crow. He usually eats things that have been dead for a while," I told her. "Trust me, he isn't very fussy about what he's eating for the most part. As mom said, 'You can take the crow out of the woods, but you can't take the woods out of the crow.' I've seen him eat road kill because he liked the taste of the rotting meat. Most of the time though he eats things like corn salads. The meat's meant to be a treat."

"Still ... raw meat? Gross," Jamie said and gave a disgusted shudder.

Shadow gave me what I could only describe as a humorous wink. *You just don't know what you're missing.*

I simply shook my head but was able to avoid laughing so as not to disturb my client. "Come on. Let me see how bad your cooking is."

We sat down for a late dinner and I was able to choke down her cooking, and even managed to smile through it. It was just as bad as I had feared. She must have taken cooking lessons from Casper, our camp's cook, the food was that awful. Still it could have been worse. It could have been K rations. Next time either I would cook, or we would order from a decent restaurant.

After dinner I suggested that she get some sleep, since I had to make a few calls to set up something special for her two tails. I needed to question them and I needed some place quiet where I could work at least one of them over for a while without being disturbed. I needed a favor from the owner of my favorite bar.

I picked up the phone and dialed the number for the Mystic Wolf. After the fourth ring someone at the bar picked up. "Mystic Wolf. Can I help you?"

"It's Jason Black. I need to talk to Brisbane." Brisbane was the owner of the Mystic Wolf. The bar wasn't so much a bar as it was a pocket dimension where Brisbane was God. The bar had some fun tricks that would make my job a hundred times easier.

"Hold for a second."

"Hey you old Sherlock! What can I do for you?"

"I need to use the private room and have some painter's cloths on the floor. It's going to be messy."

"The bar is neutral territory Black, you know that." Brisbane didn't need to remind me that he didn't care who you were as long as you were buying and didn't get rowdy, but I had to do something he would bend the rules for.

"I'm doing this to help a client; she has a problem."

"What kind of problem?" Brisbane asked.

"She's got two Shadow Men following her," I told him. "I need to know who sent them, and trust me, they're not going to give up that information without a little persuasion."

"Understood." I knew I could trust Brisbane to do the right thing. "I've never had to deal with them, but I understand that they're very nasty pieces of work. Do you have any idea who might have sent them?"

"I'm pretty sure they were summoned by the Ladies of the River." I had no reason to hide the truth from Brisbane; no sane practitioner of magick wanted anything to do with those women. "What I'm going to try to get out of these two is the name of who asked the Ladies for help."

"You're going to take on the Ladies? Are you nuts?" Brisbane asked, probably alarmed that I was even thinking of trying something so reckless.

"I damn near wiped those magick whores out back during prohibition," I told him. "I guess I didn't finish the job or a few from more southerly climes moved north and started up the group again. Whatever the case is, I'm going to kick them out of the Cities again."

"Okay I'll have the room ready for you." It was comforting to see that I knew the bartender so well. "Just make sure the Ladies don't find out about the Mystic. I really don't need them poking their filthy noses around here."

"Don't worry. After I'm done with them there is a good chance that none of them will still have their breathing licenses," I said, trying to reassure my friend.

"Just make sure that they don't come here. I don't need any trouble, though I know we can handle it here. I still want this to be considered neutral ground."

"Don't worry, your name will never be mentioned."

"Make sure of it. I'll have the room ready tomorrow. Just make sure you clean up after yourself."

CHAPTER 4

The next day I took Jamie across town to a good restaurant, seeing as I had next to nothing for breakfast in the house. The restaurant was mostly a breakfast place though they supposedly had good lunch specials. Still a large platter of hash browns topped in eggs, cheese and almost too much bacon was all I needed at the moment. I waited until she was done with her French toast covered in strawberries and whipped cream to tell her the plan for getting rid of the Shadow Men.

"How brave are you?" I asked her simply.

"I'm not very brave, but I'm not weak by any means," Jamie said firmly. "I'm brave enough to not just let myself give up and die at the hands of those Shadow Men things."

"Good, because I'm going to need to you to be brave for the plan to work. I know how to get rid them, and it should help me find out why they're after you." I was being honest with her, to a point at least. She was going have to be damn brave not to faint from fear of what was going to happen.

"What am I going to have to do?" she asked.

"Not much. What I need you to do is walk into a bar without me."

"You want me to what?!" she screamed as if I had just told her that I was the next person to be tasked with killing her.

"I'll be nearby, so don't worry," I said, trying to calm her. "All I'm asking you to do is to walk into a bar without me being right there. I'm fairly certain that the two Shadow Men will follow you in. Once they do, they'll be forced by the magickal nature of the place into taking a physical form. When they're solid, I'll take them down and interrogate them."

Jamie nodded her head slowly. "I think I can do that. Are you sure this is going to work?"

"Yes. According to the owner of the bar, they've never had Shadow Men in the place before. It's a fair bet that they won't know that they'll become solid as soon as they walk through the door," I told her.

"What did you mean when you said the 'magickal nature' of the bar'?" she asked.

"The bar exists in a pocket dimension," I told her. "Everything that enters the bar must take a solid form. Also, for the most part, people can't change their form without using a physical disguise. So I know I can take them."

"I hope you can do all of that," Jamie said, sounding as if she was trying to convince herself that I knew what I was doing.

"Trust me. I've been doing this for over a century. I can do this."

"When are we going to do this?" Jamie asked nervously.

"Here's the plan." I laid out the whole plan from where she was going to leave my company to when I was going to start interrogating the Shadow Men. I told her that I was going to have her stay in the company of some friends of mine in the bar.

Now I just had to make a couple of calls. First to the Countess Blood Wolf, the leader of the Court of Night. The second call was to another shamus, a femme fatale friend of mine named Scar Face Sarah. Before we left I asked the waitress for a doggy bag so that I could save some of my breakfast for Shadow. Kind of hard to bring a crow into a restaurant, even if you promise the staff that he'll stay on your shoulder the whole time. Made me wonder, not for the first time, if I could get him a service animal vest. Where would you even find something like that? Not really worth finding out since he would probably throw a massive fit if I even tried.

CHAPTER 5

"Don't bother following me in here. I'm meeting a real detective in this place, not some crack-pot loony like you," Jamie yelled at me as she slammed the door to the car in front of the Mystic Wolf.

I quickly stepped out of the car "Be reasonable! You won't last a day without my help," I pleaded with her.

Jamie flipped me the bird and headed into the bar where Sarah and the Countess would be waiting for her. I slid back into my car and waited a couple of minutes for the Shadow Men to make an appearance. I didn't have to wait long. As soon as they headed in, I jumped out of my car and followed them in.

They must not have noticed the reshaping of reality around the bar, most likely because they constantly existed in two dimensions at once. I lost track of them myself as I was hit by an earful of colors and a blazing sight of sound. The joys of shifting dimensions is during the jump your senses get badly confused. It's particularly bad at the Wolf because the gate is stable so it gets a bit polluted with everyone's emotional energies and a lot of people leave quite drunk. When I saw them again I could tell they had quickly spotted Jamie and then, just as quickly, saw everything around them. They didn't have a chance to turn before I pistol-whipped the one closest to the door. The second one turned around to see what the thump behind him had been. As soon as his chin was in sight, I gave him a love tap with a solid left hook that sent him sprawling to the floor unconscious.

"What happens now?" Jamie asked.

"Interrogation," I said with a wicked smile. "Why don't you go with the Countess?" I indicated the short, brunette teenager wearing a beat-up, old army jacket. "I promised to let Sarah watch."

Jamie left with the Countess as Brisbane came over to where Sarah and I were standing. The giant of a man looked at the two Daemons sprawled out on the floor of his bar and then at myself and Sarah. "Come on. I'll get you to the back room I promised to let you use," he said. He then picked up one of the Shadow Men, threw it over his shoulder and started walking towards the back of the bar. I quickly scooped up the other Daemon and followed in his wake.

There had been some muttering by other patrons regarding neutrality, but once they noticed that we were dealing with Shadow Men the muttering ceased. No one likes these bastards. No one.

As soon as Brisbane opened the door to the back room, we threw the Shadow Men into chairs and I locked them down with some handcuffs I had brought just for the purpose of interrogating Daemons. I gave one of the Shadow Men a few solid slaps to wake him up while Sarah did the same to the other. Once the two Daemons were vaguely conscious, they tried desperately to get fee of the handcuffs and leave as soon as possible. Shadow Men aren't particularly tough. They're assassins. They went in, did the job, usually with pretty nasty results to send a message, and then left again. Now I had the two of them handcuffed to chairs with locks they could not slip through I was at the obvious advantage, meaning that they were in uncharted territory. They had no idea what was coming but it looked like they were sure that they weren't going to like it.

"Don't bother struggling," I said in a casual, almost friendly tone of voice. "Those cuffs have held a lot stronger Daemons than you in their time so don't waste your strength."

If anything, the concept that I had done this with other Daemons increased their frantic struggling. I decided to let their obvious fear play to my advantage by ignoring it. "Now I'm not going to bother asking for your names, for two reasons. First you wouldn't give me your names for anything. And second, my friend over there wouldn't be able to pronounce them even if you did give them up." I said indicating Scar Face.

"What do you want?" The one on the right asked.

"Well, I need to ask you a few simple questions. You answer them, I let you go back to whatever Hell you crawled out of. You don't answer me, or even worse, lie, and… well, I have to clean up a mess." I looked over at where Brisbane was still standing off to the side. "Isn't that right?"

"Well none of the staff is going to do it for you."

"What do you want to know?" the other one hissed.

"Let's start off with who hired you?" There was no malice in my voice. I really was going to give them the friendly option of answering of their own free will and then just letting them slink off to whatever infernal dimension they had come from.

"You know we can't tell you that." The Shadow Man on the right probably realized that I knew they couldn't willingly answer the questions I was going to be asking. "We can't break our contracts."

"Brisbane? Get a mop. This probably going to get a little messy." My voice started friendly then quickly drew down into the malice that showed I was about to seriously enjoy hurting someone.

"Sorry boys, this is your own funeral," Brisbane said. "Do yourselves a favor and cooperate, because I'm sure that if you don't … well you'll see."

I took off my jacket and put it neatly on a nearby table and rolled up the sleeves of my shirt. Turning my back to them I loosened my tie, reached into my satchel and pulled out a few things to aid in the interrogation. First I picked up a set of enchanted, silver knuckle dusters.

"Now this is going to go a little slower than I'd normally go," I told them without turning back to face them. "You see, Sarah here asked me to let her watch. So I'm basically giving her a lesson on Daemon interrogation. And you? Well you two are going to be the subject matter of today's lesson."

I heard both of them swallow hard and gave them a three count to come to grips with what was about to happen and how much pain they were about to be in. I turned back to face them, walked up to the Shadow Man on the right and massaged my hand with the silver knuckles. "Now I'm going to ask you again. Who hired you?"

"I can't tell…" was as far as the Daemon got before I smashed my fist into his gut. I then pulled back and with a solid hook to the jaw, knocked him to the floor still bound to the chair. There had been an almost pleasant sound of breaking bone to accompany the hit. Had he been Human, they would have needed to wire his jaw shut for a month after a hit like that. This guy though would heal up fast enough to allow me to work him over for a very long while and get results.

I turned to look at the other Shadow Man. "Now let's try you. Are you going to cooperate?"

"I can't tell you anything. I can't break my contract." His voice was pleading with me not to do what he knew I was about to.

"Now that's really too bad," I said, sounding a little disheartened. I pulled back my fist and slammed it into the bastards face straight on.

I turned back to the Daemon on the floor and set his chair up straight again. A bit of bluish blood dripped from his mouth. Prying open his jaw, I saw some teeth were missing and spotted them on the ground. "Now I'm sure that must have hurt a lot," I said, and then slammed my fist repeatedly into his gut. I put my weight down on the chair and gave him a solid right hook to the side of the temple. "I'm sure that couldn't have felt very good either. Now back to my questions. Who hired you?"

"I can't…"

"Okay Sarah," I called back over my shoulder. "This is one of the reasons it's hard to interrogate two Daemons at the same time. They tend to heal up fast enough to be ready to withstand the next round of abuse before you're done working on the other."

"Duly noted," Sarah replied, pretending to take a note on an imaginary notepad. "So what are you going to do about it? Are you going to kill one of them now as an example to the other?"

"In a sense, yeah." I pulled out the Ace of Spades with her magazine of banishing rounds, aiming it at the Daemon who had been watching his pal take the beating. "Now what I'm about to do to your friend over there is going to be pleasant compared to what I'm about to do to you if you don't start to cooperate."

"Like a bullet is going to kill him," the Daemon laughed.

"Who said anything about killing him?" I asked. I pulled the trigger.

The bullet hit the Shadow Man dead center in the chest and then started to go to work. The bastard started screaming as the banishing round slowly sucked him inside out as it sent him back to a Hell that I didn't really bother to care about. He wouldn't be back anytime soon.

"Wow. That looked painful." Sarah said, faking a shiver.

I leaned over the remaining Daemon who was staring at the place where his friend had just been sitting. A look of total panic made its way forcefully across his face. "How did..."

"Oh that?" I shrugged. "Old trick I learned back about eighty years ago. Banishing rounds can be pretty messy as you just saw. But I assure you that it was pleasant compared to what is about to happen to you."

"Please. I can't tell you. I can't break my contract."

I jackhammered my fist repeatedly into his gut and the slammed a solid hook into his temple. "Now I'm well aware that you can break your contract. Yes, I'm aware that it will mean that you will never be able to return to this world. However, you should know that if I were to let you go without you giving me the answers I want, I would make sure that you would never want to come back. I'd just hunt you down and you'd go through all of this and then some again."

"I can't..." I hit him square in the chest and heard bones crunch. He screamed and dark, blue-green blood spurted out of his mouth.

"You're not going to be able to get any answers out of him if you beat him to death," Scar Face said.

"Don't worry, this isn't going to kill him. I'll let him sit there long enough to heal up a bit," I said.

The Daemon's breath was ragged and the diseased-looking blood dribbled out of his mouth. I turned my back on him and waited for the sounds of his breathing to even out. I took off the silvered knuckles and put them back in the bag. I hadn't really expected to get any answers out of him with those, they were just to soften him up a bit. I then pulled out a nasty looking scalpel with ancient runes etched upon the edge of the blade. As the Daemon's breath evened out, I turned around and smiled at him.

"Now let's start again," I said, showing the Shadow Man the scalpel. "Who hired you?"

CHAPTER

An hour and a clean shirt later, I dropped into the seat next to the Countess in the corner booth she was sharing with Jamie. "Hi Yvette. Have you been regaling my client of wild tales of court life?"

The Countess snorted. "You know that stuff bores me. No, I've been scaring off the people trying to take Jamie down onto the dance floor."

"Anyone I should be aware of?" I asked.

"No one really," she said, as she did a triple tap on the top of the table and jerked her thumb right.

I simply nodded, and took a quick look round. 'The Fiddler' was sitting a couple tables away with a pair of Neanderthal looking gunsels, if I was judging the cut of their jackets right. A good tailor can make it hard to see if a guy is packing an armpit full of artillery, but the tailor for these guys wasn't that good.

The Countess and I had worked out signals like that over the years, back when I helped her form the Court of Night.

Decades ago, while the world was immersed in the horror that was World War II, there had been a secret war, the Knights' War, that had pitted occult forces of the Allies against those of the Axis. In an Allied raid on a Nazi research lab, led by me in '43, we discovered them trying to mix Vampirism with Lycanthropy to create super soldiers. From the looks of the lab, there had been dozens of unsuccessful attempts, only one scared, seventeen-year-old Jewish girl had survived. That was of course, my close friend Yvette. After that raid and a little rehabilitation, I turned her into one of the nastiest Nazi killers the Allies ever had.

After the war was over, I offered her the choice of staying in Germany or coming home with me to the States. Shortly after we arrived, we discovered that the U.S. had been flooded with refugee Vampires and Lycanthropes, mostly from Eastern Europe. They had fallen into an underground war fueled by a mix of speciesist hatred and distrust of others from various parts of Europe. Yvette decided that to keep things from bubbling over, she was going to take control of the whole mess herself. For decades we put enough bodies into the ground on both sides to allow Yvette to step into the power vacuum and form the Court of Night.

The two of us had stopped counting which of us owed the other a favor and we just helped each other whenever one needed the other. Right now I was pretty sure I was going to need her help. I was in the tight spot of needing to track down the people after Jamie, while keeping her safe at the same time. Thankfully, the Countess could help; she had a small army that I could bum a couple soldiers from for a few days as bodyguards.

"So where's Scar Face?" Yvette asked. She and Sarah tolerated each other for my sake, but neither of them actually liked the other.

"She's on her second Corpse Reviver," I said. "She needed a couple of stiff drinks after we cleaned the place up. That Shadow Man was a real bleeder, screamed a lot too."

Yvette snorted derisively. "She never did have a strong stomach for blood from what I recall."

"She didn't go through what you did, no. Doesn't make her weak though." It irked me when Yvette talked like this; she always seemed to want to prove a point.

The Countess Blood Wolf was a major player on the National scene and yet she seemed to have always had an issue with Sarah, who was still not much of anyone on any sort of scene. There was nothing I could do to put a stop to it, and I was fairly sure the problem wouldn't end until Sarah died. As far as I was concerned, as long as the two of them kept the dislike of each other civilized I would just make do. Yvette would never actively do anything against Sarah for my sake. At least Sarah knew it would be suicidal to act against my friend from the Knight's War.

"All I'm saying Jason, is that even though she may not carry a badge anymore Scar Face still has the moral compass of a cop," Yvette said. "It's going to get her in trouble. There is going to come a time when she'll hesitate to pull the trigger. I don't want to see you get hurt."

"Let me worry about that," I said as harshly. I wanted her to ease off for now.

"So, what did you find out from those two Shadow Men following your client?" Yvette asked.

"Just what I already knew," I said. "They were summoned by the Ladies of the River. Unfortunately, the one I kept around to properly question didn't know who had hired the Ladies."

"Bad business if the Ladies get involved," Yvette said. "Are you sure he wasn't lying to you about not knowing who had hired them?"

"With what I did to him I know he would have told me if he could," I said with nasty smile. "Used the scalpel on him."

"I remember seeing you use that thing before, and you're right. He would have told you." Yvette knew what I could do with that thing and it was a nasty piece of work.

"Look I need a favor," I said.

"Name it." A few minutes ago she had sounded like a jealous ex-girlfriend. Now she sounded like what she truly was. Someone who was in the business of having peoples' legs broken.

"I need to borrow a couple of your toughest enforcers to keep an eye on my house for the next few days." Yvette's goons make the toughest guys from any of the organized crime syndicates look like kittens. Which was why many syndicates and cartels contracted with her for soldiers. She kept tabs on who was working for whom and kept groups of Werewolves and Vampires who were working for differing clients from killing each other. It was bad for her business if her workers were to kill each other.

"Anyone in particular?" she asked.

"Can you spare Black Hat and the Dentist?"

"They're yours," she said with a smile. "But I want something in return."

I never liked it when she gave me a condition, it never led to any good. "Okay Yvette, what do you want?"

"A trip with you up to the North Shore," Yvette smiled. "Two nights."

"Yvette, you're seventeen..." I started.

"Don't give me that. I've been seventeen for over eighty years now." I hated this part. "We've put a lot of bodies into the ground together. What're a couple of nights going to hurt?"

"You're how old?" Jamie asked. I guess she had finally started to come to grips with the Mystic Wolf. At least enough to really start paying attention without looking like a deer caught in the head lights.

"Eighty-nine," replied Yvette. "Look pretty good for an octogenarian, don't I?"

"Are you a Daemon like Black?"

"Hardly. I'm half Vampire and half Werewolf. I was one of the Nazis' many attempts at creating a super soldier. I was the sole survivor of that particular project."

Jamie looked at me in shock. "You put me in the hands of a... a..."

"No she's not a monster. Well maybe in the classical sense of the word, yes. However, she is a lot less of a monster than many quote unquote normal people out there," I said, trying to calm my client. The last thing I needed her doing was insulting one of my closest friends.

"But she just said that the two of you had, well..." She didn't finish the sentence and let it hang in the air for me to answer.

"Oh that. After the war she came to live here. At the time the Vampires and Werewolves in North America, most of whom were foreigners, were in a constant state of war. With my help we culled both sides deep enough for Yvette to step into the leadership role for both groups and force a sort of peace treaty," I explained. "And so far it's worked fairly well."

"How long ago?" Jamie asked.

"Oh, the court has been around for almost forty years now," Yvette said. "And before you ask, I didn't bother to keep count of the number of corpses we left in our wake."

"Well, I have to go check in with a friend of mine," I said, getting up from the booth. It was time to check in on the Fiddler and see what had interested him enough to try to dance with Jamie even though she was sitting with the Countess. "Yvette, can you take Jamie back to my place? You still have keys right?"

"Right next to the keys for my own home," she said with an obvious smile. "I'll call Black Hat and the Dentist and have them stake out your place. I'll stay with Jamie until they both get there. And don't worry, I'll make sure the Dentist knows exactly what you'll do to him if he tries to have a drink."

"Jason are you sure..." I didn't let Jamie finish the sentence.

"Don't worry, you'll be safer at my place with those two guarding you than with me out on the street," I told her. "I'll call you in a little while."

"Okay," she sighed.

"Come on dearie. I'll take good care of you," Yvette said, sliding an arm around Jamie. She then turned to look at me. "Remember ... two nights."

"I'll make a reservation for the nicest place I can find once I'm done with this case." The things I go through to wrap up a case.

Once I saw Jamie and the Countess get to the door, I turned my attention to the Fiddler. One of the men he was with got up and followed the two ladies out the door. That left the Fiddler with only one gunsel, and he would be easy enough to deal with. As I walked over to have a friendly chat with the hitter, I slipped my hand into my coat and wrapped my hand around the grip of Ace of Spades. I approached the Fiddler from behind him. I had never seen his help before so I was fairly sure he wouldn't know my face, or the reputation that went along with it. Once I was within touching distance of my target, I yanked my heater from her holster and jammed it into the idiot's ribs. The goon went for his gun but halted when he realized that I could plug his boss and then kill him before he could draw.

"Well Francis, it's good to see you again," I said. "Now be a good boy and tell your monkey to take a hike. The way he's grabbing his chest has got me nervous and my hand always starts shaking, along with the finger on the trigger."

"Hit the bar and get me a whiskey neat. You want anything Black?" the Fiddler asked casually. If the guy was nervous, he wasn't showing it.

"Double shot of bourbon," I ordered.

The gunsel didn't make a move. "Didn't you hear me?" Francis asked harshly. "I said a whiskey neat and my friend here will have a double shot of bourbon."

His man nodded and left the table. "Seems like a nice kid. Bit dumb though," I commented.

"A primitive I picked up a couple months ago," Francis said. "They learn fairly fast, but aren't much better than monkeys. However, they do like hurting people, which is all I really need them for."

"Well, be sure that the one you just sent to follow my client doesn't run afoul of the Countess Blood Wolf, or the guys who'll be meeting up with her soon. It might be hard to replace the guy."

"True enough I guess," he said. "But you'd be surprised at how easy it was to acquire both of them in the first place."

"I'm sure I would be. You're too cheap to risk expensive help," I said as I sat down across from the hitter. "So what's got you interested in my client?"

"The question should be: 'What is going on with her that warrants you getting help from both Scar Face and, more importantly, the Countess?'"

"That's a dangerous question to be asking," Sarah whispered into the Fiddler's ear having snuck up on him from behind.

From the look on the Fiddler's face my companion had jammed her own heater into the man's back.

"No need for that, Scar Face. I'll step off. But keep this in mind, you're not a real player on the scene," the Fiddler said. The professional hitter gulped heavily and made a slight lurch forward as Sarah shoved her rod harder into his back.

"Maybe I should do something about that right now," she said.

"Call your bitch off Bla..." was all Francis got out before Sarah pistol whipped him.

"Dumb ass," Sarah said, spitting on the unconscious hit man.

It was about this time that Francis's gunsel showed up with the drinks. I took my bourbon from him and gave it a quick sniff. The idiot had tried to doctor the drink on me. I grabbed the thug by the back of his head and gave his face a hard bounce off the table.

"What did he do to deserve that?" Sarah asked when I gave the primitive a rib breaking kick in the side.

"He tried to slip me a Mickey," I said. "Now let's go."

"So where to now?" Sarah asked.

"The Shadow Man confessed to being hired by the Ladies after you left. So now comes the hard part of tracking them down."

"Any idea where to start?" Sarah asked.

"Well, the last time they had a base of operation they were holed up near the 35W bridge," I told her. "Now I doubt that they'd be dumb enough to go back where I could easily find them, but they're still going to be near the river."

Regarding the mess the two of us had just made, I grabbed a passing Succubus waitress and asked her to apologize to Brisbane for me. The Succubus looked at the Fiddler splayed out across the table, his face buried in his dinner. She merely shrugged and kicked his chair out from underneath him. "He's a lousy tipper," she said before walking off. I couldn't help but laugh.

"This way," I said motioning Sarah toward the door that led to the mortal world.

"So how are we going to find the Ladies of the River?" Sarah asked again.

"That's where Shadow comes in."

"Of course!" Sarah clapped her hand to her forehead. "He'll be able to fly up and down the river and spot the magickal signature coming off of them, and then he can show you where they are."

When we got to my car Shadow was already perched on the hood. "Reading my mind again?" I asked.

As easily as if it were a dime store pulp novel, he replied smugly.

"There haven't been any dime stores in decades," I reminded him.

Says the man who just stepped out of 'The Big Sleep', Shadow replied. I often forgot that the idiot crow was a big Raymond Chandler fan.

"Point taken." I replied.

So what do you want me to do?

"How would you like to track down the Ladies of the River." It wasn't a question and Shadow knew it.

You have got to be kidding me! Shadow screamed in my head. *Do you have any concept of the number of diseases in their familiars? Those wretched things are more polluted than the river.*

"I'm not asking you to do battle with them." This was going to get irritating, I just knew it. "All I need to know is where I can find them."

I still don't like it.

"I don't care if you don't like it," I hissed at the bird. "This is a direct order. Go find the Ladies of the River."

Your mother would never have made me do this, Shadow sulked.

"In case you haven't noticed, I'm not my mother," I snarled.

Yeah, yeah. I've noticed.

"Good. Now get going," I said, taking a swipe at him.

"I'll never get used to that," Sarah said.

"What? Me talking to Shadow?"

"Yeah. I mean I can see you talking to a bird, and while I know that he's talking back to you, I can't hear it."

"I'm sure you'll get used to it sooner or later," I said with a shrug.

"So now what?" Sarah asked the logical question.

"We head towards the river, find a place to park and wait until we hear from Shadow," I replied.

"Until you hear from him," she said.

"Whatever."

CHAPTER 7

We had been parked near the 35W bridge for nearly two hours when Shadow reported back. *Found them. At least I think I have. There is no way that I'm going any closer. Remember, their familiars can sense me almost as well as I can sense them. If I got too close, I'd be in a lot of danger.*

"Not a problem. Just wait until I come for you, then you can wait it out safe in the car," I told him.

From where I'm perched the Ladies are between me and the only real way for you to get here. I'll just stay put until the coast is clear, Shadow replied. It was a sensible plan. Shadow is loyal. Not terribly brave, but loyal.

"I'll see you soon," I told him. I turned the engine over and the car crawled out of its spot on the side of the interstate. Soon we were merging seamlessly into the light traffic.

I looked over at Sarah who seemed a little on edge. "You don't have to come if you don't want to. In fact, I'd almost prefer it if you didn't," I said.

Sarah glared at me. "What's that supposed to mean?"

"Look Sarah, what I'm about to do is going to be messy business. I'm going to be shedding a lot of blood tonight. And when I say blood, I mean Human blood. Not like the blood of the Daemon I was cutting on earlier." I was remembering what Yvette had told me earlier. Sarah was still a cop deep down. Tonight, I was going to perform butchery. I didn't need my friend to see that side of me. This wasn't going to be the first time I dipped my hands shoulder deep in the gore of Humanity, and by the Gods I knew it wouldn't be the last time either.

"I..." She didn't finish the sentence. There really was no need for her to do so.

Sarah was silent for the rest of the trip. The silence sat there like a fog, no real substance, but still able to obscure anything out there. An hour later I took the car off the main drag and down a side road that led closer to the river. I shut the lights off and let my Daemonic senses show me where I was going.

As soon as we got close, I shut the engine off and we coasted another hundred yards or so. I slid her to a stop behind some bushes.

I reached into the back seat and grabbed an old friend of mine from prohibition.

"A Tommy Gun?" Sarah asked in almost disbelief.

"Yep. Used this girl all throughout the gangster wars. These babies are what made the Twenties roar," I said with a wicked grin.

When I got out of the car I took my whippet out from behind the seat. I eased my trench coat off and slung the short strap of the sawed-off twelve gauge under my right shoulder Bonnie and Clyde style. I put my trench coat back on, obscuring the gun from sight. The whole point of the whippet is that you'd be able to carry something as fierce as a Remington twelve gauge as easily as if it were a pistol in a shoulder holster. It had taken me a little while to get used to carrying it, but once I had I made sure to always have it with me when I knew I was walking into a fight.

I then made sure that Ace of Spades was securely tucked away in her holster under my left shoulder. That little girl had seen me safe through two world wars. With a little love and care, she'd always be there for me when I needed her.

I had been armed this way the last time I had rid the Twin Cities of the Ladies of the River back during the Great Depression. In fact, these were even the exact same guns. The Colt in its shoulder holster, the whippet under my right, and the Tommy in my hands. I was as ready to spill a lot of blood as I was ever going to get.

"Be careful," Sarah said as I closed the car door. I simply nodded. She would be safe here; I didn't want her getting too close to this. She'd be just one more thing for me to worry about.

"How many are there, Shadow?" I asked my familiar who looked to be several hundred yards away.

Thirteen, just as you'd expect, the crow replied.

Covens of witches, both good and bad, always tried to form into groups of thirteen. I never knew exactly why since my mother had never been able to give me a suitable answer herself, and she had been an old school good witch. There were various theories, the dumbest one being that it was part of the spread of Christianity over pagan Europe, with revisionist idiots pointing to the fact that Jesus had twelve apostles with him making thirteen. It's of course complete and utter nonsense since the number showed up all over the world, well before Judaism had been created. Whatever the reason, all that mattered at the moment was that I was facing thirteen magick whores.

I closed my eyes and took a deep breath. I opened my eyes halfway through the long exhale. Now was the time to send these cockroaches of the magickal world to the Hell that had been reserved for them. I casually rested my Thompson on my shoulder and nonchalantly walked down the path towards them. The Grim Reaper was about to get busy.

The night was cold, even for spring. The thirteen witches were grouped close around a couple of trash can fires. I spotted them before they saw me, which played to my advantage. Their first warning of my presence came from the barking of a pair of mangy, mongrel dogs that I immediately knew to be familiars. The dogs were fairly large, but I knew they'd probably be half again as large if they were eating on something other than the garbage the witches subsisted on. The second warning cry, though it was no longer needed, came from the ragged trees that grew around this part of the bluffs by the river. A small murder of crows was belting out the raucous cries. The thirteen Ladies of the River turned to look at me and I knew, and I was sure that they too knew that this encounter was going to end in bloodletting.

"What do you want, creature of the pit?" one of them asked me. I figured that since she had spoken first she must be the leader of this coven of cockroaches. By the look of her she wasn't much long for this world, two maybe three months max. However, it really was only idle speculation on my part; in a few minutes I'd be putting all of them out of the world's misery.

"Now, now, that's not a very nice way to start what I hope to be a pleasant conversation. I was hoping that we could keep this friendly." They obviously knew I was lying. There was no way they'd let another Daemon, even a half-Daemon such as me, walk away if they could help it.

"Hardly friendly if you're carrying a gun like that," their leader spat.

I quickly surveyed the group and spotted the witch Jamie had described heading left. "I just need to ask a couple of simple questions and then I'll leave. Simple as that. No need for things to get messy." The other witches were breaking off, but they were still close enough that a sprayed barrage from my Tommy would cut all of them down.

"Ask your questions," the leader finally said after a pause. She was obviously stalling. They were starting to surround me like a pack of wild dogs on anything that looked tasty.

"You recently summoned up a couple of Shadow Men to stalk and kill a client of mine. I want to know who hired you," I said. I dropped the Tommy from my shoulder and shifted it to a two handed grip. I was starting to get nervous, they seemed to know what they were doing.

"What makes you think we had anything to do with a summoning of any Shadow Men?" the leader asked, lying through her decaying teeth.

"Oh that's easy. One of them told me to stop the pain after I cut on him long enough to get him to break his contract." I smiled evilly.

The leader shrugged. "Seeing as there's no denying it I may as well tell you. We were hired by Landers Goldweight."

I was honestly surprised that Landers was involved with any of this. Last time I checked the guy was nothing more than a two-bit magick shylock. If Jamie was involved with that little piece of sleaze she wouldn't have been so surprised to have had Shadow Men after her. No. There was someone else involved.

"Why is he after my client?" I asked.

"He didn't say, but he did say that he might need another job from us soon. However, that doesn't really concern you," their leader said.

"And why's that?" I asked even though I already knew why. I could feel the crackle and pop of dark energies polluting the air.

"Because you're not going to leave this place alive," she cackled. It wasn't a good cackle, she hadn't had enough time to practice and she would never get any more. However, since the rest of them were laughing it left me with plenty of time. Idiots.

"Suit yourself." I grinned as I squeezed the trigger.

The gun jumped to life with a rattling roar sounding like a thousand Daemonic typewriters. It was that very sound that had earned the Tommy one of its more sinister monikers, 'The Chicago Typewriter'. My first burst caught their leader full in the chest cutting her almost in half. I spun a half circle round and with a few pulls of the trigger rattled off enough rounds to cut down another five witches. The polluting energies of the witches fractured as the terrifying sound of the furious Tommy shattered their concentration.

As I kept turning I could see that the remaining Ladies were trying to run, knowing that their magick was no match for the death I was writing across the landscape. It would do them no good however. Bullets ripped through their backs, their blood painting the ground. They were no better than cockroaches and I was an exterminator come to clean the cities I loved of their filth.

Then came two of the crows. Most had died when their mistress had lost her breathing license, the others I didn't care about. But these two were diving towards my face, obviously trying to rake out my eyes. I dropped the Thompson and rolled for the ground leaving the crows catching nothing but empty air. As I rolled I reached high into my coat and grabbed my whippet from under my right shoulder. I brought it to bear as I came to my knees. When the crows came in for a second dive, the gun bucked hard as I pulled the trigger twice. The crows disintegrated in explosions of blood and feathers, hit by the twelve gauge shells mere inches from the muzzle of the sawed-off shotgun.

Out of the corner of my eye I saw that one of the mongrel dogs was still moving and he was coming fast. I didn't have enough time to bring the shot gun to bear on the dog. I let go of the shotgun with my left hand and grabbed the charging dog by the throat as it jumped high at me. Squeezing the dog's neck, I lifted it easily as I came to my feet. The dog kept snapping at me, trying in vain to bite into me with its diseased mouth. I reached under my left shoulder and yanked out Ace of Spades and put two rounds into the frenzied beast's scrawny chest.

I slid the Colt back into her holster and casually tossed the carcass of the beast away to survey the carnage. I had barely started looking over the area when a sudden weight landed square on my back. The hit knocked me flat on the chest. My left hand was down my side at an awkward angle. My right hand was still on my gun with my chest pinning it down in such a way as to make it impossible to get any good leverage. Somehow I had missed one of these whores and I was soon going to be paying a harsh penalty for my mistake. What truly amazed me was how much she weighed. On their diet, even the largest of them shouldn't have weighed more than a hundred pounds. This one felt to weigh a couple hundred; I couldn't shift her off.

I twisted my head round and saw a rusty, magickally diseased butchers knife pull up and I knew that it was soon going to end up in my neck. My one regret was that I was letting Jamie down, and that soon she would be paying for my failure.

Just as the knife was about to fall I heard two loud cracks and the witch's weight decreased ten-fold, then simply slumped off my back. I rolled to my side and upon standing saw Sarah holding a .357 revolver and shaking. I approached her from the side and eased the gun out of her still fully extended hands. "It's never as easy to put a couple rounds through a person as it is shooting silhouettes down at the range," I said gently.

"She was going to kill you," Sarah was still badly shaken up by it. "It was just like what happened to me, but in reverse. It was... it was..."

Sarah collapsed into me, bawling like a child. I put my arms around her and just held her for a couple of minutes. Maybe Yvette was right about Sarah. There may come a day when she might hesitate and not pull the trigger when she needed to. However, today had, thankfully, not been that day. I brought her over to a large rock and set her down. "I have a little clean up to do," I told her.

Looking around I saw that all but two of the Ladies of the River were already starting to crumble in on themselves. I took my Colt back out of her holster and shot those two in the back of their heads. It was a merciful end for the wretches. Soon all of these witches would crumble into dust no longer of any use to the Daemon of the Mighty Miss.

Sarah was still shaking when I walked back over to her. I pulled my hip flask, a friend for well over a century, out of my pocket, unscrewed the top and handed it to her. She could use a couple drops of the medicine to help stop the shaking. "Here, this'll help. Trust me."

Sarah took a quick swig and gave a shudder. "I always forget you drink cheap bourbon," she complained.

"We all have our vices," I said with a slight smile and a shrug. A little conversation would help just as much as the alcohol. "That tastes pretty close to what I had to drink during prohibition. I just acquired a taste for it."

She took another, much longer pull from the flask and gave another shudder. "Feeling a little better now?" I asked.

"Well enough, I guess." She stood up slowly and headed back to the car. She seemed to have successfully pulled herself back together. I was again reminded of what Yvette had said. Sarah was going to have to develop a thicker skin if she was going to make it in the world I had introduced her to.

"Shadow," I called into the air. "I want you to meet us by the car."

Way ahead of you, he answered.

I surveyed the scene again. By this time all of the bodies of the Ladies of the River had crumbled. It was odd in a way. If they died naturally they left a withered body, but if they died violently it was like this, crumbling to dust that would just blow away. All that was left of them now was bullet riddled clothing. Someday another group like this would probably infect the area, but I would worry about that later. For now, I had washed their blighted presence from the land. Now it was time to find out how that two-bit shylock Landers Goldweight fit in with all of this.

Walking over to the car, I saw Sarah scratching the top of Shadow's head. I guess she was finally starting to come to grips with the familiar and how much he had helped us tonight. "Enjoying that, bird brain?"

Yes, and you're going to make her stop aren't you, the bird complained.

"You bet," I told Shadow. I then turned my head slightly to look at Sarah. "Come on let's get going."

I lit a cigarette and took a couple long drags before I got into the car. I put her into gear and started her up the path to the main drag. I felt Sarah's hand come to rest on my leg. "Thanks," she said cryptically.

"Why?" I asked confused. "I should be the one thanking you. And thank you, by the way."

"Because seeing you there, pinned down about to die like that, a knife through your neck, it reminded me of that night," she said. "It was fourteen months ago, and it all came flooding back to me when I shot her. I just don't remember if I thanked you properly for that night."

"You've thanked me more than a few times." I patted her hand gently and just held it for a while. As we got back onto 35W I took my hand away from hers and put it on the steering wheel to merge seamlessly into traffic. My only hope at this point was for Sarah to not say she loved me. Having to deal with spending two nights on the North Shore with Yvette, who would not accept anything but sharing a bed with me, was going to be hard enough. I didn't need to hear a similar request from Sarah.

"So what's next?" Sarah asked, thankfully breaking my train of thought.

"We're going to talk to a shylock named Landers Goldweight," I told her.

"What would a loan shark be doing that would make him go to a group of witches like the ones you just wiped out?" Sarah asked. It was a logical question since she didn't know what kind of stuff Landers was in the business of lending.

"Landers isn't exactly a loan shark, well not a normal one," I said.

"But you just called him a shylock, I thought there wasn't a difference," Sarah asked confused.

"Well, in this case there's a very important distinction," I said. "In the circles I have always traveled in, and which you do now, a shylock is someone who lends magickal power. So, in a sense, Landers is a loan shark of magickal power, and the interest rates he charges are preternaturally high."

"What do you mean?"

"Landers goes after his borrower's soul if he doesn't receive payment," I told her. "Before I started shooting, the leader of the Ladies told me that he said he might need their help again."

"Which means that Jamie wasn't the one who was doing the borrowing," Sarah said in sudden realization. "He can't receive payment from a corpse, not even the soul if he's not right there."

"Exactly." She was learning fast. I knew she'd have a fast learning curve when I took her under my wing. Her superior told me while she was in the hospital recovering, that it was a shame she'd have to leave the force. "Jamie's death was meant to be a big ass warning to somebody."

"So how are we going to find out who he is after?" Sarah asked.

"Simple. I'm going to kick in his door and ask him," I said with an almost manic grin.

It was at this time that I got a call on my cell. The ringtone belonged to Yvette. I pulled the phone out of my jacket pocket and slid my thumb across the screen to answer it, "Hey Yvette, what do you need?" I asked casually.

"One of goons that I contracted out just showed up at your place. He was talking with some Neanderthal looking guy. When he headed up the walk to your house he saw Black Hat. He turned to walk away but he didn't get far before 'the Dentist' grabbed him," she said, skipping the pleasantries.

"Let me guess, you have him working for Landers Goldweight," I replied.

"How did you know?" There was a sound of total amazement in Yvette's voice.

"I'll explain when I get there," I said.

"So what do you want me to do with him?" Yvette asked.

"Have him call his boss and tell him there's no one's there, and that he's going to wait," I said after a second.

"And after that?"

"I'll be there in thirty minutes give or take. Just sit on him until then," I said.

"Understood. I'll be here waiting for you." Normally when she would say something like that it would have been with a romantic lilt in it. Thankfully she knew when to be serious.

"Thank you. I'll see you in thirty," I said as I hung up.

"What's next?" Sarah asked.

"You'll see." With Landers' heavy in Yvette's possession, we had the advantage of the situation over the shylock. First rule of being a detective, try to know, or at least be able to fake knowing, the answers to any question you're about to ask. If you have the answers it'll unnerve them enough to be truthful regarding any other questions from you. Also, if they lie to you, you'll be able to find out why they're lying.

CHAPTER 7

"Where is he?" I asked as soon as I walked through the door.

"He's in your Trophy room." Yvette's smile was wicked, and with good reason. The trophy room could unnerve even hardcore horror fans, because everything in there is real.

She then looked past me and saw Sarah walking through the door after me. "Hello Scarface," she said coldly.

"You're looking well, Blood Wolf," Sarah replied in an equally cold voice.

"Where's Jamie?" I asked Yvette.

"In the library."

"Sarah, go join Jamie," I ordered. I needed to separate the two girls before Yvette killed Sarah, which would force me to kill my old friend.

"But I wanted to..." Sarah started to protest.

"Go!" I barked. "I'll tell you all about it later."

"She really needs to learn her place," Yvette said as soon as Sarah was out of the room.

"That chip on your shoulder must weigh a ton," I snarled at Yvette.

"What chip?" Yvette sounded shocked with the tone I had just taken with her.

"The one you put there as soon as I took Sarah under my wing and started training her," I said.

"She's no good for you," Yvette said. There was a sense of longing in her voice that irritated me at the moment. "She'll get you hurt."

"I'll worry about that when the problem comes up," I said. "In fact, if she hadn't been with me tonight you'd be looking at me in a coffin."

"What's that supposed to mean?" Yvette asked, obviously confused.

"She double tapped one of the Ladies just as the bitch was about to put some sort of magickally diseased knife through my neck."

"Oh." The revelation that Sarah had saved my life seemed to take all the wind out of Yvette's sails. "If you'll excuse me, I've got to have a little girl to girl chat with Sarah."

The Countess walked down the hall towards the library. Hopefully that would buy me some peace between those two. At least for a while, not that I expected it to last. Now to deal with Goldweight's hired muscle.

I headed to the trophy room, which had things best not spoken of. I don't let most people in the place; only magickally powerful individuals can handle being in there for more than fifteen minutes, give or take, without going insane. Unless you were invited, this was the last place you ever wanted to be. Cursed items from all over the world had come to live here. Much of the wood furniture came from the Suicide Forest in Japan. Torture tools of the Spanish Inquisition had made their way here. Those were some of the more pleasant items. I was particularly proud of the collection of shrunken heads I had acquired awhile back. I saw my prisoner, who had taken Human form, sitting in a chair with a look of pure terror on his face. On one side of him sat the Dentist, who looked impeccably clean as usual. As befitting his moniker, his smile was blazingly white with a set of menacing fangs. He was dressed as if he were about to go to the opera. Knowing him, he'd probably take some young lady there out on the town and then have a drink, her treat.

On the other side of him was Black Hat. Dressed like a blue-collar construction worker, he was in a partial Werewolf state, looking much like Lon Chaney Jr. Black Hat had gotten his name from the black stocking cap he always wore; according to him he had been wearing it when he had first turned and had just grown attached to it. He had been a cage fighter, and apparently a good one before he had gotten bitten by a Werewolf.

You couldn't imagine two more unlikely friends than those two. They liked to work together. This was odd, considering one was a Vampire and the other a Werewolf. The relationships between both groups had verged on full out war before Countess Blood Wolf had slaughtered her way to the control of both sides. The remnants of that unease were still there and she sometimes had to remind them that they were all working for her now. However, these two were close friends and were two of Yvette's best enforcers.

I didn't know the werewolf between the two of them, but that didn't mean much. He did look tough though, which was probably why Landers had hired him in the first place. In this case, however, I was more than willing to lay a hundred down with my bookie that he was all bark and no bite.

I pulled up a chair and sat across from the bruiser. "So let's have a nice conversation," I said in a friendly voice.

"As I'm sure you have realized by now, I am a close friend of Countess Blood Wolf. So, you seem to have found yourself in an awful situation." There was no reason that this conversation couldn't be civilized, after all, I had given the Shadow Men a chance to cooperate. Here the situation was better. I didn't have to ask him who had hired him, and by now he would have realized that I was a friend of the Countess. He was in no situation to lie to me without very severe consequences.

"Now, let's go over the facts. First you were contracted out by the Countess to work for Landers Goldweight. I know that at the very least you were told to track down a girl named Jamie Cross, who is my client. Now from here, I will ask you some simple questions. If you answer truthfully, I let you keep your breathing privileges, if not, well..." Black Hat gave the werewolf's shoulder a painfully hard squeeze.

"I'll talk! I'll talk, just don't let them hurt me." As I thought ... all bark. Of course, having a pair of notorious hitters on either side of him and his contractor in the house probably took all the bite out of him.

"So, my first question is, how did you know where my client was?" I asked, keeping the tone of my voice friendly.

"Mr. Goldweight got a phone call. He didn't seem to like what he heard. He then gave me a picture of the girl and her name, and the address to this place, and told me to come here. I was told to simply wait and keep an eye out for the girl," the werewolf said.

"Did you recognize the name or the number?" I asked. It didn't really matter since I already had a pretty good idea of who had tipped them off.

"The voice sounded familiar but I couldn't quite place it." The guy was eager to help. Of course Black Hat's claws in the guy's shoulder had probably helped. I really didn't care who had made the call, I had a good feeling that the tip had come from the Fiddler.

"Let's get to the real heart of the matter," I said. "Why is Landers after my client? Remember, right now honesty is the best policy. And I assure you that it will be very beneficial for your health."

"Here's what I know. Mr. Goldweight had someone come by the office a couple of weeks ago. The guy said that he wanted help with some sort of interview that was coming up, something about a big promotion, some sort of bullshit like that." The werewolf had started to sing. "Mr. Goldweight says that they should be able to work something out. He then starts interviewing the guy about all sorts of shit."

"What sorts of shit?" I asked.

"The usual sort of crap. Stuff about family, where he likes to eat, his golf handicap. How the hell should I know? I didn't pay attention," he said shrugging.

"Why didn't you pay attention?" I asked. This sort of stuff was always important when dealing with someone who brokered any sort of power, especially magickal power.

"Hey look, I'm just muscle. I don't get paid to take notes. I..." The werewolf yelped in pain as Black Hat squeezed hard into the stool pigeon's arm.

"Play nice or I get mean and feed you your own arm," Black Hat snarled less than an inch from my interviewee's ear.

"Okay, okay, I'll talk." This guy wasn't much on brains but he was obviously familiar with Black Hat's well-earned reputation for liking to hurt people.

"Now back to this customer of Landers'. Did you catch anything like the name of the guy? Maybe you can give me a description?"

"Yeah I can do both for you easy. His name was Eric Fish. He was a pretty tall guy and he looked like he was in pretty decent shape, but I wouldn't swear to it since he was wearing a suit." The guy was starting to sing like the proverbial canary, and I would lay more than even odds that it was all the more beautiful because it was a performance inspired by the gracious threat of Black Hat. The guy may not have taken notes on the conversation but he knew more than enough about the guy to be able to spot him in a hundred-man line up. I'm sure the reason he could remember what the guy looked like so well was in case he needed to track down someone who had skipped town instead of paying up.

After a ten-minute serenade, I had a pretty good idea of what the man who had borrowed the power from Landers looked like. He was a tall man somewhere between six-six and six-eight. Hard features, almost as if he had been chiseled out of stone, the werewolf had said. The guy had blue-green eyes, and his black hair, showing just a touch of gray, was cut short, not a crew cut but still short. He then went on to describe some of the finer details, from the height of his cheek bones to the exact shape of his nose. I eventually cut stoolie off at the part about the college class ring.

"Okay, now you are going to stay put for a while, while I take care of a few things. Once I'm done with that, you and I and everyone else here are going to move this conversation to your boss's office." As I stood up to leave I looked at Black Hat and the Dentist. "He's been a good boy. So don't rough him up." I heard a sigh of disappointment from Black Hat once my back was turned.

I also heard a sigh of relief from Landers' goon. He had given me everything I had needed so there was no need for violence.

When I got to the library it seemed that the Countess had made some peace with Sarah. In fact, they had gone so far as to having a civilized, if somewhat tense, conversation with each other. I didn't know how long it was going to last but for now I was going to enjoy it. "I need to ask you a couple questions Jamie," I said, interrupting the flow of the conversation.

"Anything," Jamie said eagerly. "Sarah said that you had a lead on who contracted those Ladies of the River people to kill me."

"Yes we do have a lead, which is why these questions are going to be so important," I started. "First, do you know anyone named Landers Goldweight?"

Jamie closed her eyes and cocked her head to one side. "No, not that I know of. Why?"

"Didn't think so." I really hadn't expected her to know the sleaze. "How about an Eric Fish? He's supposed to be a tall guy, short black hair, and blue eyes."

Jamie didn't even close her eyes this time. "I know exactly who you're talking about, but his name isn't Eric Fish it's Derek Fynch. He has a slight speech impediment that always causes people to make that mistake." Well at least the werewolf wasn't an idiot for names.

"So how do you know him?" I asked her.

"He's my boss." Then a light sparked behind her eyes. "Are you saying that it was my boss who asked me to be killed? That sounds a bit extreme for me turning him down. Sure, I threatened to go to Human Resources for harassment, but wanting to kill me?"

"Actually, it isn't your boss who wants you dead. I'm fairly sure that the person who ordered your death meant it to be a very big and messy warning to your boss," I told her. "Do you know if your boss was up for any sort of promotion?"

"Actually, now that I think about it, I'm fairly sure he was. He made some vague promises that he could get me a promotion if I went out with him. I didn't think too much of it at the time because when he said that, he didn't have the authority to give me a promotion."

"I hate to tell you this, but you seem to be nothing more than collateral damage in a nasty piece of work," I told her.

"So, what got me involved in this whole mess?" Jamie asked.

"Well, your boss got involved with a type of shylock who deals in magickal power..." I started before Jamie interrupted me.

"What's a shylock?"

"A loan shark." Kids these days have no sense of what they're missing now that the classic slang of the Roaring Twenties through the forties is no longer being used. Next I'll probably have to explain what a zip gun is. "Anyways, this shylock, a mean piece of sleaze named Landers Goldweight, probably felt that your boss hadn't paid his debts in a timely enough fashion. So, to make it well known to Mr. Fynch that he wanted his money, he was going to have you killed in a suitably gruesome fashion as a warning."

"So you're saying I was going to be killed because my boss didn't pay up to a loan shark?" Jamie asked in a justifiably shocked voice.

"Pretty much so. Don't worry. I'm going to get all of this sorted out." This wasn't the first time, and it certainly wouldn't be the last time, that a shylock used a trick like this. I've seen cops clean up these types of messages for more decades than I cared to count, but this time was different. This time I was being paid to keep the message from being delivered. I knew what Landers was after, or rather who he was after. I was simply going to make a trade. Jamie's safety in return for a guy who was probably scum anyways.

"So what're the plans Jason?" Yvette asked.

I thought about what the next move should be. "Do you have a limo that can take seven passengers?" I asked her.

"Of course. I take it we are going to be paying Mr. Goldweight a little visit then?" the Countess replied.

"Of course. I was thinking we could move this little party to his greasy little office," I said.

"He's come up a long way if you're still thinking of that run-down office building in the warehouse district. How that place stayed open with all those code violations is beyond me," the Countess said. "He's got a corner office in one of the newer high rise office buildings in downtown Minneapolis."

"High risk, high paying loans aren't limited to just banks then," I mused.

"Hold that thought," Yvette held up a hand. She pulled out her cell phone and called one of her people to bring 'round a limo and a change of clothes. "And don't forget my work clothes."

I looked at her and raised an eyebrow. "You really are serious about making an impression aren't you?"

"You of all people should know that it's important to dress for success," Yvette said. "Now I don't know about the rest of you, but I plan on getting Landers properly worried."

All of a sudden I realized that she was going to be changing into her 'I'm the biggest bad ass here' clothes. Normally I only saw her in those clothes when she was going to set an example to her followers about what it meant to cross her. Normally that meant she would rip the offender's arm off and then feed it to them. When she was dressed like that, she looked like a high-priced dominatrix looking ready to kill someone very painfully instead of playfully slapping them around. The leather of the outfit was tanned Werewolf hide, studded with Vampire fangs. Truly nauseating when you knew the history behind it.

I decided that I too could use a change of clothes after my rather messy encounter with the Ladies of the River. The limo arrived thirty minutes after Yvette called for it. Once it arrived she quickly changed and was ready to go.

When we got into the limo, Landers' goon was sitting between the Dentist and Black Hat. On the other side, Jamie sat next to Sarah. Yvette sat next to me in back. I saw Sarah's distinct glare when Yvette's hand seemed to all too casually make its way onto my lap. The brief peace between the two of them wasn't going to last, and as headstrong as the two of them were, I knew I was going to just have to suffer through it.

"Does Landers have any other muscle than just you?" I asked the werewolf.

"No one but me," the werewolf said. It was an obvious lie from the way he said it.

"Dentist, if you would be so kind," Yvette said sweetly.

The Dentist pulled a pair of pliers out of an inner coat pocket. He forced the werewolf's jaws open. "Please try not to bleed on this suit, it's dry clean only," the Vampire said as he casually wrenched out a canine.

The Werewolf screamed in pain but was smart enough to try his hardest not to bleed on the Vampire's expensive tuxedo. Jamie looked away, quickly burying her face in Sarah's shoulder. Sarah didn't even flinch, but considering what she had seen me do earlier in the evening, this was tame by comparison.

"Now are you going to tell us the truth or is 'the Dentist' going to have to look for some more cavities?" Yvette asked sweetly.

"He's got a pair of Incubi in the office with him at all times. They never leave. I don't think their contracts allow them to," the werewolf whimpered.

"Oh don't be such a baby," Yvette said, patting the werewolf on the knee. "You'll grow a new tooth soon enough, at least as long as you do exactly what I tell you to do."

"Anything you say Countess," the werewolf whimpered, fresh blood drooling down his chin.

Yvette turned her attention to me. "Incubi. Those are pretty nasty pieces of work. Are you prepared to handle them?"

I simply gave Yvette a withering glare.

"Sorry, I shouldn't have even bothered asking," Yvette conceded. "So what exactly is the plan?"

"Simple. Black Hat kicks the door in and I put a banishing round into each of those scum sucking Daemons." Never did like those types of Daemons, probably because the Nazis were so fond of them, and anything that the Nazis liked has to be viewed with suspicion. Plus they're all serial rapists, so it sort of goes without saying why I hate them.

"Then I'm going to grab that two-bit shylock Landers and pound on him until we come to an understanding."

"What is it with you and beating people up?" Jamie asked.

"In the circles you have found yourself thrown into Jamie, violence gets results," I said. "Here it gets you names and motives. And tonight it's going to get you off the hook for someone else's mess."

"I just think you enjoy it," Jamie said.

"Maybe a little more than I should," I conceded. "Mom always did say I was a bit too much like my father in that regard. Though for as long as I can remember, dad never touched my mother with anything other than a loving hand."

"Well considering that you're here, he must have touched her with something more than just his hand at least once," Sarah said, trying to make a bad joke. She then quickly shut her jaws when I glared at her. It was a standing rule with my friends and associates that all matters regarding my family were off the table, unless I brought it up. There were to be no questions, no pushing for more information, and definitely no jokes.

"Is there something I should know?" Jamie asked.

"Yes. What I've already told you about my parents is all you need to know. Everything else is off the table." I then turned my attention back to Sarah. "Isn't that right Sarah?"

"Sorry Jason," Sarah said in a quiet voice. She realized that she had crossed the line. I wasn't so much mad as I was irritated.

The rest of the ride was fairly quiet. Not that Sarah and Jamie weren't talking, but everyone else sat in stony silence. I'm fairly sure that the only reason Jamie was talking to Sarah was to keep her mind elsewhere. I didn't blame her. After all, she was on her way to meet the man who had put a contract out on her head. Had I been in the same shoes as my client I probably would have been scared too, but she managed to put on a brave face. I had to admire her. A couple of days ago she had been like most people, oblivious to this magickal underworld of the Twin Cities. And now she was sitting in a limo with people who normally would have been the villains in a horror movie. What was probably the weirdest part of that was that we were, with one exception, the good guys. True, the only reason that Black Hat and the Dentist were being good guys was that they were acting on Yvette's orders. Still we, the monsters, were going to be saving Jamie's life.

When we arrived at our destination I was impressed with what I saw. Apparently what Yvette had told me about Landers' large step up in society wasn't an exaggeration. The last time I had endured the displeasure of dealing with that louse, he had been working out of dilapidated building in a disreputable part of town. Back then his only muscle had been a brutish thug armed with a gun and an axe handle. The area had become the kind of place that had earned Minneapolis its name Murderapolis, which at times was very justified. This new place was a world away from there, it was in a clean part of downtown, the kind of area where the cops did the rounds of kicking vagrants off the street corners.

"This is the place," Yvette said as we exited her limo.

"Let me guess. His office is on the thirteenth floor?" I asked, not that it was really a question.

"Of course, where else would a guy like that have his office?" Yvette smiled.

I took Ace of Spades out of her holster and swapped out its current magazine with one fully loaded with banishing rounds. I chambered a round and put the gun back in its holster. The Incubi in Landers' office were in for a painful one-way trip back to whichever Infernal realm they had been summoned from.

When we entered the office building, I made a quick survey of the building's business directory. The place was infested with the offices of lawyers and business consultants. It was under the listings for financial consultants that I found Landers Goldweight's office. If it weren't for the seriousness of the situation, I would have laughed, but in this case it wasn't anywhere near funny.

As we took the elevator up to Landers' office, the shylock's muscle was still uncomfortably squeezed between Black Hat and the Dentist. The two of them were quietly menacing the Werewolf, whose name I still hadn't bothered to ask. Neither of them actually had to say or do anything to make it well understood that they had no qualms about hurting people. They're used to inflicting pain upon people, and usually it was not out of any sort of malice, but simply because it was part of their job description.

When we reached the door to Lander's outer office, the glass to the side of the door showed that the lights had been turned off. "Are you sure he's in there?" I asked the Werewolf as I grabbed him by the collar and pulled him close enough to smell his fetid breath. That was the problem with many Werewolves; sure, they could hide what they were on the outside, but often times they couldn't hide their smell. This one needed a box of breath mints.

"He's in there," the Werewolf yelped. "He never leaves."

I looked over at Black Hat. "If you would be so good as to knock," I said, motioning to the door.

Black Hat kicked the door so hard that the metal of the frame twisted as the door ripped away from its hinges.

As soon as I entered the outer office I could hear alarms going off in the inner office. It took me less than a second to realize that these alarms were designed to go off in case someone of power entered the office, and most of us fit that description. The only one who didn't was my client. Even Sarah would have set the alarms off because of the magickal eye I had given her to replace the one that she had lost.

Four Incubi in well-tailored suits showed up, which was their mistake. Just as they started to rush I put a banishing round into each of them so fast that you would have thought this was an action movie. The fact that there were more than the two Lander's rented muscle had told us about meant some dire consequences for him.

As the Daemons were being sucked painfully inside out I heard Yvette tell the Dentist to teach Landers' goon why it was a bad thing to lie to her, but not to kill him. She must have been in a good mood. I switched magazines in the Colt, no point in using expensive banishing rounds on a Human like Landers. Once again I motioned to Black Hat to kick in the inner office door, which he seemed more than happy to do.

As I walked into the inner office, that short, bloated toad of a shylock Landers made a huge mistake and gave me both barrels of a side by side 12 gauge. The two shells didn't do much to me, but they did ruin a perfectly good dress shirt, and I became fairly pissed when I realized that my trench coat hadn't been spared. I was mad because that coat had been tailor made to hide the shoulder holster and had cost me a few grand.

I grabbed the shot gun out of Landers' hands and hit him with the butt stock, which sent him sprawling. I then vaulted the desk and grabbed him off the ground by his collar and slammed him into his high backed office chair.

"I'm sorry Black! I didn't realize it was you!" he yelped in fear. He had already realized that he had just put me in a very foul mood. "I just heard the shooting out there and got scared. It was nothing personal."

"Yeah, yeah, whatever. You pay for a new shirt and coat and I'll forget the shotgun bit." I said sourly. I really had liked that trench, but I had to expect that kind of thing in my line of work. "Now back to the business at hand."

"What can I d..." Landers was cut off mid-sentence by a scream of pain as the Dentist removed one of the goon's teeth. "What the hell was that?!"

"That would be the Dentist working on that idiot you hired from me," Yvette said as she came to rest against the door frame. I hadn't heard her come in, but then again, she was one of the few people who could consistently get the drop on me.

"Dear Christ! Not you too!" Things just weren't going Landers' way tonight.

"Don't bother getting religious on me..." I started before I was interrupted by another scream. "It doesn't suit you."

"Okay, what do you want Black?" Landers asked. "You've kicked in both of my doors and the Dentist is removing Mikey's teeth, so I'm assuming this isn't a social call."

"Well it has to do with my client." I motioned for Sarah to bring in Jamie. "Now I have it on very good authority that you hired those whores known as the Ladies of the River to kill my client."

"Who told you that? It's a wild pack of filthy lies." Even if I hadn't already known the answer to the non-question, I wouldn't have believed him for a second. He always was a lousy liar.

"The Ladies told me themselves, right before I shot the shit out of them," I said, a happy note in my voice.

"Oh." Landers' face dropped so much that it looked as if he had aged a good twenty years in a couple of seconds. "Wait a second. Are you trying to tell me that you killed all of them?"

"My second time cleaning house of those cockroaches," I said with a smile.

"Why doesn't that surprise me? Everyone knows that you're a nasty piece of work, Black," Landers said dejectedly.

"What can I say? I need to keep my reputation going for being one of the biggest hard asses around. You know, the ultimate hard-boiled detective and all that," I said with a shrug. "However, that still doesn't answer the question of why you put a contract out on my client's head."

At about this time another scream came from the outer office. "Now, I'm going to ask you a simple question. Lie to me and I'll make a dental appointment for you."

"Shit! Okay, okay, whatever you want! I don't want that blood sucker looking at my teeth!" The sound of panic in the shylock's voice sounded like he was willing to be cooperative.

"Here's the question. Why do you want my client dead? I know she didn't come to you. So why do you want her dead so much that you were willing to work with the Ladies?"

"An idiot client welched on his debt, so I needed to let him know that I wasn't pleased." Well I had been right, not that I was surprised about that. "He had told me about this dumb broad at his job that he had a thing for, said that once he had that promotion he was after he would give her a promotion if she went out with him. Well, I can't get money out of a stiff, may as well try juicing a rock. So, I decided the best way to scare him into paying up would be to make her death as messy as possible." He turned to look at Jamie. "Look it wasn't anything personal you understand. It was just business."

"Don't worry, I understand," Jamie said so sweetly that I did a Loony Toons style double take. She held a hand out to Sarah. "Do you mind if I borrow your gun?"

Sarah pulled her .357 and handed it to Jamie. I had to admit that I was impressed. My client was quickly learning how to play by the rules of the circles of society that she had so recently been thrust into. She expertly cocked the gun and walked behind the desk to where I was standing over Landers. "No offense, but this is just business. I hope you understand," she said as she put a bullet into each of Landers' knees.

The shylock was screaming in pain, holding his shattered and bleeding knees as Jamie walked back over to Sarah and returned the gun. "Thanks for letting me borrow that. I've had the worst urge to shoot a bad guy since I found out what was going on," she said.

"Feeling better?" I asked her.

"Much."

"That bitch just..." Landers started before I jammed my heater under his jaw.

"I would really think hard about what you're going to say next," I snarled.

"Understood," Landers said with a hard swallow. "Perfectly understood."

"Okay Landers, I'm going to make you a deal," I said ominously.

"Can I at least put my knees back together before we talk?" Landers asked.

"Sure, I really don't care," I shrugged.

"Thank you," Landers pulled out a vial of some green ooze. Opening the vial, he poured the contents onto the remains of his knees. In a minute the blood and fragments of bone had disappeared and his knees were once again intact. "Okay then. What's the deal?"

"I hand over Fynch to you. You can collect whatever you want out of him, it's none of my concern."

"And in exchange?"

"You disappear," I said. "I don't care where you go. I just want you out of my city."

"That seems like an awfully steep price," Landers said.

I leaned in so close that I could smell his breath. "Let me put it this way Goldweight, you were going to kill an innocent person in order to collect from someone who welched on you. That I will not tolerate," I snarled. "If you stay in this city that green stuff you used on your knees won't help you heal where I put a bullet in your hide. Understand?"

Goldweight looked away from me and seemed to sink into his chair. "Perfectly, Black. I'll be more than happy to leave since you asked me so nicely."

I slapped him lightly on the cheek a couple of times. "Good boy, good boy."

"So, how are you going to get him for me?" Goldweight asked.

"Simple." I shrugged. "I'm going to kill Ms. Cross."

It was so quiet that you could have heard a pin hit the desk, since the carpet would have kept the pin from making any noise if it hit the floor. "You're going to do what?!" Jamie shouted the question in disbelief.

Yvette started laughing hard. "That's always going to be a classic."

"What do you mean?" Jamie asked, still sounding panicked. "I paid you to keep me alive. What do you mean you're going to kill me?"

"Don't worry. I'm not actually going to kill you. I'm just going to make it look like you were turned into a rather bloody mess," I said. "Unfortunately, I'm going to have to pretty much destroy your apartment, but that is the way things are going to work."

"Well, as long as I'm not actually going to be dead it shouldn't be too bad," Jamie said evenly. "How is this going to sit with the law?"

"Don't worry I'll take care of that. I've faked people's deaths in the past." I then turned to look at Landers. "So what do you want out of Fynch?" I asked.

"He owes me $500,000," the shylock said. "Three hundred from the initial loan, fifty in interest, and another fifty as down payment to the ladies, and another hundred from having to deal with you."

"And if he doesn't have the money?" I asked.

"I'll settle for his mortal soul," Landers sneered. "That bastard has caused me a lot of trouble since it got you involved."

"Well, I can handle that," I said. I then smiled at Jamie, Yvette, and Sarah. "Come on ladies, it is time to get ready to make a mess at Jamie's place."

Yvette stopped and turned to glare at Landers. "Before we go, I have one question?"

"Will it get you out of here if I answer politely?" Landers asked.

"Why did Mikey show up at Black's palace? There was no way you could have known Jamie would have been there."

"Francis the Fiddler called me and told me he had one of his boys follow the girl."

"How did he know who to look for?" I asked, realizing I may have to ventilate Francis just on principal.

"I keep him on retainer," Landers said. "I told him that it was possible she had gone to you and just to keep an eye out. He must have been mad that I had started outsourcing with the Court and kept out the fact that she was with the Countess."

"You are an idiot," the Countess said. "However, you're a decent client. Black will get you your money, but then you and I will have to have a pleasant talk about Mikey's future employment with you."

Landers turned green at the thought of having a pleasant talk with the Countess. I can't say as I blame him. During the Knights' War, her having pleasant conversations with Nazis often meant she would string them up with barbed wire, then rip out their intestines with her bare claws. She was almost as good at torturing people as I am, but when she shifts into her debased Werewolf form, she looks like Hell itself has taken physical shape to walk the Mortal world.

As we left I saw Lander's goon on his hands and knees looking for all of his teeth. I must have gotten so wrapped up in my conversation with Landers that I had stopped hearing the Werewolf's screaming. "Come on boys," Yvette said to Black Hat and the Dentist. "We have to go make it look like someone got butchered."

"So where to next, Black?" Yvette asked me as we headed down to her limo.

"Can you lend me four liters of blood?" I asked Yvette. "I want this to be as messy as possible."

"Oh that's easy," Yvette said.

"All from the same person?" I asked her.

"Of course. Would ruin the plan if there were multiple DNA samples in the evidence."

"Do I even dare ask why you would have so much blood from just one person?" Sarah asked the Countess.

"Oh it's nothing illegal, I assure you," Yvette said with a smile. "Some of my followers develop a taste for one donor over another. Since I have so many Humans who want to be part of the Court, they have to give blood for a while before I approve their change. So, yes, I can easily get enough blood from the same person to have enough for the illusion of a messy death."

"Still, it's getting late," I said. "We should probably let the Humans get some decent sleep before we do this."

"Good point," Yvette agreed.

"I'm not tired," Jamie protested.

"When was the last time you got a decent night's sleep?" I asked my client.

"I admit it's been a while, but I'm still awake enough to do this."

"No you're not. Now sleep." I slowly waved my hand in front of Jamie's face and she immediately fell asleep. I knew she wasn't going to be happy when she woke up, but she really did need the sleep.

"I should get some sleep as well," Sarah said. "Can you drop me off at my place?"

Yvette tapped on the window to the driver and had Sarah give him the address to her apartment. After we dropped off Sarah, we dropped off Black Hat, then the Dentist, then we headed to my place. Yvette said she was going to drop me off before she went home herself; I knew that was going to be a lie. She was going to stay in the house and keep me up talking about old times. She really could be a pest at times.

CHAPTER

"That was a dirty trick," Jamie said when I woke her up twelve hours after I had put her to sleep with a little charm.

"You needed the rest," I said calmly. "You've had a rough few days, and while I may not be a doctor, even I could tell that you needed some decent sleep."

"Yeah, yeah whatever." She didn't seem up to arguing with me, or she had realized that there was no point in not admitting the truth. "So what's the plan?"

"We're going to take a trip to your apartment so you can collect whatever you need in the immediate sense of time, since the police are going to cordon off your apartment for a while." Last time I had to do this for a customer it took over a week before they could get back into their house, no sense in making things harder on her than necessary.

"What do I tell my neighbors if we run into any of them?" It was a sensible question.

"Tell them you are going on a much-needed vacation, after a very stressful time at work the last few days." Jamie nodded. She seemed satisfied with the solution to the problem.

Twenty minutes after we arrived at Jamie's apartment, my client was heading out to her car with the spare keys to my house and carrying a couple suitcases. She was meeting Sarah there so that she would have some company while we destroyed her apartment. Black Hat was on hand to help; 'the Dentist' hadn't come since this wasn't really his style.

I gave the Werewolf free reign to have fun. He took on his half-wolf form and started shredding everything with his claws, and smashing through furniture, throwing over tables and bookshelves, and putting holes in the plaster. We then liberally smeared blood throughout the place, making sure it looked logically placed to fit with the shredded upholstery and carpet. Much of the blood was smeared around by Black Hat using his now oversized, fur covered hands as paint brushes. After thirty minutes of smash and destroy, Black Hat and I left. After making sure no one was around to hear it, I had the Werewolf kick in the door. All in all, it had taken a little over an hour to get Jamie packed up and for the Countess's hitter and myself to create a big enough mess to make everyone think my client was very much dead.

CHAPTER 9

Jamie, Sarah, Yvette, and I were watching the evening news when we saw the story about Jamie's apartment. The police had called my client's phone, which I had told her not to answer. We were going to keep her under wraps for a few days, at least until I had turned Fynch over to Landers. After the story aired I called a homicide detective in Minneapolis. I was fairly sure it wasn't going to go well.

"Detective Rogers, homicide."

"It's Black," I said.

"Can this wait, Black? I'm up to my nose in the Cross case," the detective said. "I'm sure you heard about it. Or have you been ignoring the news?"

"That's the reason I'm calling you," I said. "I need information about it."

"It's an ongoing investigation, Black, so don't bother asking. Now step off my case or I will arrest you."

"I'm still on your shit list, aren't I." I couldn't say I was surprised. I had solved several of his cases by going over his head and made him look only borderline competent.

"You bet you are," he seethed through obviously clenched teeth. "Now what do you want."

"I'm fairly certain I know who ordered the hit, I just need your help in tracking him down."

"What do you mean hit? That place was straight out of a nightmare. I've seen shit like it before and I'm almost dead certain there's a serial killer out there that no one is talking about."

"I have it on good authority that this was a pay for play hit. So how about it? You give me what I want I'll give you what you need."

"Why should I help you? If it was a hit, I should be able to find out who ordered it easily enough." Stupid and cocky. Truthfully I always wondered how he had made it to homicide in the first place.

"Tell you what. I'll make you a deal. You do exactly what I tell you to do and I'll give you all the evidence you need to wrap this up all neat and tidy. You'll get all the glory of solving this. No one will know I was involved."

"What do you really get out of this Black?"

"I'm working for a third party that wishes to remain anonymous at this time. As I said, you will get all the glory in the press, and on the force. My client gets the satisfaction of knowing who the killer was."

"Fine, then I'll work with that deal. What do you need?"

"I need you to track down Ms. Cross's boss. I'm almost dead positive that he is the key to this whole mess."

"You think he's the one who ordered the hit?"

"I never said that, did I? I just need you to find him for me, so I can have a chat with him."

"I can talk to him myself. Why should I let you have the fun?"

"Simple, I can make him crack faster than you can, and I won't even have to work him over. You see, I have a lot of evidence that could tie him to all sorts of problems. Don't worry, I'll hand all of that over to you as well, but I need to speak with him alone first."

"Deal. I find him for you, then I'm going to give you three hours to talk to him before you hand him over. Not a minute longer or I arrest you and your client for obstruction."

"Fine by me. I just want you to find him before he skips town."

CHAPTER 10

It took three days for the cops to find Fynch. During that time Jamie learned, much to my annoyance, not to draw to an inside straight. Still, I was taking enough of her money to not really want to steal any more playing poker. One nice thing was that she proved to be interesting to talk to and it still amazed me how well she adapted to the new world she had been thrust into.

I was bluffing with nothing more than garbage, ace high, when Rogers called me. "What have you got for me?"

"Fynch is holed up in a flea bag motel on West Seventh, a couple miles out of downtown St. Paul. That Pepto pink place. You know the one I'm talking about?"

"Yeah, I know the place." The motel was nothing more than a place to bring hookers. They changed the sheets too infrequently and charged by the hour. To rate the place as a flea bag was to give it higher marks than it deserved because fleas died ten steps into the door. It was close to the airport and the person running the place knew where to get well-made fake IDs.

"I'm going to go pick him up. Tell the guy who found him not to tail me when I take him out of there."

I headed out the door and got ready for a fun visit. More kicking down doors for fun. I pulled up in front of the motel and walked to the office, which was manned by a dope fiend named Franky Callaghan. His face barely changed when he first saw me; it took a few seconds until my face finally registered in his baked brain. "Shit! Black, what do want here?"

"Fynch, he showed up here not too long ago. What room is he in?"

"I don't know who you're talking about. No one named Fynch here." He lied to me.

"Maybe not anymore, but only because you set him up with that forger, Shutterbug," I snarled. "So what room is the low life shit in. He tried to kill my client and I intend to make sure he spends a long time in prison. Either you give him up to me now or I make it my business to shut this cheap roach motel down. I'll make sure you have no money to get your next fix of black tar. Now give him up."

"Crap! Okay Black. No need for threats like that. Room six. His new name is Howard Fischer," the dope fiend said.

"Key."

Franky handed me a key on a filthy key chain. "Here now, please don't bring the cops down on me."

"Next time don't play stupid with me, though in your case I'm more than willing to bet that you weren't acting." I picked up the key chain and headed over to room six.

I knocked on the door. "Mr. Fynch, Landers is looking for you. Now come on out or do I have to come in after you?"

There was no sound coming from the room so I opened the door slightly so as not to break anything when I kicked the door in. I heard an explosive "Oomph" from behind the door and a lamp crashed to the floor as the door rebounded off of Fynch's chest. I grabbed him by the arm and forced him up. "Come on Fynch. Up on your feet. Landers wants to talk to you."

"Let me go, I can pay you. Just tell your boss that you couldn't find me," he said desperately. He reached into his back pocket, grabbed his wallet and pulled out ten 'C' notes, which he waved in my face.

I knocked the hand out my face. "Save the money for Landers. You're going to need it."

"I'll double it, just let me go."

I jammed my heater into his ribs. "Sorry, we're going to talk to Landers. You see, right now Landers is sitting on evidence that says you're the guy who killed Ms. Cross. Now you hand over the money to him and he hands over the evidence on the guy who actually ripped her up."

"I don't have the money," he said.

"Well, well, well. You're just going to have to give up what you put up as collateral. Now come on. Let's go." I grabbed his shoulder and marched him to my car, never taking my heater out of his ribs.

Twenty minutes later we were in front of Landers' office door. I dragged Fynch into the office and shoved him into the chair across from Landers.

"That was a nasty business you did, wasn't it?" Landers asked him.

"I didn't do anything, that was you and your goons."

"You were the one who welched on our deal. I had to let you know I was displeased with you. If you hadn't been dumb enough to run from me, she would still be alive. So it really was you that killed her." He popped his knuckles. "Now, I'm going to offer you a deal. You pay me what you owe me and I don't hand over the 'evidence' that you made a mess of her."

"I don't have the money," Fynch said.

"You know I don't believe you." Landers kicked his feet up on the desk. "You see, I had another detective look over your accounts. So, what's in that safety deposit box at that small bank on Grand?"

"I don't know what you're talking about," Fynch said.

"You aren't in a good position," Landers said with a smile. "You see, my friend here called the police and told them he'd be able to hand over the killer in three hours. That was almost two hours ago. Now, what's in the box?"

"Gold," Fynch said quietly. "But not enough to pay all that I owe you."

"Well, then you know what I want," Landers said with an evil smile.

"How are you going to collect my soul when you weren't able to give me enough influence to get that promotion?" Fynch said defiantly.

Landers smiled. "It's not my fault you are that worthless. All I can do is stack the deck in people's favor. If you were worth anything you probably would have been able to get that job."

"Well let's get to work," I said. "I think it's time for you to talk." I grabbed Fynch round the head with both hands and ran through a spell that would make him tell us exactly what we wanted to hear. The recording was for the cops in case Fynch decided to get uncooperative with them.

I had a sorcerer friend who would act as Fynch's lawyer as well just to make sure everything went well. He would also collect the idiot's soul for Landers and that wrapped everything up neatly. Except for Rogers.

The detective was pissed as hell when he found out that the third party who had hired me was the same person whose death he was investigating. He was only half relieved that she was alive, but—it meant no glory for him. So, I was still on his shit list. I'd have to do something about that later, maybe get him out of homicide and on crossing duty in front of an elementary school.

CHAPTER

I was sitting in my office when Jamie walked in with the remainder of what she owed me, which was another two-fifty. I didn't want her money. I was hoping she would be willing to do something else for me. "I want to ask you a question," I said, handing her back her check.

"Um ... sure," Jamie said nervously. "What do you want to know?"

"I need a secretary. I was wondering if you would like the job," I said. "I'll pay you more than what you're getting paid now. So what do you say?"

Jamie looked at me in what appeared to be a slight state of shock. "You want me to what?" she asked.

"I would like to hire you," I repeated.

"But why me?"

"For several reasons," I started. "First, you're levelheaded. You know when to keep your cool and how to handle my friends. Second, you seem to have adapted well to this new circle of society, which you were so rudely thrown into. Most importantly having spent so much time with you over the last few days, I feel that we have formed some sort of bond and that we could work well together. So what do you say?"

Jamie cocked her head to one side and closed her eyes for a few seconds. Over the last few days I had come to realize that not only did that mean she was trying hard to remember something, but also that she was just giving something some serious thought. I held my breath as I waited for the answer. I really was hoping that she would say yes; she was just what I was looking for in a secretary. She was smart, calm, and could handle the people I dealt with. And she was very attractive, though I was fairly sure she wouldn't sit on my lap while taking dictation.

While Jamie was thinking. the phone rang in the office. Jamie picked up the handset. "Black Shadow Detective Agency, how can we help you?" Jamie asked as if she had worked for me for years.

Jamie nodded a couple of times. "I'll pass on the message." She then turned to look at me. "That was the Countess Blood Wolf. Your ride is here."

I sighed, two nights with a woman who wanted to be more than friends. This was going to be a dreadful two nights. Still, it could be worse. "Don't worry boss. I can manage the phone while you're on vacation," Jamie said with a smile.

"Welcome aboard."

THE MISSING APPRENTICE CAPER

CHAPTER

The August afternoon was almost unbearably humid as I sat in my office with my feet up on my desk, listening to the game on an antique radio. Close at hand I had a low-ball glass that had contained two fingers of bourbon an inning ago. On the perch just a few feet away was my familiar, a crow named Shadow, who had been passed down my family line for centuries. I was bored from not having had a case in three weeks. I wasn't hurting for money, considering. I owned the building my office is in. I was just bored.

The St. Paul Saints were up to bat in the bottom of the sixth against the Winnipeg Goldeyes, and had a comfortable lead. The home team had been in a bit of a slump and I was hoping this game would snap their six-game losing streak, especially since I had a hundred bucks on the line. I've always rooted for any team that held the name of the St. Paul Saints ever since the first one had formed back in late nineteenth century.

The Saints' catcher, Rich Mecardo, struck out just as the phone in the outer office rang. I heard my secretary answer the phone. "Black Shadow Detective Agency. How can we help you?"

I went back to listening to the game knowing that Jamie would page me if the phone call required my attention. Jamie's a good kid, she's just the kind of secretary a guy like me needs. She's level headed, brave, and I can trust her to think on her feet. And, she's always calm around my friends and clients, which was the main reason I hired her. There is also the fact that she's very pretty and has never commented on the seven-year-old Sports Illustrated swimsuit calendar that hangs on my wall showing the month of September. Never once.

I hit the intercom button as soon as it buzzed. "A Maurine Wells for you on line one. Says she has a missing persons case for you."

"Thanks, I'll take the call." I then looked at the mostly empty bottle on my desk. "And Sweetheart? Could you stop by the pharmacy and pick up a couple of bottles of cold medicine? Take it out of petty cash."

"Yes boss, I'll go over to Grand Street Liquors for you," she said sarcastically. At least she had stopped complaining about me calling her sweetheart.

I picked up the hand set of my phone and punched the button for line one. "Investigator Jason Black speaking."

"Hello Mr. Black," came a feminine voice. "My name is Maurine Wells and I was told that you might be able to help me."

"Depending on what your problem is, I'll do my best," I answered. I was hoping that her problem was one I could help with since I was starting to go a little stir-crazy. "Now, my secretary tells me that someone has disappeared?"

"It's my son, James..." There was a definite break in her voice. "He's disappeared and I have no idea what's happened to him." Something about the way she said it though sounded forced. As if she was trying to sound more worried than she was.

Now, I'm not one to take pleasure in another's misfortune, but this was going to get me out of the office and for that I was glad. "I take it you've talked to the police?"

"Oh yes. The detective took a look around my son's room and said he found some stuff that made it seem like it would be your type of case," she replied.

I wondered what kind of stuff her son had and why the police had sent her to me. Very rarely will a detective send someone my way, at least not openly They have too much pride for their own good sometimes. "What kind of stuff did they find that made them send you my way?"

"Well, the detective said there were some books on my son's shelves that were about magick or something." It had to have been Wallace who had gone out to her house. He was the only detective on any of the local forces who could even spot true books of the occult. Which was odd, since he had no ties to the Court of Night. He hung out at the Mystic Wolf and had studied a little magick. He knew a couple spells that were useful in his line of work. He also knew enough to get himself in trouble, but was smart enough to come to me if he got into that sort of territory. The weird thing was the last time I talked to him he was in homicide. What had he done to get stuck in missing persons?

"This detective, was he on the older side of middle age, and a bit on the heavy side?"

"Why yes. How did you know?" There was some surprise in Ms. Wells' voice.

"Wallace stops by to pick up a couple of my business cards every once in a while." At least one detective from just about every town and city in the Metro area had a couple of my cards floating around. Those cards were my main source of advertising. When I feel up to it and something major happens, I'll occasionally tick off the police by showing up to a fresh crime scene to start handing out the cards myself. Doing that always makes me the first suspect, but that's just the way things work.

"Now, before I come over to your place to start the investigation, I need to know one important thing. How old is your son?"

"He turns seventeen in a couple of months. Why?"

"I just needed to know if I was looking for a legal adult or not. It gives me an idea of what I can do once I've found him."

"I just want him back home," she said in a frail voice. "I'll pay you whatever you want."

"I'll come over then to start my investigation," I said.

"Please do. I haven't left here since he disappeared."

"Where is 'here'?" I asked.

"It's 416 Summit Ave," she said, which made me very happy. The entire length of Summit is a filthy rich part of town, meaning the kids who live there tend to have the means to get themselves in all sorts of interesting trouble.

"Give me half an hour and I'll be there with my standard contract," I told her. I switched off the game, and got ready to go out. Opening my gun safe, I pulled out my shoulder holster. Putting it on, I felt the comforting weight of my Colt, Ace of Spades, nestle up against me. I also pulled out a couple of magazines with different types of bullets, one of blessed silver, the other cold iron. I then slipped into my light suit jacket and carefully lifted my fedora off the coat tree. Despite the fact that it was the twenty-first century, the old noir detective style had never gotten out of my system.

I grabbed my satchel which contained all the tools of my trade and put a copy of my rich person contract in it. I keep several different 'standard' contracts on hand. I charge by what I think people can afford. Since this woman lived on Summit I picked out my thousand dollars a day contract with a five-day retainer. She had the money to pay me, so I was going to take it. I also had contracts for much less, for people who had little to spare.

I once took a case for a quarter for a little girl whose father had vanished. Turned out the dad had been disappeared by a cult, not a pretty ending to the case. The police still don't know what happened the night the five men involved had been ripped apart and their bodies smeared across the room. There had been bullet casings all over the place. Not one bullet had even touched me. It had been labeled as a cold case some seventy years ago. Just wish I could have done more for the kid.

Shadow landed on my shoulder and broke into my thoughts. *I know you always think about that case when you take on a case involving a child, but you have to let it go.*

"You say that all the time."

Do you think this case will work out? Shadow asked, speaking directly into my mind.

"I can always hope," I replied. "Sure it's probably nothing more than a spoiled rich kid running away to get attention. But it's possible he's gotten in way over his head and fallen in with the wrong crowd. But with any real luck it will be something completely different."

If I had any use for money, I'd lay twenty to one odds that the kid's a simple rich-shit runaway. Shadow could be a pain and sounded like my bookie at times. However, he was always helpful in his own way, plus he had been in the family for more generations than I cared to think about. In fact, he could no longer remember how old he was himself.

"I wouldn't take those odds," I replied. "He probably is just a runaway. But it's a case and I've been sitting on my ass for far too long. Now let's not keep Ms. Wells waiting."

Before I left the office I scribbled a quick note on the memo pad on Jamie's desk to let her know the address of where I had gone. She was always worried about me and bitched her head off if I didn't let her know what was going on. As irritating as those chewing outs could be, I loved her for 'em. Showed me that she was just about as loyal to me as any familiar could be. She could also do some things that no animal familiar could ever do, no matter how clever. Shadow couldn't organize a spread sheet for the life of him.

CHAPTER

Fifteen minutes after leaving the garage, I parked my '41 Buick Special outside of Ms. Wells' house. I gave the home my best appraising look and figured that even in the current crappy housing market this place could still probably sell for well over a million. The Victorian mansion was fairly large, not as big as some of the houses on the street, but big enough.

Shadow hopped off his perch on the front seat of the car and landed on my shoulder. *What do you think boss?*

"Well, if he lives here, his mother almost definitely has the kind of money that would give the kid the means to buy his way into some serious trouble." It was obvious to both Shadow and I that any kid who lived here may be the kind who sometimes needs to do something extreme to get attention. Maybe the mother worked so much that she was never home. Or, just as likely, she had become such a socialite that she was more interested in her parties than her own kid. For me, it really didn't matter the reason he was gone. I was just being paid to find him, and as long as the check cleared, I'd do just that.

I walked up to the front door, which was enhanced with a stained-glass transom window, and knocked. When the door opened, I found myself looking at a woman who appeared to be in her mid to late forties and had not aged gracefully. She was fairly heavy and her face was showing definite signs of aging, a fact that she was trying unsuccessfully to hide with make-up. Her shoulder length black hair was shot through with grey. It was possible that when she was younger she had been pretty, but I doubted it.

"Mr. Black?" she asked in the frail voice that had come from the phone. I could feel her appraising look run over me. From the perpetual five o'clock shadow, to the grey fedora that hid a white streak running through my black hair, I looked every part the noir detective.

"I take it that you are Ms. Wells?" I asked in return.

"Yes. Please call me Maurine. Thank you for coming so quickly. The police detective who came to check things out said that if anyone could help me it was you. I've barely slept since my son disappeared. I need you to find him." She gave Shadow an appraising look. "Um, what's with the crow?"

I could feel Shadow glare at her as I said. "He's my partner, Shadow, sort of like a police dog in a K-9 unit. He sometimes spots things I miss. Don't worry though, he's house broken and won't make a mess. He comes with me on every case."

"Okay." Maurine seemed nervous. "I guess if that's what it takes to find my son."

I trust her about as far as I can throw you.

I nodded in reply. Something didn't seem right but I couldn't place my finger on it. "Well how about you show me his room so I can start my investigation. But before that I need you to sign this contract." I pulled the contract out of the satchel and let her scan over the fine print. After two minutes of reading she signed her name next to the 'X'.

As I walked into the house I saw several pictures of a young teenager on the wall. "Is this James?" I asked.

"Yes it is, but they're a couple years old," she said. "However I do have a more recent picture of him."

"That would be great," I said.

My client handed me a photograph. The kid looked as if he had been up for a couple of days when the picture had been taken. His brown eyes were red from fatigue, and there were dark circles under his eyes. Truthfully it looked almost as if he were addicted to something that no one should be putting into their system. The only thing that looked right about him was his hair, which was neatly parted to the left. "Handsome kid," I lied.

"Thank you. He's always been a little charmer with the girls." Again there was something in her voice that didn't sound right.

I looked around the first floor for a few more minutes, not that I really expected to find much. In truth I was just trying to make it look like I was doing everything I could to earn the $5,000 check in my pocket. The first floor was tasteful, if you find wasting money on overpriced crap tasteful.

"I'd like to see your son's room now," I said after fifteen minutes of poking around.

"Please follow me."

I followed her to the second floor where the bedrooms were but I had no need for her to show me which room belonged to her son. The scent of magick coming from his room was palpable to my half-Daemon senses. I opened the door immediately found the source of the magick.

In a bookcase on the left wall was a shelf containing books on the occult. Not just the modern stuff written by new age hacks, but the real stuff. There were three books that sent chills down my spine to know that a kid had somehow gotten a hold of. *The Circles of Darius*, *Riding the Soul*, and *The Book of Daemonic Tongues* are books that should never be seen by anyone without many years of serious experience in the occult. There was a fourth book I didn't recognize, which was odd. I thought I knew all of the major books on the ancient occult out there so I was confused and I definitely didn't like the look of it.

The newest of the books, *Riding the Soul* hadn't been published in English since the mid-eighteen-hundreds, and this was the Latin translation, which was even older.

The Book of Daemonic Tongues was worrying in that it meant that the kid may have tried to summon a Daemon and would have the misplaced belief that he would be able to control it. Only the most experienced of summoners should even think of trying such a thing, at sixteen he'd get ripped apart if it had appeared.

The oldest, *The Circles of Darius*, had last been published in England about a hundred years before the first thirteen colonies became the United States. Truthfully the English translation is a lousy one, but the original was written in Aramaic and there are few people nowadays who can read that ancient language. I have copies of all of the translations of the book. Some are better than others, but the English is the worst. Even though it's a bad translation, it is good enough to be trouble since the pictures of the different circles themselves are accurate.

I flipped through the fourth book looking for a publishing date, or even a name. I was willing to guess it to be from early eighteenth century. Eventually I found a name, *The Lost Letters of the Angels*. I skimmed through it and was surprised with what I saw. It was a dictionary translating the oldest known human language into the vocabulary and spelling of Victorian era English. The weird thing was that at the time this book looked to have been written, no one had even known this language existed so how was it possible that it could exist? I showed the books to Shadow. "What do you think buddy?"

That I'm glad I didn't put any money down with you. This kid could be in some very serious trouble. He was only confirming what I was already thinking. *There is no way he would run away and leave those four books.*

I had to know if any books had been taken by Wallace, though I doubted he would have taken them if he had referred her to me. The books weren't direct evidence of anything, but sometimes Wallace was a bit too curious for his own good. I took out my phone and punched in his number.

He picked up on the third ring. "Hey Jason," he said, having obviously checked his caller ID. "Are you at the Wells' place?"

"Just got here a few minutes ago. I need to ask you a question."

"Sure," he said with an audible shrug. "What do you need to know?"

"Did you take anything out of the kid's room?" I asked him. "There are a few books here that are really bad news and I need to know if anything is missing from the collection."

"You know me better than that Black." His tone betrayed his annoyance that I'd even ask such a question. "I would never remove evidence that you'd need for your type of work. I took a quick look around his room for any hints of where he might have gone. As soon as I saw those books I knew it was your type of case and left. Other than that I just took the basic facts and a couple of recent pictures of the kid."

"I just had to ask, Kevin. I'm going to take a look around here and see what I can figure out. How about we meet up at the Mystic Wolf around ten and compare notes."

I could almost see the police detective nod before he answered me. "Okay. But you owe me a drink for doubting me."

"Done and done. I'll see you at ten," I said as I ended the call.

I took out four large pieces of white silk from my satchel and wrapped each book and placed them in my satchel. If the kid had done the proper ritual to make them his, I could use them to find him. I wasn't sure what I'd do with the books after that. They were far too dangerous for people to get their hands on, especially *The Circles of Darius*. That one I'd probably destroy outright. The other three I'd probably keep in my private collection. I might find a serious student of the occult who could possibly use them. Until then I needed them as they were.

Now that I found the books on magick, I needed to find the altar where he may have practiced what he found in them. I looked around the room again and found nothing of interest, so it must have been somewhere else.

"What do you think Shadow? He had to have had an altar somewhere in this house, I doubt he'd go somewhere else."

Well, he would have wanted to go somewhere where he wouldn't have been disturbed, and where it wouldn't be likely to be found even when he wasn't there. The idea was fairly obvious and I kicked myself for the inability to think like a teenager. I hadn't been this kid's age for well over two centuries.

I looked over at Ms. Wells. "Is there any part of this house where you seldom go?"

"Well, I haven't been in the attic since early January when I put away the Christmas decorations," she said.

Sounds good master, Shadow said with a dip of his head to emphasize his point.

"Where is the door to the attic?" I asked.

Maurine turned around and pointed to a door directly across the hallway across from James's room. "It's up those stairs."

When I opened the door to the stairs I knew I was on the right track as I was immediately hit by the smell of stale incense smoke, dragon's blood to be exact. The use of dragon's blood was not an unexpected choice, since it's a commonly used incense for occult purposes. To my Daemon born senses, I could get a hint of old, weak magicks. Now that I had an idea where it was, it was time to find the altar. At the top of the stairs, I stopped and took a pendulum out of my coat pocket to help me find what I was looking for since the smells were so old they had diffused throughout the room. "Find the altar," I whispered to it.

Walking into the middle of the attic, I held the pendulum at arm's length and slowly turned around watching how large an arc it described. The larger the arc, the closer I was to the altar. Like any attic it had its typical junk; boxes of stuff that should have been thrown out years ago, and knick-knacks that probably still had meaning for their owner but not enough to keep them on display. Probably a couple pieces of art that had once decorated the refrigerator when James was younger, back when he was proud of the finger painting that only he could tell was a horse. Call it the cynicism of old age, but I couldn't see myself holding on to crap like that. Then again, I'm not a parent.

As I made my way into a back corner of the attic my pendulum was swinging wildly so I knew I was close. I shoved a clothing rack full of dresses that looked like they were from the early eighties out of my way and found the altar. It was a large coffee table covered by a black silk cloth. On it there were a couple of pictures, one of Ms. Wells. The other picture was of a man who bore a striking resemblance to the picture I had seen of James.

The picture of Ms. Wells had been written on with a quill pen using what appeared to be blood. The writing was so grammatically incorrect that it was barely understandable, and the handwriting was like that of a third grader just learning cursive. Still, it was legible enough to show exactly what it was: a rather nasty, blood magick curse against James' mother. Because of the quality of the writing and grammar there was no way the curse would have worked, no matter how much blood was used. But the intent was clear.

The picture of the man I took to be James' father was draped with dove feathers that were held in place with blood. Again, the charm was poorly written and grammatically incorrect, but the intent was still clear; the kid wanted to protect his father from something. The weird part was that the charm looked as if it was to be used against magick. What worried James concerning his father wasn't quite clear, but he was obviously worried about something. It was somewhat odd using blood magick to form a charm of protection, but not unheard of since, a person's own blood can make magick easier to cast.

So the question became, what did the kid have against his mother? "What do you think Shadow?"

Well this kid is more than a little pissed off at his mother. He wants her dead.

"No shit, tell me something other than the obvious."

Well let's assume that the guy in the picture is James' dad. Maybe he wants to go live with him, so much so that he'd kill his mother to get his way. It was an obvious assumption. *But the spell of protection makes no sense.*

"It could be that the father isn't doing well in some way or another and the kid is doing all that he can to help. He may just be using the wrong spell."

I guess that could be a possibility, my familiar agreed. *But what if the charm is the correct one?* he asked.

"Then I guess he feels that his father is under some sort of magickal attack and he is trying to do everything he can to help. Still, that doesn't explain why he wants his mother dead." I pondered the question of why for a while, but decided that I could find out the answer when I found the kid.

I took the two pictures of the kids parents and put those in my satchel, along with the books. I decided that I was going to have to toss the kids room to see if I could find any more clues as to where the kid might have gone. It was likely that Wallace hadn't done a thorough check of the kid's room before he spotted the books so there were probably still some clues that were worth checking out.

Once I was back on the second floor I warned my client that I was going to be making a huge mess out of her son's room. She seemed about to object but I told her that it was all necessary if I was to have a chance to find James. I didn't tell her what I had already found, no reason to tell her that her son wanted her dead. My client quickly agreed to let me toss the place since it could lead to clues that would safely return her son to her. Once again I got an odd feeling from her, but I still was having a hard time reading her.

"Where should we start?" I asked Shadow when we entered James' room.

Well in movies and television kids tend to hide things they want to keep secret under their mattress. I decided to follow my familiar's advice since he watched that kind of stuff more than I did. I'll take a good radio show over anything on TV any day.

I flipped the mattress over and had a look. Nothing. The next thing I did was rifle through his dresser. Not much was in there other than a couple of old dirty magazines. Hormones ... I next searched his desk. In the top drawer I found his wallet, yet another sign that he hadn't run away. The wallet yielded up my first solid clue, a paycheck stub from my friend Felix's occult supply store. The check was for thirty-two hours over a two-week time frame, with a fairly large hourly wage. I should have guessed that Felix was probably involved as soon as I had seen those four books. Not many people would have access to the three books I knew let alone the one I didn't, but Felix was definitely one of them. The question then came to one of what Felix was doing with an employee as young as James? In order to answer that question, I was going to have to ask Felix directly, making his shop my next stop.

The next thing of interest in the desk was the kid's cellphone. It was locked with a pattern password so it didn't do me any good at the moment, but I had friends who could crack the password. If James was anything like other kids he would have just about his entire life on the phone. In the old days a Rolodex or address book were great leads. Cellphones were even better because they not only served as address books, they also kept a record of who you called and when you called them. With it I'd be able to track down the people the kid had recently talked to.

After another twenty minutes of searching, I didn't turn up anything more of interest. I was happy to have found that check stub; it was a solid lead, and should be very useful in tracking the kid down. Before I left the house I decided to ask my client a couple of more questions.

"Did James have a part time job?" I asked. It would have been hard to explain away that much time unless my client was oblivious to what her son did with his time.

"Not that I'm aware of," she said. "But now that you mention it, he did seem to have more money than what I give him as an allowance, and his dad really sends money to him, only a couple times a year."

"Now, what about his father?" I asked. "Does he have a good relationship with his father? Is it possible that he may have gone to see him?"

"They're barely on speaking terms," she said. "Ever since that bastard left us for his trophy wife and moved back to Dublin, they really haven't had much to say to each other. Truthfully, I think the only reason James has anything to do with the man is because of the money."

Fat lot she knows. My guess was that James either had more contact with his father than my client wanted to admit, or he had found some way of talking to him behind her back. "What's your ex's name? Do you have a phone number I can reach him at? This is just so that I can rule him out as a suspect in James' disappearance."

"The bastard's name is Dylan, Dylan O'Malley, and no, I don't have his phone number. He pays child support on time so I never have any reason to get ahold of him." Her tone was positively venomous. "If you want his number it would probably be easiest to go through the courts. If you need me to I'll be happy to sign any paperwork they need for a release."

"Well that should be all I need from you at the moment. I'm going to make some calls and see if I can turn anything up, and then I'll do some shoe leather investigating," I told her. I was going to keep her in the dark about certain matters until I knew more about what was going on. With that spell that the kid had tried to cast against his mother I wanted to tread carefully. My duty was not only to my client but now to her son as well. Things were running deeper than I had first suspected. A simple runaway wouldn't be too bad, but this wasn't that. "If you can think of anything else that may be of help to me give me a call."

As we left Shadow asked me a question, the answer to which should have been obvious to the feather brain. *Where to next master?*

"I'm going to go have a chat with Felix," I told him. "If the kid was hiding his job with my old friend I want to know why."

Sounds reasonable, Shadow agreed.

CHAPTER

We got into the car and were soon heading down to Dinky Town in Minneapolis. The college district had always been good business for Felix; more than a few students sought help from him when it came to passing their exams. He had moved his shop twice since it had first opened, each time for expansion, but it had never left the street it was on. It was in a great location and had become a bit of an institution in the area. We got there with about ten minutes to spare before it was closing time, which was perfect for my needs. I didn't want anyone to overhear my talk with Felix, especially if I had to rough him up a bit to get the information I needed.

As soon as a couple in their mid-fifties walked out of the store, I walked in. I stepped over the laser beam that triggered the bell and quietly padded down the stairs to the basement store. Using a little magick, I altered the probability of being seen by anyone to virtually nil and entered the back room of the shop, which was cut off from the rest of the store by a simple curtain. There was no need for Felix to lock up inventory since it was a well-known fact that everything in the store was jinxed—and the jinx would only be lifted by paying for it. In fact, there was even a sign that read, "All Shoplifters Will Be Ritually Cursed." They always thought it was a joke until the jinx took effect and they were cursed with bad luck until they returned and paid for whatever it was that they had stolen.

I left Shadow in the car, since he's allergic to the type of incense that Felix is always burning. The incense was there to hide the smell of some of the mustier books that had been around for a long time. The books you had to know about if you wanted to look at them. It also covered up the odor of some of the more interesting ceremonial components that were used by more powerful magick users.

When I heard Felix lock the door I waited for him to return to the register to make my presence known to him. "Hello Felix," I said coolly.

"How did you do that?" Felix asked in a stunned voice.

"Showing up in your store like this?" I asked. "It was fairly easy."

"No, knowing that I was about to call you," Felix said. "You did know that I was about to call you, didn't you?"

Now it was my turned to be confused. "Why were you about to call me?" I asked him.

"I've got a missing persons case for you," he said.

"Let me guess, a kid named James Wells." I doubted that he could have meant anyone else.

"Okay if you didn't know that I was going to call you before you showed up, how did you know who was missing?" he asked, clearly puzzled.

"I've already taken the case from his mother," I told him.

"Let me guess, you found his pay stubs." The tone of his voice made it clear that it wasn't a question.

I merely nodded. "So you don't know where he is either," I said.

"Wish I did, he's been missing for six days, both from work and from training. He was supposed to be at the ceremony last full moon but he didn't show," Felix said. "I got worried then. He's never missed a training night before, not even when he was running a fairly high fever. But to not even call! To put it mildly, I was fairly pissed, but then he didn't turn up for work two days, and still no call. He's been so excited about everything, from training to work, that I'm dead certain that something must have happened to him."

I was getting an odd read off of Felix; there was something he wasn't telling me. What was going on with this kid that was causing people to be less than truthful about him? Whatever it was, I was getting increasingly worried about him.

"Well you're not the only one who's worried about him," I said. "His mother has hired me to look for him."

"That fat old cow?" Felix spat. "From what James has been telling me about her I'm surprised that she called you. I don't know all of what's going on between them, but I know it's not pretty."

"I can show you exactly how un-pretty it is," I said. I took the two pictures out of my satchel and placed them on the counter next to the cash register. Felix examined the two pictures for a while he then took off his glasses and rubbed the bridge of his nose.

"Can't say I'm pleased with him if he wrote that spell," he said. "His grammar is atrocious and the handwriting looks as if he has palsy, which he doesn't. I thought I taught that kid better."

"You're not mad about the fact that he tried to make a curse that nasty?" I asked with a fair amount of surprise.

"Only slightly, however I can't say that I'm the least bit surprised," he said slowly. "If only half of what he has been telling me is true about his relationship with his mother, and I'm fairly sure he's left a lot out, then I definitely can't say that I'm surprised."

"What sort of stuff has he been telling?" I asked.

"Well, for one thing, she's apparently been trying to drive a wedge between him and his father. The kid has been able to get around that to some extent, but his mother has made it hard for him." Again it felt like he was only giving me half the truth.

I was surprised, in this day of modern technology blocking communication between people was getting harder. From cellphones, messaging apps, and only the Gods knew how many email platforms. "What has she been doing?"

"Well apparently she had a friend of hers hack all of his email accounts, save for his work account. I'm positive the only reason that one hasn't been hacked is that it was put together by Gregory Dante," Felix said.

"As in the Silicon Slave 'Inferno's Plague'?" I asked him. Dante and I knew each other well enough to say 'hi' when we passed each other at the Mystic Wolf. We traveled in different circles so our paths had never crossed and both of us liked it that way. Whenever I needed the help of a technomancer, I would call on a woman known in the world of Silicon Slaves as "Hell Fire's Dame." I had helped her out a few years ago by tracking down a friend of hers who had suddenly disappeared off the grid. Because of that I knew I could trust her to some extent. All things being fair though, because this was Dante's work, it'd be easier to go straight to the source for what I needed.

"That's the one," Felix confirmed. "He's a regular and I hired him awhile back to help me upgraded my website. I was having trouble with the old one being too slow and hard to update. So Gregory put a new one together in a few hours that would probably have taken a regular programmer a couple of weeks to build. As part of it I asked him to make an email service for the business, and lo and behold the damn thing is pretty much impossible to hack."

"Good for the kid then," I said, more to myself then to Felix. "Can you get me access to it?"

"You'll have to talk to Inferno's Plague for that. And use that name; he hates being called Gregory."

"How do I get ahold of him?" I asked. "He and I don't run into each other much at the Mystic Wolf."

"I'm surprised you see him there at all, he doesn't get out much. Here, let me get you his phone number," Felix scribbled a thirteen-digit number on a piece of paper. "You'll have to text him. He doesn't like talking on the phone."

"Why am I not surprised?" It wasn't a question and Felix knew I wasn't talking to him. "Anything else I should know about Inferno's Plague?"

"Nothing really, just tell him that you're working for me and not the kid's mother. Other than that I can't much help you," Felix said. "Just do me a favor and find him. He's a good student with a lot of natural talent. I'd hate to hear that something happened to him."

"I'll do what I can," I said and then left the shop.

So we're going to text Dante now I take it? Shadow asked as soon as I got back to the car. He had obviously used my ears to listen in on the conversation.

"Am I really that easy to listen in on?" I asked him.

Master you're an easier read than all those dime store pulp novels you used to read way back when, the crow said.

"Eavesdropper," I muttered.

I need to find out what's going on some way, the crow said. *Your mother never complained about it.*

"How many times do I have to remind you that I'm not my mother?" I asked him. The question was futile since I knew that he would always compare me to her.

I'll make you a deal. Start treating me more like your mother did and I'll stop, the crow said with only a little humor in his voice.

"Stuff it, bird brain," I told him. "Now leave me alone for a second while I text Dante."

I took out my cell phone and slowly typed a message to Inferno's Plague. It took me almost five minutes to write something I could have said out loud in thirty seconds. I had to go back and retype several words because of hitting the wrong 'buttons'. Damn I hate smart phones. Whoever came up with the brilliant idea of texting should be dragged out into the street and shot.

"Inferno's Plague, I need your help. James Wells has disappeared and I need to get into his phone and email. Please let me know where I can find you and how much this is going to cost me.' It took me two texts to tell him what I need from him. Stupid technomancer.

After a few minutes I got a reply. "Mystic Wolf 8. Will tell you then."

That worked into my schedule just nicely since I was going to meet up with Wallace there at ten anyways. I checked the clock on the dashboard and saw that it was twenty past seven—I would have plenty of time to get to the bar.

CHAPTER 4

I arrived at the Mystic Wolf at quarter to eight and found a seat at the bar. After a couple of minutes, the bar owner's daughter, Sam, who was a bartender herself, spotted me. "What'll it be Jason?" she asked.

"Two fingers of bourbon, neat," I ordered.

What about me master? Shadow asked.

"Can I get a couple ounces of raw steak as well for Shadow?" I asked.

Sam looked at the crow and gave a slight shudder. "That shouldn't be a problem, but wouldn't he like it cooked at all?"

"No, he likes it raw," I told her.

"Whatever you say." I saw Sam punch a few buttons into a computer cash register and then walk to the back of the bar to pour me a couple shots of bourbon.

While she was getting my drink I looked around the bar, which tonight had taken the form of an old blues and jazz club. On stage was a new band, The Strange Heroes, kicking out some pretty good tunes. I hadn't seen them before. I wondered if they were new to the area or just a group of talented kids who had finally summoned up the courage to send a demo to Brisbane, the chief God of the bar's pantheon, in hopes of getting a real gig. Without a doubt they had another in with the bar owner, because unless my guess was way off, they were directly connected with the Court of Night. The guitarist / vocalist was definitely a Vampire and looked a bit like Brian Setzer when he had been with the Stray Cats, right down to the guitar. Slamming his way through a great drum solo was a werewolf in full Lycanthropic form. The only surprising thing was that slap bass was being played by an empty set of clothing. Either someone had recreated the potion that had created the invisible man, or it was a Ghost that liked getting dressed up. Either way it was odd that it was playing music with members of the Court. Still, it didn't really matter since they were pretty damn good; I'd pick up their CD before the night was over.

As much as I was enjoying the music, I wasn't there to listen to them. I was here to meet up with Dante and he wasn't here yet. It was still early though, and from his rep, 'Inferno's Plague' had a habit of showing up late to appointments.

Soon enough Sam put a lowball next to me with my bourbon. "Want me to put this on a tab or are you going to pay as you go?"

I reached into my wallet, took out my credit card and handed it to her. "Start a tab, I'm going to be here for a while." Sam took the card and swiped it, then handed it back to me.

I kept my eyes on the door for a while and at quarter past eight saw Dante walk in. I polished off the bourbon and walked over to where the technomancer was standing. "Hello Inferno's Plague. Thanks for coming," I said, holding out a hand for him to shake.

Dante looked at my hand for a few seconds as if trying to remember what it meant to shake hands. He finally shook it and then made a rather odd remark. "Don't get out much anymore. Sort of forget certain things." When he finally looked at me long enough for me to get a good look at his eyes, I noticed that they looked like the snow you get on old TVs when they're not getting a signal. Guess that's what happens to technomancers after too much time plugged into a computer grid.

"Join me in a drink?" I asked him. "I'll even pay."

"Um, yeah, a drink." Dante looked confused for a few seconds, making me wonder when he had last unhooked himself from the grid long enough to go anywhere. He motioned to get the attention of a bartender. "Plain club soda," he ordered as soon as Sam got to us.

Sam shrugged at the unusual order but said nothing as she grabbed a highball glass and the drinks gun, then hit the button for the carbonated water. As soon as the glass was topped off she handed it to the Silicon Slave. "There you go. Now who's paying?"

"Put it on my tab," I said quickly before Dante did something weird to the registers by paying the tab without pulling out an old-fashioned credit card.

"Let's find a table," I said to Dante.

"I'll have someone take the steak over to your table in a bit," Sam said as we left the bar.

As soon as we found an empty table I motioned for Dante to take a seat, then sat down across from him. "So, the Wells kid disappeared?" the Silicon Slave asked.

I nodded. "So it seems."

"So where do I come in?" Dante asked, in a distant tone of voice. "I barely knew the kid other than that he works for and is an apprentice to Felix."

I hadn't expected Dante to know much about the kid, but that wasn't what I needed him for. "I need your help getting into his electronics," I said. "His phone has a symbol lock on it so I have no way of unlocking it. Plus, I need access to his email, which according to Felix, you made just about un-hackable."

"And so, you came to me," Dante said, with an almost amused voice. "Don't you usually work with that tramp Hell Fire's Dame?"

Great, just what I needed, Dante was going to start a pissing contest with another Silicon Slave who wasn't here. "Well, I'm not about to bring someone to step on your territory," I said, trying to keep on Dante's good side. Whenever Silicon Slaves get into pissing contests, parts of the net start screwing up for the better part of a day. For the most part these guys don't play well together. It's a completely different story when they team up. Then they can really put the hurt on someone ... and anyone they ever had any contact with.

"Okay, I'll do it for you, and I'm going to cut you a deal since you're working for Felix," he said in a tone of voice I didn't trust. I was sure that whatever he was going to charge was going to be the going rate, reduced because I was working for Felix, but also raised because I usually go to a competitor. We may know each other well enough to say hi to each other, but we weren't friends. Still, I needed his help and he knew it. Maybe I should have gone to Hell Fire's Dame and let her hack him so that she could prove a point, but that would have made me an enemy of Dante's if he ever found out who had hired her, and I really didn't need that kind of bullshit.

"What's the damage total going to be?" I asked in a resigned voice.

"A thousand." Dante smiled, a smug smile that I wanted to slap off his face with the butt end of Ace of Spades. But I was at his mercy. My friend would have done it cheaper to prove a point but this way was quicker.

"Deal. Now let's start with the phone," I said.

Dante held out his hand. I was about to give him the phone until he said, "Payment first."

I handed over my credit card. "If you take out one cent over the thousand we agreed upon, I'm going to trash the most important piece of hardware you use."

"I could easily replace any computer of mine you destroy," he said haughtily.

"I was talking about the one between your ears," I said with a rather nasty smile.

The way Dante swallowed made me realize that he had indeed been thinking of doing just that. "There is no reason to resort to threats," he said a little too hastily.

"Good." Having just made things clear I handed him my card. He looked at the front of it, then flipped it over to look at the back and returned it to me. "Don't you need a card swipe?"

"Those are so passé," he said dismissively. "Now let's see the phone."

I gave him James's phone. Dante looked at it for a second and then blinked. Suddenly the screen came to life and random patterns flashed across the screen so fast that I could barely discern one from another. Soon the patterns ceased to flash and one held. It was then replaced by a blank pattern screen. Dante handed it back to me. "Enter whatever pattern you want on it now," he said.

I drew a quick pattern on the phone and once it was accepted I put it in my pocket. "Okay, now what about the email?" I asked him.

"Do you have a microphone on your computer?" the Silicon Slave asked me.

"Of course, I'm not a complete luddite," I said in a slightly annoyed voice. "I may be old but I keep up with the times."

"Fashion not withstanding," Dante said and smiled.

"Just remember who's paying," I reminded him.

Dante handed me a small digital voice recorder and a piece of paper with a website, an email address, and two letter-number combinations with the word *audio* between them. "Okay here's what you do. Type in the first part of the combination, then after the prompt which says 'combination not accepted,' play the audio recording, then enter the second password. Simple as that."

"Cute," I said. "Anything else I should know?"

"Yes, you only have two shots at either number. If you screw it up there is an automatic data dump, if that happens you have to come to me. And of course, there will be a fee." The smile he gave me was sleazy enough to make me want to hit him for the second time in the last two minutes.

"Remember what I said about destroying hardware if you try and screw me on this," I told him with my own smile. I didn't trust him. You should never trust a Silicon Slave with too much information. The main thing you sometimes had to remind them was that their bodies were helpless when they were jacked up into the web and trying to screw you over.

"No tricks Black," he said, raising his hands slightly in a sign of surrender.

One of the Succubus waitresses, a middle-eastern looking girl who went by the name of Sasha, arrived with Shadow's steak. "Here you go.

One raw steak," she said sweetly and with a sly wink that earned her a better tip. "Can I get you two anything else?"

"I'll have another double of bourbon," I said. "But my friend here was just about to leave. Wasn't he?"

"Guess I was," Dante said, getting up out of his chair. "Catch you later Black."

"Good bye," I said to his retreating back. "And good riddance," I muttered once he was out of ear shot.

"Never did like that guy," Sasha said.

"Oh?"

"He's a lousy tipper. Not at all like you," she said breathily, maybe two inches from my ear, once again increasing the size of her tip. There was a reason Brisbane had hired Succubae to work as waitresses.

"Sweet of you to say," I smiled. "As for my drink?"

"Just a couple of minutes, sweetheart." She flexed her wings, stirring a light wind which felt like a hand caressing the back of my neck. I closed my eyes and reminded myself of what the two women in my life, that both wanted to be more than friends, would do if they had just witnessed this.

It was an hour wait for Wallace to show, during which time I listened to the band sing several songs, including a pretty damn good one about a voodoo priestess of New Orleans. I actually happened to know the lady they were singing about. She was an interesting character I had met once while tracking down a guy who had turned the sister of a client of mine into a proper zombie. She had been most helpful and kept good rum in stock.

Sasha had made two more passes at me while I was waiting for Wallace, which was truthfully getting rather annoying by the time Wallace showed. "Kevin. Over here," I called with a wave of the hand.

"Hey Jason, how is it going?" Wallace asked sliding into the chair across from me.

"Not too bad. How's the wife?"

"Well, she's still my wife," he said. The detective's marriage had been rocky for the entire twelve years I had known him.

"Going to end it?" I asked.

"It's really up to her, but it looks that way. She moved in with her sister about three weeks ago," he said with a noncommittal shrug.

"Didn't know things were that bad between the two of you," I said. It was a just a supportive lie. I probably knew better than he did how bad it was. I also knew that she wasn't staying with her sister.

"It's probably worse than that," he said after a brief pause. "At least the kids are all grown and moved out so I won't have to pay child support. Still, she'll get half of everything, but at least I won't have to listen to her constant nagging about fixing the sink, or whatever else she can think of."

At that time the waitress returned with another bourbon for me and a menu, having apparently spotted the police detective. "Well, hello Kevin. Can I get you something to drink?" she asked with a smile that showed two rows of pointed teeth.

"A red, if possible off the tap," the detective said.

"Not a problem, sweetie. I'll let you look over the menu while I get your beer." She gave Wallace the menu and left with a little shake of her rear and twitch of her whip-like tail, which Wallace followed with his eyes.

"Wouldn't mind getting some of that," he said.

"Isn't that what got you in trouble with your wife?" I asked him.

"Hey I may have looked, but I never touched. My wife just never believed me. Now that we're probably getting divorced, I can start thinking about it more," he said, and I knew he was telling the truth. I knew the private dick his wife had paid to follow Kevin around and he had admitted to me that Kevin was clean, but as long as the checks kept clearing he would keep tailing the poor sap. He also told me it was the police detective's wife who was the one stepping out at night when she was supposedly at her sister's. I just didn't have the heart to tell my friend about it.

"Well, either way I'd stay away from any of the waitresses around here. They're damn easy on the eyes, but you can't trust them," I said.

"Can't trust who?" Sasha asked returning with Wallace's beer.

"You."

"I'm wounded, Jason. How could you possibly say such a mean thing about me?" She threw the back of her hand to her forehead in melodramatic fashion. "Even if it is true." She gave an almost innocent giggle, the effect of which was ruined by the bat-like wings and horns.

She then got back to her more professional demeanor and asked Wallace what he wanted to eat. Kevin hadn't decided yet. She told us she'd be back in ten minutes and left. I watched my friend stare lustfully at her retreating ass and cleared my throat. "I'm going to warn you one last time. Don't." My voice was flat, I wanted to make sure he understood that I was serious in my warning.

"What would one night hurt?" he asked me. "Surely one night wouldn't be that bad?"

"They're a drug. You start off saying 'one night won't hurt', and then you get hooked, and you'll pay just about any price to spend another night with them," I told him.

"Then why does Brisbane hire them if they're that dangerous to his customers?"

"He gets a cut of their tips, and those tips are huge," I said simply. "He also keeps them under some control. They may tease and flirt, but they know that if they bed one of his Human customers, he'll send them back to whichever Infernal Realm he hired them from. They like it up here, and there is a catch in their contract that can nullify that clause."

"And what's that?" I didn't like the almost hopeful tone in Wallace's voice.

"They have to pledge total loyalty to one Human, in a contract signed in their blood, with their true name on the seal. It's the only way to protect any person they decided to spend a lifetime with." It was nearly unheard of, but it had happened once since The Mystic Wolf had opened.

"Ahhh." It sounded as if Wallace had finally come to terms with how things worked with these girls. His face then turned more professional. "Well let's get to why we're both here," he said.

"James Wells," I said. "Did you dig up anything about him after you left his mother's place? Or did you just dump the whole matter in my lap?"

"I figured that since you were buying, I'd do at least something to earn the drink. So I did a little digging."

"What do you have for me?" I asked, probably a little too eagerly.

"Did you know his dad lives in Dublin?" the detective asked me.

"Yes, according to the mother he ditched out on her and the kid for a trophy wife and moved back to Dublin," I said.

"I did some digging on the father, though I wasn't able to get a hold of him directly." I could tell that he was building up to something that could be interesting.

"So what did you find out?"

"He owns a fairly large construction company in Ireland, which belonged to his wife's father," Wallace said, taking a sip of his beer. "The thing is, it has been going through a rash of problems. A lot of it looks like sabotage, but not in the normal sense."

Wallace was going somewhere with it. "I got the Dublin police to send me the records of what had been happening on those job sites. At first it looked like it was just kids playing dumb pranks on the company, but the attacks are getting increasingly malevolent."

"How so?"

"At first it was childish stuff like pouring sugar into the gas tanks of earth movers and the like. Next it was pulling spark plug leads. Then after a while it was damage to safety systems on equipment," Wallace explained. I must say he had gotten good at going with gut instinct. "So far no one's been killed, but there have been several near misses. The most recent thing to happen was that the break lines on James's father's truck were cut. Before you ask I did check out incident reports of the competitors. So far nothing has really happened to them, at least nowhere near the scale of what that his company has seen."

I wondered again about the charm against magick the kid had tried to cast on behalf of his father. "Are the construction sites near any sort of sacred site as seen by local folklore?" It wasn't unheard of for fair folk to do that kind of sabotage if they felt that their homes were going to be destroyed.

"Checked into that as well, and the answer is a resounding no. Truthfully, I'm at a loss for an explanation."

"Well, I found something that maybe of interest on that note," I said.

"Oh?"

I reached into my satchel and pulled out the picture of the father I had found on James' altar and handed it to Wallace. The cop looked at it and turned it round a couple of times before looking at me. "What does it say?" he eventually asked. "I'm sure I should be able to read it but I can't."

"I really didn't expect you to be able to read it," I said, just as our waitress arrived to take Wallace's order.

The Succubus looked down at the picture and then looked at me in surprise. "Please tell me that you didn't write that," she said giving me an accusatory look. "It's horrid."

"Of course not," I said.

"I should hope not," Sasha said.

I grinned at her and pulled out the picture of Maurine. "If you want bad, try looking at this one."

The Daemon looked fit to be tied. "That is vile and disgusting! Whoever wrote that should be ashamed of themselves!"

I was mildly shocked by Sasha's reaction to the curse, she was from an Infernal Realm after all. "I'm surprised that a curse against one's own mother would upset you so much," I said.

"Who cares about the curse?! I was talking about the penmanship and the grammar; it's horrid! Whoever taught this kid must be completely incompetent." Maybe I shouldn't have shown her the picture, but I had to admit it was fun watching her fume over it.

"Felix was displeased with it as well," I told her.

"I should have known it would have been that fop," the Daemon huffed. "He doesn't tip well, he's rude, and he's resisted all my attempts to flirt with him. I mean seriously, a body like this," she said indicating a body that only a Succubus could possess, "and he doesn't even give me a second look. Do you have any idea how that makes me feel? I have feelings too you know. And it not just me, he's like that with all of us. Truthfully, I think there is something seriously wrong with that guy."

"There is, but it's not my secret to share," I said. "Now if you'd be so kind as to take Kevin's order?"

The Succubus immediately cut off the sulk and was all smiles as she took the detective's order. After he ordered a bacon double cheeseburger with the works, she left with a wiggle to show that she was back into her usual good mood.

Wallace turned his attention from the Succubus to me. "Now that our waitress and her over-the-top personality are gone, I have to ask what's written on those two pictures."

"Well, the picture of the mother has an attempt at a rather nasty curse on it," I said.

"Just how nasty?"

"He wants his mother dead," I told the detective.

"Now that's a call for a counselor if ever there was one," he said trying to make a joke of a dark matter. It was a bit of a defense mechanism for him to deal with anything upsetting. "How about the picture of the father?"

"Well, as far as I can make out, it's supposed to be a charm of protection against magick," I said. "But as you may have gathered from our waitress's reaction, it is very poorly written and useless. But it was done in earnest. Originally I thought the kid had made a mistake in the wording of the spell, more than just the bad grammar and poor handwriting. However, with what you just told me about the quote unquote accidents that have been happening to the father's company, James may have been trying to use the correct charm after all."

"I don't quite follow," Wallace said.

"There may be some sort of magickal force at work causing those accidents. It is also possible that the kid's mother is involved in some way with the accidents. If that is the case, then the reason for the curse becomes obvious," I said.

I did of course realize I was making some big assumptions on the matter. It was just as likely that the mother was not involved in any way, but the kid thought she was. At the very least, the kid wanted to see his dad, which he was being prevented from doing by his mother. And, the 'accidents' were quite possibly plain old corporate sabotage by another company. In this kid's impressionable mind though, they may have smacked of an occult force. "However, there is another explanation that is equally plausible and in no way involves the supernatural."

"I'm all ears. If it can be explained away to my captain without me having to bring in the supernatural, I'm all for it."

"Let's put together the facts as we know them to be without making any sort of assumptions," I began.

"Okay," Wallace said, "makes sense."

"Fact one: James has disappeared. The reason is unknown, however, some of the evidence supports an idea that the disappearance was not voluntary," I said.

"I assume the evidence you are using to support that is those books on the occult, which were the reason I had the mother call you?" Wallace asked.

"Correct. Second fact: In the attic of the house I found an altar with the pictures of James' parents. On the picture of the father was a blood magick charm against the supernatural; on the picture of the mother was a very nasty blood magick curse against her, nasty enough to show a desire to kill her. Now the spells were so poorly written that there was no possible way they could have worked, but that doesn't matter. What does matter is the intent for which they had been cast."

"Okay then. What comes next?" asked the detective.

"Fact three: after I found those pictures, I tossed the kid's room and found a pay stub from Felix's store. I went there and questioned Felix on the matter. According to Felix, he was about to call me himself about finding James. He also told me that, not only did he work for him as an employee, but he was also an apprentice. But he hasn't seen the kid in a week. Now, if Felix is telling me the truth, it means he isn't responsible for the kid's disappearance. I'm pretty sure that he might be hiding something, but for now I'm going to give him the benefit of the doubt. What I learned from him was that the kid did hate his mother and was trying to get in contact with his dad, but his mother was making it difficult for him to do so. The mother had her friend hack all of James' email accounts, with the exception of the one he had at the store. There are two possibilities for this, either she didn't know the account existed or she was unable to have it hacked because it was set up by a Silicon Slave."

Wallace nodded. "Either way it makes sense. What else do we know?"

"Fact four: as you've dug up yourself, someone has been sabotaging the father's company. Now if you were to ignore everything that has been happening here, it wouldn't be a hard sell for it to be industrial sabotage."

"So now that we have established all of this, what do we do?"

"You eat your burger sweetie," Sasha said, placing Wallace's dinner in front of him.

"I just ordered that burger a couple minutes ago," Wallace said in a shocked voice. "How did you get back here so quickly with it?"

"The kitchen exists on a separate timeline. Brisbane doesn't want people having to wait for their food for twenty or thirty minutes, so the place exists within a pocket dimension of another pocket dimension," she slid into a chair next to me. "So what are the two of you sleuthing?"

"Shouldn't you be waiting tables?" I asked her.

"I'm on my half and a friend of mine called to let me know she wasn't coming in tonight so I thought I'd come spend a few minutes with you." She covered one of my hands with one of hers and I couldn't help but think of what would happen if Countess Blood Wolf walked in at this moment.

"A kid disappeared, and his mother wants him back. So does Felix for that matter," I told her. Who knew? Maybe she would catch something that the two of professional detectives missed.

"You're saying the mother of that kid who wrote that pathetic curse wants him back?" The Succubus sounded surprised. "I know if it was my kid who wrote that, I wouldn't want to have anything to do with him."

"I wasn't even aware you could have kids?" It was a joke of a question.

"I wasn't being literal," she said. "Still, if I was reading the intent correctly, and the kid's handle of the language was better, not to mention the penmanship, it may have done some damage."

"Okay, I have to ask. What was that written in?" Wallace asked. "Since I've started hanging around Black I've seen all sorts of strange alphabets, but I didn't recognize that one."

"Oh, it's Sumerian," she said. "Archaic Sumerian in the Eme-Sal dialect to be more precise. Wait ... you did say the kid is a boy right?"

"Yes, he's a boy." I had no idea where she was going with this. "Why do you ask?"

"Agh Felix is an idiot!" The Succubus threw up her hands in frustration. "You don't teach a boy Eme-Sal, you teach him Eme-Gir! The next time that fop comes into this place I'm going to give him a piece of my mind. It's not enough that he's rude, doesn't tip or resists flirting, but he has to go and screw up a kid's education. I mean I'm sure the kid's penmanship and grammar will improve, hell even my English grammar needs a bit more work, but he's teaching him the wrong dialect for a boy. There is no excuse!"

"This seems to have got you pretty worked up," I said, truly taken aback by her reaction.

"I hate to see a kid get a second rate education, which is why I'm in school," she said. Now I was truly taken aback. Since when do Succubae go to school?

"Dare I ask what you're going to school for?"

"Elementary education," she said as if it should be obvious. "You don't think I want to wait tables my whole life, do you?"

"You have got to be kidding me!" I couldn't believe what I was hearing. I couldn't help but think of what kind of teacher she would make. Of course you wouldn't be able to keep most of the dads, and probably quite a few of the mothers, from going to parent / teacher conferences.

"If all goes to plan I should start my student teaching in January," she said proudly. Wallace whistled the opening chords of *Hot For Teacher* and I kicked him.

"Brisbane is actually letting you out of the Mystic Wolf to go to school? I thought he'd have kicked you back to whatever Hell he hired you from if you tried something like this."

"How do you think I got my G.E.D.? Sam helped me study for the test," she said rather smugly. "When Brisbane realized that I was quite serious about becoming a teacher, he supported me on it one hundred percent. He even lets me stay after my shift so I can use the internet connection here for doing my homework. Do you have any concept of how difficult it is to get a mortal world net connection in another realm?"

"Well then let me say that I'm glad you seem so passionate to do something so far out of character for a Succubus," I said.

"Why thank you," she said with a smile that showed off too many needle like teeth for my comfort. I didn't like to think of what it would be like to French kiss one of them. You'd probably shred your tongue if you did. "Now back to this case of yours. What can you tell me?" she asked.

I quickly ran through the details of the case for her. She sat back and closed her eyes for a couple seconds, had she cocked her head to one side she'd have looked much like a Daemonic version of my secretary. "Do you know for certain if the kid has much contact with his father?" she finally asked.

"From what Felix told me, the kid has some contact, but I'm not sure how much that is since I haven't had a chance to check the kid's email yet." I was pretty sure I knew where she was going with this.

"If I was you, I'd take a look at those emails before you do anything else, other than maybe getting a hold of the father." Then a light flashed in the Daemons eyes, a certain sign of a eureka moment. "Kevin, when did the really nasty stuff start happening to the father's company?"

"It was about six days ago when things started going from juvenile to deadly." It was as far as the detective got before I jumped in.

"Do you think that the kid's disappearance might be connected to the attacks?" I asked the Daemon.

"It's a workable theory, isn't it," she said.

"I don't get it," Wallace said.

"Think about it," Sasha said. "It's possible that something happened to the kid that has made it easier for the attacks to happen. Like he's being used by something to get closer to his dad."

"Are you thinking that someone sacrificed him?" Wallace said.

"If it wasn't for the fact that she hired Black, I'd lay good money on the mother." What the Succubus was saying made sense. I also agreed with her that it didn't make sense for the mother to hire me if she was the one responsible for the kid's disappearance. However...

"Well, whatever the case is, I'm going to put a tail on the mother, just in case she is involved. You want the job?" I asked Wallace.

"Sorry I can't do it," he said shaking his head. "Unless the mother starts making a big stink about it with the chief and goes to the media, I doubt much is going to get done. So far the chief wants to treat this as a runaway and let it sort itself out."

"I'll hire Sarah then." Sarah was a shamus like myself, though she was still fairly new on the scene.

Sasha looked at her watch. "As much as I'd like to keep talking, I need to get back to the tables. I'll talk to you sweeties later," she said kissing both me and Wallace on the cheek.

As the Daemon walked away, I watched Kevin stare after her lustfully. "Go home Kevin and forget about her. Leave her a big tip and leave it at that."

"A guy can dream," he said in a wistful tone of voice. He then looked at his watch. "Well I need to get home so I can get some sleep."

He dropped a twenty on the table, which was of course meant for Sasha since I was buying. *If his wife had just seen him drop that kind of tip on a waitress, things would have blown up,* Shadow said.

"Well you and I both know that it wouldn't matter since she's got another stallion in the stable," I replied.

Are you ever going to tell him about that?

"Not if I can help it," I said. "Wouldn't do any good. If his kids were still young enough to be living at home and there was a custody battle, then yeah, I'd tell him in a heartbeat. But that's not a factor now. I think it would hurt him too much to tell him."

Shadow looked up and stared out the door which the detective had just passed through. *I guess you're right. I never did understand you Humans enough to figure out that bullshit. Before I became a familiar I had a mate. I would have never cheated on her, and she would never have cheated on me. But you Humans. I will never figure you guys out.*

"Hell I've never figured us out either. Why do you think I stopped doing divorce cases? Humans treat each other like shit, and they want me to find out just how bad it is." I looked around the bar for a bit and as soon as I saw Sasha, I let her know I was heading out. I dropped a hundred on the table. With what I had gotten for myself and Kevin, as well as the drink I had bought Dante, the tip probably amounted to nearly a hundred-and-fifty percent.

On my way out I stopped by the merchandise table and picked up a copy of the CD of the band, who were kicking out a damn good cover of *Stray Cat Strut*. I took a quick look at it and noticed that it had been produced by Empty Grave Productions. I had almost forgotten that Countess Blood Wolf had talked about getting into the recording business. I thought it was mostly going to be for Silent Song Bird, a very talented, and very poor, Werewolf guitarist. Apparently she was going to produce a few other bands connected to the Court of Night. I paid my five dollars, threw another ten into the tip jar by the stage and headed out.

I slipped the CD into the car stereo, once again thinking how a collector would go insane if they saw the top end stereo in a '41 Buick Special. I pulled out of the parking lot and eased into traffic. Ten minutes later I parked the car in my garage.

As I got out of the car, I thought back to what Sasha had said about the kid having possibly been used as a sacrifice. I then thought back to my initial interview with the mother when I had gone to her house to start my investigation. Something had seemed wrong about the situation. I was fairly sure that my client was lying to me, or at the very least, feeding me a lot of half-truths. Still, why bring me into the midst of this if she was the one who had gotten rid of the kid? It made no sense. I guessed I'd just sleep on the matter and maybe something would strike a chord when I wasn't being hassled by consciousness. I just hoped it wouldn't keep me up all night.

CHAPTER

By the time I woke up, I was no closer to an answer than I had been when I had gone to sleep, but at least I had gotten enough rest to think about it clearly. I looked at my watch and saw that it was just after seven. Sarah wouldn't be in the office for another two hours, give or take, and I decided that I'd call her around nine. I did a quick mental calculation and realized that it was around one in the afternoon Dublin time, which meant that I would have a decent time trying to get ahold of James' father. I decided to call him from the office.

After a quick shower and some breakfast, I headed to the office and made sure that I had the file Wallace had given me with the father's phone numbers in it. By the time I got to the office it was about eight thirty. Jamie wouldn't be in for at least another half-hour. I also knew that Sarah didn't usually get in to her own office until around nine, so there was no reason to call her yet.

I was about to call the father when I realized it might be a good idea to check James' email first. If the dad lied to me about how much contact he had with James, I wanted to know about it before hand. I turned on my computer and, taking out the slip of paper with the website and passwords, along with the voice recorder, I got ready to check the kids email.

Five minutes later I had gotten past the second password, and had gone from being in a decent mood to completely pissed. The file had been wiped. Either 'Inferno's Plague' had backstabbed me or someone had hacked the email, and I wasn't about to rule out either possibility. Knowing that my client had hacked her kid's other email addresses I knew that her friend was at least a halfway decent hacker, but now I had reason to believe that they were a Silicon Slave. Since I may be dealing with another Silicon Slave, there was a good chance that all the data on the kid's phone had been compromised. I quickly drew out the symbol I had used as a password on the phone and was immediately pissed. The phone was completely blank. The damn thing had been hacked. Only a technomancer can hack another technomancer's work, which meant that either there was another Silicon Slave involved or that I was going to have to shoot Dante. Now I just had to find that little shit.

Thankfully, my friend Hell Fire's Dame had given me a little present that was perfect for finding Dante. I had no idea of how the thing worked, but I knew what it did. All I had to do was get ahold of Dante over a voice connection, and then hit a button. The little box would send out some sort of signal that would knock whoever was on the receiving end flat on their ass for a few hours. It would also give me a location on that person. I've used it enough times to know that it works; now I just had to get Dante to call me.

I took out my cellphone and hooked up the little box to the phone and sent a quick text message to Dante. 'Inferno's Plague. Something happened that I need help with. Call me.'

After about a minute I got a call. I heard Dante yawn. "What do you want Black? I was about to go to bed."

"Don't worry, this'll just take a minute," I said and hit the button on the device Hell Fire's Dame had given me. I heard a yelp of pain followed by something hitting what I guessed was the floor. I then looked at the address the device gave me and knew I could get there in forty minutes if the traffic was with me, about an hour if it wasn't.

"That little shit better not have crossed me," I said to no one, but Shadow answered anyways.

I'm fairly sure that Dante took you seriously when you said you'd shoot him if he double crossed you, so I doubt he was behind this. I think he was trying more to calm me down than anything else. For reasons that I had yet to figure out, Shadow had recently become concerned with my blood pressure. I think I have been letting him watch too much television and he's been seeing too many commercials for blood pressure medications.

"Well if that's the case I'm still going to need his help to recover those emails. I want to know how much contact James has had with his father of late. And you know me, I want to know if the father lies to me when I ask him," I said as I put on my light jacket and It may be August and hot, but I had an image to maintain.

You know I've never understood why people would ever lie about some matters, Shadow said as I scribbled a note on the memo pad on Jamie's desk. *Unless the father has something to hide, there shouldn't be any reason for him to hide the kid.*

I got to the elevator before I answered him. "I don't know the conditions of any custody issues so it may be that my client's son isn't supposed to have any contact with his father. If I tell the father that his ex-wife hired me to find James, he'll clam up knowing that he would be in legal trouble if he had the kid against any sort of legal terms."

Shadow dipped his head in a quick nod. *I hadn't thought of that possibility.*

"I'm not surprised," I said. "I've never heard of any species of animals having something similar to the Human concept of divorce, let alone custody battles and visitation rights."

You Humans are simply too weird to understand.

"Normally I'd point out the fact that I'm only half-Human, but in this case it doesn't really matter." A few minutes later we were in the car heading out to wherever I had flattened Dante.

In forty-five minutes we arrived in a dirty trailer park. Dante was probably worth a small fortune, or at least could be, so I couldn't figure out what he was doing in a dump like this. In the time it took me to exit to my car and then jimmy the lock on Dante's trailer, I realized the answer. By living in a trailer, the Silicon Slave opened up the ability to stay mobile in case someone, or something, decided they were pissed off with him and came gunning for him. It wouldn't keep him safe for long, but as long as he kept moving, he could possibly stay one step ahead of whoever was after him. Like many Silicon Slaves, Dante was a bit of a conspiracy nut, but he had seen so much stuff on the net in files that no one should have access to that maybe he had actually found something.

"Shadow, do me a favor and keep a look out. I don't want any unexpected guests while I work."

Sure thing master. The bird flew up from my shoulder and staked out a perch on top of the trailer's small satellite dish.

I wrinkled my nose in disgust when I walked into the trailer. The place wreaked of long dead pizza and Styrofoam pots of ramen noodles, as well as being littered with half-eaten pastries and empty cans of energy drinks. One side of the trailer was jammed with a mass of computer equipment buzzing happily along. There were runes scribbled on most of the equipment and I couldn't even begin to guess what most of it did. I made my way to the back of the trailer and found Dante sprawled out on what little floor space there was, clothed in a pair of boxers with a couple holes in them and a grimy undershirt. What a slob.

I toed the technomancer in the side and eventually rolled him over with my foot. Bending over, I picked him up and threw him roughly onto the bed. When that didn't work I gave him a couple hard slaps. That did the trick. "Come on Dante, wake up," I said, grabbing him by the soiled shirt and giving him a couple hard shakes.

"The hell!" Dante yelped. "How did you find me?"

"I'm a detective. How the hell do you think? Now I've got some questions for you." I dragged a struggling Dante out of his bedroom and threw him into the seat that he was obviously using as a desk chair. I yanked 'Ace of Spades', out of her holster and jammed the barrel between his eyes. "Why did you cross me? I told you that it would be bad for your health if you did, but you did anyways. So what is it? Do you have a death wish?"

"What are you talking about?!" Dante yelped in obvious fear.

"You wiped the kid's emails! What else would get me this pissed off with you?" I snarled. I did not know for certain if he had wiped those files, but this kind of adrenaline rush would wake him up fast. "Not only that, but you took a giant piss on the phone and it's useless to me. Now, I'm giving you one minute to retrieve the kid's emails and fix the phone or I pull the trigger."

"Shit Black! I'm not stupid enough to cross you like that! You got to believe me!" he all but screamed. Then I smelled an ammonia stink of urine as he voided his bladder.

"Don't worry, I believe you," I said patting him on the cheek with the barrel of 'Ace of Spades' before I put her back in the holster. "In fact, I was pretty sure that you weren't dumb enough to do something so stupid as to cross me like that."

"Then why did you pull a gun on me like that?" he asked, obviously thinking that I had gone completely nuts.

"Quickest way I could think of to wake you up. Now go take a shower and change. You stink."

Dante quickly left and I mused on how effective that technique had just been. It was very rare for me to threaten someone like that to wake them, though I had done it several times to sober people up. Nothing quite like a shot of adrenaline to clear an alcohol-addled mind. It also worked well on a few other types of drugs like crack and cocaine. Throw a person around a bit, then jam a heater in their face and most people will wake up pretty damn quick.

While I heard the sound of what I assumed was Dante taking a shower, I took a look around the cramped quarters of the trailer and decided that it wasn't suitable for animal habitation, let alone Human. In other words, it was perfect for a paranoid, conspiracy nut of a Silicon Slave like Dante. That was the way it was for most Silicon Slaves. About half of them made a fortune as corporate types. Most of rest were like Inferno's Plague and made enough to survive and were scared to death of what was going on outside of the web. He could hide his tracks better than just about anyone out there, but he was always going to be afraid of men in black helicopters.

There is a Silicon Slave I usually want to fit into a small, but important, third category. Hell Fire's Dame was, at least on paper, a consultant for a small business, which kept anyone from really noticing her. She wasn't part of the radical fringe who thought the world was out to get them, and she had too many morals to be dumb enough to whore herself out to major corporations. She was a tech geek, pure and simple. She loved technology for the sake of technology itself.

After fifteen minutes of trying not to infect myself by touching anything, Dante walked back into the room looking almost presentable in a pair of sweat pants and a ratty t-shirt with only a few stains on it. "Okay Black, is this better?"

"It'll do." At least he didn't stink anymore.

"Okay, what exactly happened?" Dante ran a hand through his still wet hair. "I was having a little trouble concentrating on what exactly you were saying while you had a gun in my face. All I remember was you accusing me of doing something that I'm fairly sure I didn't do."

"James' email got hacked; all of his emails are gone. Not only that, but the phone's only worth so much plastic slag." From the reaction on Dante's face I knew he was shocked.

"Are you sure you didn't screw up the passwords?" he asked me.

"Of course I didn't. Check for yourself," I said, pointing at his computer.

Dante sat down in front of his computer and, after a series of passwords, failed to bring up the company email for Felix's. It wasn't even as far as I had gotten. After another minute or so, the swearing began. "What the hell?! What in the name of Alan Turing happened to this site?! Quick give me the phone!"

"It's worthless," I said, as I handed him the phone.

"Maybe to you but not to me." He poked at the phone for a few minutes before throwing it over his shoulder. "You're right. It's trash."

"Told you," I said rather smugly.

"Shut up and let me work!" he snapped as he turned back to the keyboard cursing up a storm. After another ten minutes of swearing, it seemed that Dante had his answer. "That bitch! She fried the whole site! It's going to take me a week to fix this muck up! Lady you messed with the wrong technomancer!" he screamed at the monitor, jabbing a finger into it.

"Who are you talking about?" I asked, perplexed.

"Kill Switch Karma! That's who!" Dante said, as if I should know the name.

"Not to sound like an idiot, but who's Kill Switch Karma?"

"One of the most notorious Silicon Slaves, corporate whore, hackers out there. She must have been hired to do this. What I don't get though is why?" While he was talking, his fingers were flying across the keyboard. "This isn't the kind of thing she'd be into. She's into corporate espionage and electronic sabotage, and as far as I know, Felix isn't on anyone's hit list. So why in the name of Charles Babbage is that corporate slut screwing with my work?"

"Is there any way of retrieving the files?" I asked. I know almost nothing about computers, Jamie does most of the computer stuff at the office. I had no way of knowing if he could do anything for me.

"It's a possibility, but I can't promise you anything. I'm going to need help, and I'm really going to be regretting it," he said.

"Who are you asking?"

"Hell Fire's Dame," he said, not sounding happy.

"Didn't you call her a tramp just last night?" I asked him.

"Yes, mostly trying to justify the fact that I stood her up a couple weeks ago." He sounded miserable.

"Oh dear," I said trying to sound sympathetic.

"'Oh dear' is right," he sighed. He then switched to another program on his computer. "Well, needs must as the devil drives."

After a few keystrokes, he was trying to get a connection to my old friend Jessica James, known in the hacker world as Hell Fire's Dame. After a few seconds, the ping was answered. "What the hell do want jerk?!" Were the first words out of Jessica's mouth.

"I need some help and you're the first person I thought of," Dante tried to say sweetly.

"And why should I help you, you little shit?"

"Come on, it was just one date, beautiful."

I tried not to snigger, it would take a fair amount of beer to see Hell Fire's Dame as beautiful. Good thing for me, it wasn't her looks that mattered in this case, it was her skill with a computer that we needed. "I really need your help. Please."

"Don't bother with flattery, I'm still pissed at you!" she snarled. I was going to get tired of this quickly.

I put myself in front of the camera. "Hell Fire's Dame it's Black..."

"I can see that. What are you doing over there?" Jessica sounded more than a little pissed. "I thought you came to me for help. What are you doing with that louse? Am I not good enough for you anymore?"

"No that's not why I'm here. It happened to be that someone named Kill Switch Karma took a big, steaming dump on one of Inferno's Plague's sites and I need to get at the information it had to help me with a case." I hoped that she would forgive me for not having her take a piss all over Dante's work, we needed her on board right now. "Please I need your help."

"Okay... but you owe me! I'll figure what I want from you later." All I could hope was that she didn't want a date. "So what do you want help with, Inferno's Plague?"

"I just need you to run interference for me while I hack into that bitch's sites and see if I can find anything that might help Black." he said.

"That's pretty dangerous," Jessica said. "Kill Switch is a pretty nasty piece of work. I don't want her to find out that I helped you hack her."

"Not to fear. Do you still have that make up gift I sent you after I, um ...?"

"Yes I still have it, but I haven't opened it up yet." Jessica showed us a small, poorly wrapped box. "So, what's in it?"

"It's a transdimensional rerouter," Dante said.

"You figured out how to make one of these things?" Jessica sounded shocked. "How does it work?"

"It's a bit complicated, I'll explain over drinks at whichever restaurant you want," Dante said.

"W.A. Frost." Expensive place. I would never have figured her as someone who would eat there.

"Fine. And don't worry, I won't stand you up again," Dante said. "Now just plug it between your modem and your computer. The prompts will tell you where to go from there."

"Hold on." Jessica ducked out of view.

"What does that thing do?" I asked.

"You know how a hacker can bounce his signal all around the world to make it hard for someone to trace him?"

"Even I know that." I've seen a couple movies about hackers so I'm not totally illiterate on the subject.

"Well, that's how I was able to trace that back to Kill Switch Karma. That arrogant slut didn't protect herself well enough." Dante gave me a rather disturbing smile. "What this does is somewhat similar, but far more difficult to trace."

"How so?"

"Well this puppy jumps the signal across multiple dimensions." I may have not liked the smile that Inferno's Plague was giving me, but I sure as hell liked what he was saying.

"I thought you couldn't get mortal world internet signals in other dimensions?" I asked, thinking about what the Succubus had said last night.

"Well you can, it's just difficult. That's why no one was able to figure out how to make these routers until just recently."

Pretty soon Jessica told us she was ready to go. "Thanks again Hell Fire," I said.

"Just remember that you owe me," she said.

"Of course. Now if you don't mind, I'll take your leave, and let the two of you work."

"I'll let you know one way or the other as soon as I can," Dante said to my retreating back.

"Good luck," I said then headed out.

I was truthfully glad to get out of that place. Dante may be a good technomancer but in many ways, he's a barely Human slob. I gave a shiver that Shadow obviously noticed.

That big of a slob? he asked me.

"You don't know the half of it," I said. "But he's doing what I need him to."

So where to now? my familiar asked me.

"Back to the office to call the father." It was really the only option I had at the moment.

Don't forget that you also have to call 'Scar Face' about following Ms. Wells. He reminded me. He probably thought I would have forgotten to call the femme fatale shamus because I had been so pissed about the email files. He was probably right too.

"Thanks for reminding me. I'll call Sarah as soon as I get into the office," I said. "I just hope that she isn't busy with another case."

CHAPTER

It was about ten-thirty when I walked into my office and saw Jamie happily humming along to a song on the radio while she worked on a spread sheet. "How goes it, boss?" she asked.

"Not bad," I replied.

"So, are we going to be working on the Wells case?" she asked me, causing me to realize I had forgotten to let her know I had taken it, and that I still had the retainer in my wallet.

"Thank you for reminding me. Pen please," I said. As soon as Jamie handed me a pen I signed the back of the check and gave it to her. "Please stop by the bank and deposit that."

She put the check in her purse. "Anything else I should get while I'm out and about?" she asked.

I thought about it for a second and couldn't think of anything else we might need. "Nothing I can think of, other than any office supplies you might think we need."

"I can't think of anything. I picked up a couple bottles of your so called 'cold medicine' yesterday so I seriously doubt that we're running low on that," Jamie said as she headed out the door. Once she was gone I headed back to the inner office.

Sitting down at the desk, I decided to call Sarah before anything else. As I waited for the femme fatale (whom I had helped get established on her own) to pick up the phone. I thought about how I had met her. It wasn't one of the happier memories of meeting some for the first time. Then again, I hadn't met any of the three most important women in my life under pleasant circumstances. In Sarah's case, it had been as frightening a moment as one could have. Back then she had been a regular patrol officer and had pulled over a guy for a busted taillight. It turned out that he was a serial killer and had almost claimed her as victim number twenty-eight. Her encounter with the bastard had ended with me putting a couple rounds in him. She had ended up with a long gash on the right side of her face that began at the forehead and ended half-way done her cheek, earning her the nickname of 'Scar Face'. It had also left her blind in that eye. She was let go by the force of course. Feeling something that I guess could be described as pity, I took her under my wing and began showing her the ways of a detective. I had also given her new sight with her milky-white, dead eye; she was now able to see the magickal world with it. It had taken her a while to adjust to what I had literally opened her eyes to, but she had adjusted quickly enough.

My musings were interrupted by Sarah answering the phone. "Hey Jason. What can I do for you?" she asked me as soon as the line was established. "And please tell me it's a date."

Not what I needed right now. She had always wanted to be more than just friends. "Sorry Sarah, this is a professional call."

"Oh well, a girl can always hope." I didn't like her tone of voice, which meant I probably was going to have to owe her a favor along with a financial payment for her services.

"Look I need to hire you to help with a case I'm working on."

"How much?" she asked me.

"How does three-hundred a day for the duration of the case sound?" That was more than what she normally made on a case, and she was well aware that I knew it.

"Well, if you came to me that does mean you really need my help. How about we say four-hundred?" She countered.

"Three-fifty and a five day retainer?"

"Add a date at the restaurant of my choice and it's a deal." She sounded almost smug about it. I had seen that one coming, of course, but I needed her abilities, and I also knew that she needed the money. Business had been slow for her lately and she was too proud to come to me for help.

"Deal." I agreed. I wasn't surprised. The last time, I had gone to another woman for help, the one Sarah saw as her chief rival for my affection, I had ended up spending two nights with Yvette up on the North Shore. May the Gods save me from women who are in love with me.

"So what do you need my help with?" she asked me. She had turned professional.

"I need you to keep an eye on my client."

"I'm not the body guard type, and you know it. So why?" she asked me.

"I don't need you to guard her, I need you to follow her around discreetly," I said. "She hired me to find her son, but I trust her about as far as I can throw a tank. I want you to tail her and see if she does anything out of character for a woman who is worried about her son."

"If you say so," she said. "What do you think she might be doing?"

"That's just it. I don't know," I told her. "I'm not going to tell you anything more about the case since I don't want my pre-judgements to affect your ability to do this job."

"I'll stop by your office in half an hour to collect everything I need from you regarding this case," Sarah said.

"That'll be fine," I said.

"And have the check waiting for me. I'm a little behind on the lease." She was probably a couple months behind. I had offered to let her partner with me, but she knew that would mean she would have no shot at me since I like to separate business from pleasure. If she wasn't working for me at all times it would keep her chances open with me.

"Don't worry. The check will be ready for you. I'll see you soon."

"Thanks," she said before she hung up.

This is going to turn around and bite you in the ass you know, Shadow said.

"What? Having my client followed?" I asked him.

No, getting 'Scar Face' involved, he replied. *It only keeps her thinking that there might eventually be something between you.*

"Mmm." I often wondered if something substantial would happen between Sarah and myself. Of course I had the same thoughts regarding Yvette. In many ways the idea was nice, being able to look forward to going home and knowing who was going to be there for you. But I couldn't see myself settling down with either of them. To me, Yvette would always be that scared teenager who I had just killed a bunch of Nazis to save. I would always remember the kid I had helped turn into the Countess Blood Wolf, curled up in my dirty jacket, crying into my shoulder with a sense of terrified freedom.

My feelings towards Sarah made a relationship with her just about as unlikely. I was her guardian and guide. I didn't know if I could, let alone wanted, to turn those feelings around. I had brought her into my world without her asking me to and I had an obligation to help her. But if we were to become an item, it would put her in even more serious danger than she was already in. Yvette was a major player on every scene and could handle anyone, but Sarah was still a nobody. If she was with me, she'd become a target.

Stop thinking like that master, it's a stupid line of thinking, Shadow warned me obviously listening in on my inner musings.

"What makes you say that?"

The last thing you need in your life is a mate, Shadow said, though I couldn't tell if he was trying to sound like a friend or a parent. *Sarah will grow old and die without you having aged a day. As for the Countess, you will always see her as a little kid. We both know that Yvette isn't a kid anymore, but that's always how you will see her. So just do yourself a favor and forget it.*

"You sound like my mother."

Well someone has to remind you of how things work in the real world.

"Still I'm stuck," I said with a shrug. "I'm too close to both of them not to be there for them, but as you said..."

Humans! I knew that Shadow would have thrown his arms up in complete disgust if he had arms.

I decided to wait on calling James' father until after I had talked to Sarah. While I waited for the shamus, I flipped through the file that Wallace had prepared for me. I was glad to see that he really had gone all out in his investigation into what had been happening in Ireland. At least it gave me a good place to start with the questioning. I knew I couldn't come out and ask him straight about the disappearance of his son so I needed to strategize about the best plan of attack. It wasn't until I heard Sarah call my name from the outer office that I realized how long I had been studying the file.

"Come on in," I said, returning the call.

"Hey Jason, it's good to see you," Sarah said in a sultry voice, as she slinked her way into my office. Gods give me strength. This was the reason I referred to her as a femme fatale.

"Hi Sarah. I've got everything you need for the job ready." I was hoping that she didn't want me to take her out. I still needed to call the dad and I was burning time that I didn't have.

"So we're going to be all business today?" she asked in a hurt tone.

"You're working for me right now and you know what that means." I reminded her.

"You're no fun." She gave me a melodramatic pout.

"I also have to make a call and I'm running out of time to make it today." I picked up the file with everything she needed for her assignment and passed her a check for the five-day retainer. "Here's everything, including the check that I promised."

"Thanks," she said as she took the check. "Just don't forget our date after this is all over."

"I'm looking forward to it," I said.

Liar, Shadow said, making me glad that I was the only one who could hear him. Especially since I was, more or less, telling the truth.

"Well, I'll pick a restaurant later. I'll go pick up the trail of your client now and I'll call you tonight in case anything happens," she said just before she left.

"Don't forget to pay your lease," I reminded her as she hit the doorway to the hall.

"They won't let me," she said. "And thanks again for the retainer."

"Don't worry about it," I said. I would have to make sure to shuffle a few more cases her way. Next time a divorce case came calling, I'd have Jamie send them 'Scar Face's way. Maybe all of them. At least until Sarah gained some more traction in the seedy magickal underworld of the metro area.

Now that I had Sarah ready to tail my client, I could call the father. It was approaching noon, which meant that it was almost six in Dublin. I just hoped that I could get ahold of the father. I decided that my best option would be to call him on his cellphone, since there was a very good chance that he wouldn't be in his office.

I dialed the international number and waited for James' father to pick up. I thought about the best way to start my interrogation of the man. I didn't want to make it sound like I was working for his ex-wife. If this turned out to involve a custody battle, the last thing he needed to know was that it was Maurine who had hired me. I decided that my best option was to say that it was James' employer who had hired me, which wasn't far from the truth. Felix had said that he had been about to call me himself regarding James' disappearance. If James was there, he would be able to tell me what he wanted Felix to know. If the kid wasn't there, it would make it seem like I had no interest in involving anyone in a custody battle.

After a minute or so, the line went to voice mail. "Mr. O'Malley, my name is Jason Black. I'm a private detective working on behalf of your son's employer. According to my client, your son has been missing for the last six days and he's worried about him. Could you please give me a call..." I left my number for my direct line and planned to call him again in an hour.

I couldn't think of another move in the case. I looked through my small library of pulp crime novels and picked out an oldie but a goodie, Dashiell Hammett's, *The Big Sleep*. I set an alarm on my cell phone to call in an hour. But I didn't have to wait that long.

I had been reading for about fifteen minutes when my phone rang. I checked the caller ID and saw that the number belonged to an Irish caller. "Hello? Investigator Black speaking," I said, hitting the button for speaker phone.

"Mr. Black?" The voice on the other end was of course Irish, as I had expected, but it was definitely not Dylan O'Malley's. This voice was female, and it was also an upset voice. "This is Katherine O'Malley. I'm Dylan's wife."

"Thank you for calling me, Katherine. May I ask you why you have called me and not your husband?"

"Dylan ..." I heard her choke down a sob. "Dylan's in the hospital."

That grabbed my attention fast. It was possible that the potentially occult corporate sabotage had just taken a turn for the deadly. "What happened?"

"The police say it was a robbery gone wrong. Whoever it was, they didn't take anything, but they did beat him into a coma." She started crying, but I needed to ask her questions before she completely lost it.

"What can you tell me about your stepson, James? Did your husband have any contact with him?" I asked her.

"Um, yes, yes he did." She was trying to focus on what I had to say in order to maintain her composure. "The kid had talked about flying out at some point. I got the impression that he didn't like his mother much." Understatement of the year.

"There was one more thing I need to know..." I never got to finish my sentence when I heard her phone drop.

What do you think happened boss? Shadow asked. Apparently he was as startled as I was by the sound of the phone hitting what I could only assume was Katherine's floor.

"Could be anything," I said with a frustrated shrug.

I was about to end the call when I heard someone scrabbling at the phone. "Jason? Are you still there?"

"Yes Mrs. O'Malley. I'm still here."

"When you find James, make sure he gets out here as soon as he can. The doctors aren't sure how much longer Dylan's got. They say he might pull through, but it doesn't look good."

"I'll make sure he knows when I find him," I told her. "I'll make sure he gets a ticket to fly out, hopefully for your husband's recovery."

"Thank you. I'll let Dylan know what you said if he comes round," she said before hanging up.

Now I was truly frustrated. James' dad was in the hospital with the distinct possibility that he wouldn't survive and I was out of leads. My only hope was that Sarah would find something.

I walked over to the white board I had recently bought for the office and started drawing a web style outline on it to track what I had. In the middle I put James; circling that I started throwing out what I knew. First was that he was being looked for by both his mother and Felix. I then thought about what I had on the kid's father from Wallace's report and wrote his name as well. Putting those three names on the board around James' name, I circled them as well and started working with what I knew regarding them. I decided to start with James' father first since I had the least to go with there.

First there was the sabotage, so I wrote that down, circled it and started adding. The sabotage had started out being annoying and then gotten to dangerous. Using the report, I wrote down a timeline. The beginning of the problems for the construction company had started a few days before the kid's disappearance, once the kid had disappeared it had started getting worse. At the tail end of the timeline I ended with the possibly fatal attack on Dylan. On another line I put down the kid's planned trip. That was all I had there. Frustrating, but I was certain I'd be able to link something in elsewhere.

I then went to work on Felix's name. The first thing I wrote down was 'master'. I then thought about the fact that my client seemed to know nothing about James working for Felix. I drew a line from 'Felix' to 'mother' and wrote, 'no known connection'. With James being Felix's apprentice, the quarter Daemon sorcerer would have been able to give me the information I needed if he was hiding the kid. He had told me though, that he was about to hire me himself, so the store owner didn't know where the kid was. The next thing I wrote down connecting to Felix was email.

All of James' email addresses had been hacked by his mother, except for the work one up until now. I drew a line from 'email' to 'mother' and wrote 'hacked'. As soon as I had tried to access the kid's work email, I had triggered something that had destroyed the website completely. A Silicon Slave—I threw up the name Kill Switch Karma—had been paid to hack the hell out of the website to cover up the destruction of the kid's email files. Now I had just talked to Dylan's wife and she said James had contacted him about coming out there. I drew a line from 'email' to 'father' and wrote 'contact'. Not much to go on. Maybe something else would connect them. Now on to the mother.

Seeing as Maurine was the one who had hired me, the first thing I connected to 'mother' was 'client'. The next fact was that I had found the altar in her house so I wrote 'altar'. Since I had found the two pictures with the poorly scrawled spells on them, I wrote 'picture spells'. From there I drew a line and connected it to 'father' and wrote 'protection from magick charm'. I then drew another line from 'picture spells' and ran it back to 'mother' and wrote 'curse'. Unfortunately, I couldn't date the spells so I didn't know where they linked to the timeline of the sabotage, however I made the rough guess that they dated early on in the sabotage and, of course, had to be before the kid's disappearance seven days ago. I ran a line from 'protection from magick charm' to a point on the time line that would fit the possibilities.

Next to 'altar' I wrote 'books' in reference to the books that I had found in the kid's room. Even though they hadn't been with the altar, they were occult so it was the appropriate place for them. I drew a line connecting 'books' to 'master'. I wasn't happy about Felix giving the kid those books, but that was his business not mine.

The next thing I thought of was the obvious bad will between the mother and the father. It seemed to me that they'd probably kill each other if they were in the same room. I drew a line between 'father' and 'mother' and wrote 'hatred'. As Shadow would have pointed out, any couple that would have gotten into that sort of problem should never have gotten together in the first place. Made me wonder if animals were just better at picking mates, or if their emotions were just not as complicated so as to cause such problems to arise in the first place. Then I considered the fact that some animals' attachments to their mates are so close that it seemed as if they'd rather die than live without their mate. I put it down to them being able to better judge compatibility. I wondered if I would ever ... I realized I had just sidetracked myself and got back to my diagram.

I took a step back from the board and tried to make sense of what I was looking at. The only thing I was missing was a firm connection between 'mother' and 'sabotage'. It looked like it was just about dead certain, but I couldn't say I had it set in cold stone. She had hired a Silicon Slave to hack James' email, which meant that she had connections in the magickal underbelly of the area. That being said, the question became, 'who else does she know?'

"Am I missing anything Shadow?" I asked my familiar, who had been silent during my writing. It was unusual for him.

Well, you still need to make a clear connection between where the parents fit in, he said. *James seemed to believe that the connection was there. So what did he see that you're missing?*

After a few seconds the answer hit me. "Who would have a connection to Ireland, and start with this kind of childish sabotage and then move up to a fatal attack?" I asked Shadow before answering my own question. "There is only one possible answer, Fair Folk."

Makes sense, Shadow agreed.

"She must have somehow contacted a group of fair folk in this area and sacrificed James to them to attack her husband. That means that most likely they are from one of the Unseelie courts," I said. Since, like most realms beyond the veil that separates the Mortal from the Magickal realms, Arcadia, the faerie realm, doesn't follow the same rules of geography. It is possible that the same court she had sacrificed James to was doing the attacks. It was also possible that there were two separate courts that had made a pact in this business. Truthfully I didn't care. The only thing I needed to do right now was get James out of the hands of whichever court had him.

"What bugs me is that I didn't know of any Unseelie court with a portal in the area, well at least not one dumb enough to cause trouble," I said.

Is it possible that one had appeared over the last few months that you aren't aware of? Shadow asked.

"I don't think that's likely," I said. "However it's the only possibility I can think of. I'm going to need the maps."

The maps were something I had created a few decades ago and kept up to date as the area changed. Using the maps, I could swing a pendulum to track down any occult changes in the area. I cleared off the top of my desk and spread the large, general map out. I took out the pendulum I used specifically for working with the maps. "Find the entrance to the Unseelie Court," I whispered.

I slowly moved my hand over the map, letting the pendulum trace circles of varying size in a mystic game of 'Colder, Hotter'. After ten minutes, the pendulum stopped circling and made a dead stop over East Minneapolis. Now that I had a general idea of where to go next, I grabbed the next map, which was a more detailed map of that area and spread it on the top of the desk. I repeated the question and started my next search.

After five minutes the pendulum came to a dead stop. "Prospect Park," I said.

Of course they'd show themselves near Witch's Hat. Shadow mentally laughed. Witch's Hat is a water tower where the roof looks like a stereotypical witch's hat, hence the name.

"That's as close as I'm going to get with the maps," I said. "Now that we have an idea of where Maurine might be going, we just have to wait for Sarah to call to confirm it."

I sat down and waited. I couldn't risk going to the court not having confirmed that Maurine was involved with them. I needed solid evidence. I rolled up the maps and put them away, and settled in to wait for the call.

CHAPTER 7

After waiting for a few hours, reading 'The Big Sleep' while Shadow listened to the radio, Jamie came in to let me know that it was six and that she was going to be heading home. Much later I had just started in on Mickey Spillane's first Mike Hammer novel, 'I, The Jury', when Sarah called. Glancing at the clock, I saw that it was ten-thirty.

"What do you have for me Sarah?" I asked, picking up the phone.

"Maurine just vanished on me," she said. "I tailed her into Prospect Park. She walked behind Witch's Hat and that was it. I walked past the water tower after a minute to see if she had just stopped there, or was meeting someone there, but she wasn't anywhere."

Bingo! She was involved with an Unseelie Court. Now I had to wait for her to leave and find a way into the court for myself. "Okay, get back to where you can see the tower without being seen and wait for her to reappear. I'll meet you there," I told her. "If she leaves, follow her and don't wait for me."

"Okay, I'll stay in the parking lot. I'm not too far from her car so she'll have to come back for it at some point."

"I'll be there as soon as I can," I told her and hung up.

"Come on Shadow, let's not keep Sarah waiting," I said. Shadow hopped off his perch and landed on my shoulder.

Aren't you forgetting something? Shadow asked.

"What do you mean?"

You'll need something to get your way into the courtroom before you talk to whichever Fey is in charge of the court, Shadow pointed out.

"Thanks! I almost forgot." I walked over to my small fridge and took out some bribe material for entrance.

Forty minutes later, I parked the car in the parking lot of Prospect Park, however Jamie's car wasn't there, meaning that Maurine had left. "Okay Shadow, take a look around," I said to my familiar as soon as he was out of the car.

Shadow jumped off and, pumping his wings hard, he made a direct line for Witch's Hat. While he was gone I made my way more slowly and kept watch for anything that might crop up. A member of an Unseelie court would recognize me for being a half Daemon and might be willing to try something, especially since they probably haven't been around long enough to have learned about my well-earned, rather nasty, reputation. As I walked, I swapped out the magazine of regular bullets in 'Ace of Spades' for one of iron.

Found it, Shadow called out to me shortly.

"Okay, I'll be there in a few minutes."

In ten minutes, I found myself looking at a ring of mushrooms, which was obviously the doorway to the Unseelie court. I looked at Shadow. "I'll be back in a few minutes," I said.

I stepped into the ring and muttered a spell in Gaelic. There was a flash of light and I found myself in part of Arcadia. Looking around I saw a couple of imps with their bronze weapons standing near their feline cavalry mounts. "Who are you Daemon?" one of them asked me in a distinctly Irish accent.

"I'm private investigator Jason Black," I said casually. I was fairly sure they wouldn't know who I was, but by the time I left they would know that it would be a good thing to fear me if they didn't cooperate.

"And what do you want here?" the other asked.

"I came to talk to your king or queen," I said.

"And why should we let you in?" the first one asked.

"Well, we can do this the easy way, where I give you a couple treats, or we can do this the hard way, where I kill you. It really doesn't matter to me either way," I said with a shrug and a rather nasty smile. "And trust me, I can make your deaths very, very painful."

The two imps looked at each other nervously. "Um, what do you have for us?" one asked.

"Fresh cream, and fresh herb bread," I said holding up a cloth bag. "I've known quite a few Fey that love this stuff, and I'm sure that you have very good taste for the finer things in life."

I could see a greedy light shine in their eyes. "Let's see."

I handed the bag over. As the first one started looking through it, I saw the other going for a knife. The stupid idiot was going to try to kill me. I grabbed the idiot by the neck and jammed my heater in his gut. "Now let's do this quick or you get to find out what it's like to be shot with a bullet made of iron," I snarled. Fey are highly susceptible to iron and it is very painful for them to even touch it let alone have it pumped into their bodies.

The Imp's eyes went wide with fright. "Not a problem, we can be nice!" he yelped.

I spun the imp around and kept 'Ace of Spades' in his back. "Now march," I said, shoving him forward.

The Imp led me down a rough stone hallway. After a couple of minutes, the hallway opened up into a large, crystalline chamber. A Goblin that was obviously their king sat on a bronze throne, surrounded by courtesans of all sorts. He wasn't a Goblin I recognized and the chamber didn't seem entirely finished so this court was still new, but that didn't matter. They had enough power to have influence back in Ireland which was what counted.

"Who are you?" the Goblin king asked.

"I am Jason Black," I said clearly. "And the longer you are in the area the more you will come to know and fear my name."

"I have heard that line before. What proof do you have that I should fear you?" the Goblin asked haughtily.

I merely shrugged and shot the Imp I was holding in the knee. The dark Fey dropped to the ground, screaming in agony. "It burns! The iron burns!" it screamed.

Ignoring the screaming Imp at my feet, I took careful aim at the Goblin king's head. "Listen to me Goblin, or the next round goes between your eyes." My voice wasn't even malicious, just calm and neutral. I'd let the screams of the Imp make the real threat. I saw the courtesans balk at the threat; even the king looked nervous.

"And what do you want with me?" he asked with a slight tremor in his voice.

"I come for James Wells," I said, leaving 'Ace of Spades' trained on the Goblin's head. "His mother made a deal with you. Now let me see him."

"So be it." The Goblin clapped his hands. "Bring the Human."

After ten minutes, a couple of Imps brought a dancing James before us, and his dance enraged me. The kid was on the verge of collapse and looked as if he had been that way for days, yet he couldn't stop the dance. "Why is he wearing the Red Shoes?!" I bellowed.

"How else is he supposed to amuse us?" the Goblin asked.

I knew I couldn't take on the whole court alone. I could kill a lot of them but they'd drag me down by sheer numbers and that would do the kid no good. "What do you want for his release?"

"What are you prepared to offer?" the Goblin king asked. "As I'm sure you know, the trade must be of equal value."

"I know the law," I said. I quickly thought of what would do the most justice and the answer was simple. The mother had done this to her son, she would just have to take his place. "I will give you the kid's mother."

The Goblin stroked his wispy beard in thought. "That has merit. But can you deliver the witch?"

"I have a reputation to live up to," I said. "As you've seen from this Imp, I have no qualms about hurting people."

"Then the deal is struck," the Goblin said. "You bring us the witch and we give the son to you."

"So be it." I walked out of the chamber and once in the entry passage I spoke a spell and left Arcadia.

So? How did it go? Shadow asked.

"Well there's an Imp down there who will never walk the same way again," I said with a grin.

And the boy?

"They have him and I made a deal to get him out of there," I said.

So what's the plan? Shadow asked.

"I make a call to Felix," I said. I took my phone out and dialed Felix's cell number.

"Hello?" Felix said rather groggily.

"Hello, Felix. It's Black. I need to get some stuff from you to get James out of the mess he's in," I said.

"You found him?!" Felix asked excitedly.

"Yes. His mother handed him over to a new Unseelie court as payment for revenge against her ex-husband," I told him. "The worst part is they put him in the Red Shoes."

"Whatever you need it's yours, free of charge," Felix said. "I want my apprentice back."

"I need half a pound of graveyard dirt, and a woman's skeleton," I told him.

"Done. I'll be at the store in thirty minutes," he said.

"I'll meet you there," I said, then disconnected the line.

"Come on Shadow we need to get to Felix's," I said.

Call Sarah and find out where that bitch client of yours is, Shadow said.

"Not a problem." I picked up the phone and hit the button for Sarah's line.

"Hey Jason," she answered.

"Where are you?" I asked her.

"I'm outside of your client's house," she replied.

"Make sure she stays there. Even if you need to keep her in there at gun point. I'll be there in an hour, give or take."

"What's going on?" Sarah asked.

"The bitch sacrificed her son to an Unseelie court," I said. "I need to pick up some stuff from Felix before I meet you there. So just keep her there."

"Not a problem. I'll see you soon."

I turned the engine of the car over and headed into Dinky Town to pick up the supplies I needed from Felix.

CHAPTER

I was fairly close to the shop and I beat Felix there. When he arrived he opened the door and led me in. If you weren't used to it, the store is fairly creepy at night when most of the lights are off. Without the constant scent of burning incense, the smells of the place get really earthy with things better not considered.

"Okay. I've got everything you need," Felix said. "It'll just take me a few minutes to get it all together."

Felix disappeared into a back room. I heard several locks click and then Felix spoke a couple words in one of the Daemonic languages, probably deactivating a guarding curse. A few minutes later he was back with what I needed. He handed over a small, rough cloth bag of graveyard dirt, and a case with the skeleton I needed in it. "Here you go."

"Female skeleton?" I asked him.

"That's what you asked for, isn't it?" Felix added with a smug look on his face.

"That's right. I'm sure you know what I'm planning on doing with it." If Felix couldn't guess, he'd have to be an idiot.

"Well, with that stuff the only thing you could possibly do is make a homunculus of the mother." It was the obvious answer and the right one.

"Yep."

"So how will 'it' be dying?" Felix asked.

"She'll be getting drunk and accidentally starting a fire," I told him.

"Of course, the real Maurine will be given over to the Unseelie court in exchange for James. And since the homunculus of the mother will be an exact copy, the cops will think that she really is dead," Felix said.

"Well, I've got people to grab and replace," I said. "I'll be back here in about two hours, maybe three."

"I'll see you then."

As I left Felix's shop, I mentally prepared myself for what I was about to do. I hadn't made a homunculus in years. I needed to get it spot on if I was going to make it work. I could have performed the ceremony without the graveyard dirt but it would have slowed down the process considerably. I needed this done as fast as possible. As long as the thing could fool the medical examiner I was good. Thankfully the main thing I was going to have to worry about was the dentals and the height. Pretty much everything was going to be destroyed by the fire. As long as those two details survived, I'd be good to go. I just needed to stop by a grocery store for the last component for the preparation of this mess.

CHAPTER 9

Half an hour after I left Felix I was standing outside of the Wells' house. I walked over to where Sarah was waiting in her car for me.

"She's still in there?" I asked.

"Of course," she said. "As you said, if she had tried to leave I'd have forced her back in at gun point."

"You want to help me perform a little arson?" I asked her.

"I've never tried being a fire bug," she said. "What do I have to do?"

"Come with me and I'll show you." I was glad she was going to help. I could have done all the work myself but it would be easier with her help.

I walked up the steps to the porch with Sarah following me. "Hold up right there," I said motioning for her to stand to the right of the door.

I put the bag of graveyard dirt and the skeleton down on the porch along with the necessary tools for the ritual. I then pulled 'Ace of Spades' out of her holster and held her behind my back. After I rang the doorbell and knocked loudly I prepared to wait. After only a minute she opened the door. I looked at her carefully and immediately knew something was wrong. She was fully dressed and not in night clothes. Instead it looked as if she had been getting ready to leave.

"What can I do for you Mr. Black?" she asked.

"I have information regarding James," I said slowly as I clenched and unclenched my hand around my gun. This was wrong, all wrong, I could feel it.

"Well come on in then," she said turning her back on me.

I walked in but I wasn't going to be stupid about it. As I walked through the door I grabbed the door frame with my left and cast a spell of silence, now no noise would leave the house. "So we have a lot to discuss."

I hadn't walked two steps into the house when I smelled the magick, but it was too late. I felt something in the back of the head, it felt like someone had hit me with a horseshoe and I hit the floor hard. As I got my hands under me to get back to my feet, I received another hard kick, this time to the side and I felt a couple ribs give. I was able to keep from screaming, but only barely. Thankfully I had held on to 'Ace of Spades' and rolled away from the direction of the kick and brought my gun to bear on the Human like figure that was about to kick me again. I squeezed off a couple rounds that I knew hit it but whatever had kicked me only laughed and landed another hard kick which rolled me at least five feet across the floor. I stopped rolling and faced the direction the kicks were coming from and, half closing my eyes, waited for the next kick to come. I was going to end this fight ... now.

As the next kick came I grabbed the foot and, pulling it in tight, slammed the butt of my gun into the knee of my attacker. I heard whatever it was screaming in pain as it fell to the floor. I was on my feet in an instant in order to take advantage of the creature's pain. I kicked the damn thing in the head a couple of times until the screaming stopped. I looked up and saw Maurine turning to run. That just wouldn't do. I fired a round into her shoulder and she dropped, screaming in pain.

I walked up to her and pistol whipped her, cutting her off in mid-scream as she dropped to the floor. I then turned back to where my attacker lay unconscious with blood oozing from its mouth. It was definitely Fey, which didn't explain why the iron bullets that were still in my gun hadn't hurt it. Iron was incredibly painful for most Fey. It was how Humans had been able to beat them back into Arcadia. Humans had been able to fight with iron weapons, whereas the poor Fey had been forced to use inferior bronze weapons. I took a second look at the Fey at my feet and noticed the iron shoes it was wearing. Damn thing was an Iron-Jack, the only type of Fey that had acclimated themselves to iron by wearing iron shoes. I gave it a couple more kicks.

Having the Iron-Jack presented a problem. I couldn't leave it here however...

I went into the kitchen and grabbed a butcher's knife. As I walked back out of the kitchen, I gave Maurine another kick as she seemed to be regaining consciousness. I walked over to a wall and carved the outline of a door in the plaster. I spoke an incantation and the door opened on to a portal that led to Arcadia. Grabbing the Fey I threw him in unceremoniously, and then closed the gateway. I'd have to have a word with the Unseelie king about this little incident.

My next move was to keep Maurine asleep. I walked over to her and muttered a sleep charm. I went back out and grabbed Sarah. "What took you so long?" she asked.

"The stupid cow had an Iron-Jack over for company. Took me a little while to send him back to Arcadia," I said.

"Ouch," she replied. "Now what do I do?"

"You still have the bag of flour I gave you?" I asked her.

"Of course, but I don't know why you gave it to me," she said.

"Old fire bug trick," I told her. "I want you to spread it liberally throughout the house. It causes the place to burn faster without being detectible like a normal accelerant, such as gasoline or lighter fluid."

"Ah."

"Okay I'm going to get my 'client' upstairs and ready for the ceremony!" I said.

I grabbed the bag of dirt and the skeleton from the porch. With that stuff in hand, I picked up Maurine, tossed her over my shoulder and headed to her bedroom. When I got there, I threw the bitch on the floor since I was sick of dragging her around for the moment. Truthfully, I was just plain sick of looking at her. I walked over to a dresser and, after rummaging through it for a few minutes, found a night gown, the buttoned up the front kind. I took the gown and lay the skeleton out in it. The next thing I did was sprinkle the skeleton with the graveyard dirt. After that I reached in to my bag of tools and grabbed a tooth extractor. I opened Maurine's mouth and yanked out a tooth and placed the tooth in the mouth of the skeleton. With that tooth there the homunculus would recreate the dental work of Maurine perfectly. My next task was to get blood out of Maurine with a ceremonial knife.

I took out a knife fitted to the job and a small bowl. I made a broad cut in her hand and squeezed a fair amount blood in to the bowl while I muttered a spell. I then took the blood and pored it over the dirt. With all of that done I was ready to complete the spell.

I closed my eyes and ran through a series of incantations, feeling the magick of my Daemonic birthright flow through my system. The incantations themselves were Human, but with the Daemonic bloodline powering them, they worked rapidly. Fifteen minutes later there was an exact likeness of Maurine laying on the bed. If you didn't know that the thing wasn't actually alive, you'd have been easily fooled. Everything was perfect, right down to the internal organs, it even breathed enough for the lungs to fill with smoke if enough of the body survived to allow for an autopsy. My next trick was to finish the final set up.

I took a bottle of vodka out of my bag of tools and spilled a fair amount near the head of the bed, next to the homunculus. Most of the rest of the bottle spilled out when I dropped it one the floor a few inches from the nightstand. Thankfully there was an electrical outlet right next to it. I put a timed fire glyph on the outlet to go off in thirty minutes. Carrying Maurine, I left the room ready to finish off the staged accidental death. I ran into Sarah who was powdering the guest room and told her to make sure she got every room on the second floor.

After five minutes she met me down stairs. "Everything taken care of up there?" I asked.

"This place will go up like a torch if this trick of yours works," she told me. "And I if I didn't know that is a homunculus up there, I'd have sworn it really was Mrs. Wells."

"That's the point," I said. "Now let's get out here. I'll meet you at my office in the morning."

"See you in the morning," she said, and then left.

Ten minutes after she left, I followed her with a limp Maurine over my shoulder. Having used a spell that would keep anyone from noticing that I was carrying her out to the car, no one even looked in my direction.

Everything go well? Shadow asked in a snide voice, which screamed that he knew what had happened.

"You already knew about that damn Iron-Jack didn't you?" I hissed at him as I threw Maurine in the back seat.

You walked right into that. Quite literally in this case. He probably would have smiled had he been able to do so.

"Shut up," I snarled. "Now let's get this bitch back to Witch's Hat."

It didn't take long to get to Witch's Hat. By the time I got there, the pain from dealing with the Iron-Jack was gone, but I was still pissed about it. I didn't have enough iron bullets for my tommy gun, so killing a shit load of Fey was out of the question. That didn't mean I couldn't screw with them, though.

When I arrived at the water tower, I threw Maurine back over my shoulder and headed to the ring of toadstools that marked the doorway. I muttered the Gaelic opening spell and stepped back into Arcadia. The first time I had arrived at this court I had been challenged by the guards, this time they ran to announce my presence as soon as I looked at them. I was happy to note that my reputation was now well formed with this court. I hadn't even needed to shoot a second Fey.

Less than a minute later, a Bogie came back out and nervously asked me to follow him in. As soon as I was in front of the throne, I dropped my former client on the ground and spoke the counter spell to the sleep charm I used on her. She looked at me with a dazed expression that quickly turned to fear when she realized where she was.

"Here she is," I said. "Now release the boy."

"Well we seem to have a problem with that. You see, we didn't actually expect you to come back," the king hesitated.

"And you killed the kid!" I snarled.

"No, he's very much alive, however I don't think we can let him go since our contract is with this witch, and not with you." The tone of the king screamed that he was scared of what he was about to say.

"I take it that is why you sent an Iron-Jack," I said in a non-question.

"More or less." The king agreed. "So I guess we'll..."

"Trying to get rid of me would be very foolish," I said, cutting him off. "You see I have a couple friends in the mortal realm that know exactly where this place is and are expecting me to show up soon. If you try to get rid of me, they'll call another friend of mine, one who controls every Vampire and Werewolf in North America. If something happens to me, she'll bring her army down upon your heads and it will be a pure blood bath down here. So, if I were you, I'd do exactly what I tell you."

The Goblin blanched at the thought of seeing that kind of army let loose on his court. "Very well, we'll take the trade."

"You can't..." Maurine started before I kicked her.

"They just did," I hissed. I then turned back to the king. "Now bring me the kid."

"Of course." The king clapped his hands summoning an Imp. "Bring the boy."

A couple minutes later an Imp brought James in. He was no longer wearing the red shoes but he couldn't walk under his own power either. I grabbed the kid before the Imp dumped him on the floor. I reached into a pocket of my coat and pulled out a horseshoe. I pressed the iron shoe against the kid's face and, when nothing happened, was satisfied that this really was James and not a changeling.

"Well, looks like I've gotten what I came for," I said to the king. I looked over at Maurine. "You were stupid for getting me involved."

"I did my part. My masters will come for me soon enough and I'll make you pay for everything that happens to me," she spat back.

"Who is your master?" I asked her.

"You have the child, now go," the king commanded.

"Not before I have my answer," I started before the king interrupted me.

"You have what you wanted. Now get out of here!" The king motioned for a couple of Bogies to take Maurine away.

"They'll come for me Black, and when I come back you will suffer!" Maurine screamed as she was being dragged off.

"Give my best regards to your torturers," I called after her. I didn't feel like trying to get anything out of her since it would mean dealing with the Goblin king and his court. However, if she did get out and some outside force came after me, all they could expect was death.

"I want you out of here Black," the king said. "Our business in concluded."

"I guess it is," I said with a shrug.

I picked up James, carried him to the entrance of the court and, with a quick charm, left Arcadia for the Human realm. I was glad to be out of there. I didn't like any part of Arcadia too much. It smelled funny and I didn't like dealing with Fey in those kinds of numbers. I can deal with Fey at the Mystic Wolf because I'm only dealing with a few at a time, but Arcadia was their home realm.

How is he? Shadow asked as soon as I returned.

"He'll be fine after a couple of weeks of rest," I said. "However, that court pissed me off." I turned around, and with a spell, flamed the circle of toadstools, effectively closing this entrance for that Unseelie court. I had a feeling that they'd come back but now they'd know not to cross me.

Well let's get back to Felix's so you can drop the kid off with him. You need to get some rest, Shadow said.

"You're probably right."

CHAPTER 10

Soon I was back at Felix's and was carrying James into the store. He still hadn't awakened, but that was probably for the best. Wouldn't want him to wake up around a stranger. Better that he sees Felix right away.

"How's he doing?" Felix asked me as soon as I walked through the door.

"He probably feels like crap and will be feeling that way for quite a while," I told him.

"So what happens now?" Felix asked me.

"Well, the mother is in an Unseelie court now, and there is a good chance that his dad is dead. Since he's your apprentice, that means, by the old law, you're now responsible for him," I said.

"Of course," Felix said. "But what does the kid owe you for saving his life?"

"Nothing. His mother's check cleared, so I've been paid," I said.

"You are a hard ass," Felix said.

"I just close cases. Nothing more, nothing less." I said.

As I was about to head out the door, my phone played my text message alert. It took me a second to realize that the number belonged to Inferno's Plague.

"We were about to nail Kill Switch Karma when this symbol popped up," it read. A second later a symbol that I hadn't seen in over seventy years showed up on my phone. It was a pair of lightning bolts, one black, the other red, crossed on a field of white. I had fought the occult members of the Third Reich back during the Knights War, but now it looked like they were back.

THE LADY K CAPER

CHAPTER

The snow was falling unseasonably wet for late November. I was loving it. Unfortunately, my secretary didn't like it one bit and had come down with a cold that had left her miserable, coughing and sneezing. She was on her second box of tissues and with her red nose, she looked absolutely pathetic. I had decided to pick her up some chicken soup from her favorite soup and sandwich shop, as well as box of organic lemon drops from Felix's store to make her feel better.

"Hey sweetheart, I thought you could use this," I said, placing the bag with the food in it in front of her.

"Eddington's?" she asked happily. "Thanks boss. You are a Godsend." I gave her a false glare, causing her to raise her hands as if to ward me off. "Not literally of course. I know you're half-Infernal and all, but you know what I mean."

"Of course I do, now eat up. Nothing helps a cold like a good bowl of chicken noodle soup. Also I got you these," I said as I put down the box of lemon drops.

"You are seriously the sweetest boss a girl could have." She then started coughing. "Gods my throat hurts."

I started to hang up my coat when I turned to ask her the question I usually ask when I've been out of the office for a while. "Any calls?"

"Nothing, I've just been playing Blackjack with Shadow while you've been out. He's lousy at it. Anything you need me for today boss, or can I go home?" Jamie asked. "My throat is killing me and I would like to do something about it."

"Sure. That won't be a problem," I said as I went into the back office.

"Oh, I put your mail on your desk," Jamie called to my retreating back.

I looked at the mail, grabbed a manila envelope and just stared at it. It obviously hadn't come by mail since there was no postage stamp on it. I stuck my head out the office door and just caught Jamie opening the door to the hallway. "You said no one came by while I was out?"

"No one, or I would have told you," she answered. "Why?"

"Oh nothing. Go on get home and rest."

"Goodnight boss." With that Jamie closed the door behind herself.

"Hey Shadow?"

Yes?

"Did anything unusual happen that Jamie didn't tell me about?" I asked.

Of course not. She would have told you if anything had. And I would have if she hadn't. Why?

I held up the envelope. On the front was simply a picture of a bald man with a bulbous nose peering over a wall. Next to the picture were three words that, back in the day, would have sent the leaders of the Third Reich and the Soviets into a panic. 'Kilroy Was Here'. The infamous super spy had been and gone, and as usual, nobody had seen him come or go; he had just left his calling card.

I opened the envelope and found a letter and five thousand in dead presidents. "Need help. Mystic Wolf, 2100 hrs. Don't bother looking for me. I'll find you." This wasn't a social call, this was business. Business with an old, and close ... well sort-of-close friend. You could have offered me a thousand times more money than the five thousand that was in the envelope and I would have turned it down without batting an eyelash. If Kilroy needed my help, something serious had happened, and it could lead to very serious trouble for more than just a few people.

CHAPTER

It was a quarter to nine when I arrived at The Mystic Wolf. The bar was relatively quiet, meaning that it was possible to hear the person next to you without resorting to shouting. The place had taken the form of an Irish pub, with Black and Tans being the special drink of the night. The waitresses had been arguing with Brisbane about uniforms again I saw, and he had lost. It looked as if they had agreed on plaid micro-skirts, with a ruffled top that started just below their breasts and gave a good sight of their cleavage, leading to off-the-shoulder short sleeves. I could tell that some men were either too distracted to look at how much they were putting down on the table for tips, or were just being very generous tonight. If these girls lived in the mortal realm they would have made enough in tips for a month's rent on a really nice apartment tonight. I once asked what they did with all the money they made since I don't know of any Infernal realm that takes U.S. currency. I found out two things: first Succubae love fast cars and expensive jewelry. Second: someone big was planning some sort of power play in the relatively near future. Of course, the term "near future" is all relative, and whomever tried that stunt would be in for a nasty surprise when it clashed with the Countess Blood Wolf and the

Court of Night. Still I was keeping tabs on the situation to see when and where things were going to blow.

In one corner I saw Bear and Coyote getting liquored up while comparing different brands of Fire Water. Alcohol was one of the worst things that the white man brought to the Americas. Even their Gods hit the sauce too hard at times. Coyote is a weird one to say the least. According to some he is the creator, according to others he is the trickster, though that was usually when he was drunk, like tonight. Some people wondered why Brisbane let Coyote into the bar when he was acting as the trickster; he explained that it was the same reason he allowed Eris Discordia and Loki into the place. It was preferable to let them into the bar without resistance, rather than worry about them gate-crashing. Of course, last time Loki tried to come in during a temporary ban of Norse Gods, Brisbane had used the bar as a giant pinball machine with Loki as the ball. In the Mystic Wolf, Brisbane is the chief God with the rest of the employees being lesser Gods and Angels, and everyone else is brought into line so that Gods can't push around the humans. Of course, Humans tend to give the Gods—and others like Dragons and Faeries—a wide berth. Inside the bar, Gods are weakened. Outside the bar ... well, they're Gods.

I looked around the bar and found a booth in the back to slide into to wait for Kilroy. I was only waiting for a couple minutes when a Succubus arrived for a drink order.

"Hey Sasha!" The Succubus was about to start student teaching next year, but for now she was still waiting tables.

"Good evening Black. Hey Shadow, still hanging around with this bum?" Shadow dipped his head in response. "So how is that apprentice of Felix's doing?"

"Not bad. He's still having nightmares about his time in Arcadia. Other than that he's holding up well."

"So what brings you here tonight? Need my help solving a case again?"

"Not at the moment, but I'm meeting a client here in a few minutes."

"Well, can I start you with a drink?"

"Double bourbon neat," I ordered. "But please wait until after I'm done with my client before you bring it."

"No problem." She left knowing that if I wanted to be left alone that it wasn't a good idea to just hang around.

I had been waiting for a few minutes when I looked at my watch. When I looked back to the seat across from me, I saw Kilroy looking at me. "How do you do that?" I asked. I couldn't do that even with all the magick I had been trained in. There would still have been some trace of me, but not so with the legendary Kilroy.

Kilroy smiled. "Old family secret. I couldn't train you in it even if I wanted to. Which I don't."

"Understood." I wasn't disappointed by his comment. Everyone has their secrets. There were things I could do which I didn't teach to the rest of the allies under my command during the Knights War. Mostly it had to do with what was required of one. Many people in that war held dark secrets that could have destroyed lesser men. We were a motley bunch of magick users, and true knights of old. Some were descendants of Merlin or were from the Arthurian court. Others were half Daemons like Kilroy and myself, or Lycanthropes, or Vampires. There was even the odd revenant out to avenge their deaths at the hand of the Nazis. We were all deadly, and almost all of us had secrets no sane person should know. "So why have you asked me to meet you here?"

"My granddaughter has disappeared and I need to find her."

"Sounds simple enough," I said. I've never had problems working missing persons cases before. "I'll need all the information you can give me on her, of course, and I'll start looking for her right away."

"Well, to start, I should tell you that she is true to the Kilroy name." I just stared at him. If you had given me the choice of any type of assignment I would want to do, probably the last would be a missing persons caper for a being like Kilroy.

Kilroy and the others like him, for example Britain's Mr. Chad or Australia's Foo, are not fully human. They are all partly daemonic beings similar to me. They are all descended from the same divine Daemon. Divine daemons have powers that Infernal Daemons, like my father, simply don't possess. Of course, the opposite is true as well. Despite what many people think, for the most part Infernal and Divine Daemons have very few problems with each other. With Daemons they have mostly a "live and let live" way of handling each other. Of course, when you get to the inner workings of the governing body that controls almost all Daemonic beings, they are just as good at backstabbing each other as any group of Humans.

"So how did she end up with her abilities?" I asked. "Was it a case of your father showing up for a night of fun?"

Kilroy gave me a hard look. "Dad's not that kind of Daemon. He stuck around for a while before he left. Did your father?"

"As a matter of fact he stuck around until shortly after my mother was burned at the stake, and a little while after that. I was well into my twenties when he left, and we still get together every year to remember my mother on the anniversary of her death." I hate it when people think all Infernal Daemons are always the "love 'em and leave 'em" type. Besides a lot of Divine Daemons are like that too, they just don't have as bad a rap. "Now let's not get into a pissing contest about who had the better fatherly role model. You've been my friend long enough to know that it's all a bunch of racist bullshit anyway."

"Off the table then," Kilroy said with an almost forced laugh. "To answer your question though, no, dad wasn't involved. Apparently her power just showed up one day. I've been trying to train her as best I can, but she got cocky and started working for the government before I felt she was ready."

"And now you think it's gotten her into trouble?" I asked, not that I didn't already know the answer.

"I haven't been able to get ahold of her. I did some digging with the help of some of our old friends and they've never even heard of her." That was worrying, between the two of us we could dig out just about anything known in government circles. Hell, I could probably get top level clearance to Area 51 if I wanted to. Of course, I had resources that included the Court of Night, which opens a whole hell of a lot of doors.

"Are you certain that these guys are real government types?"

"I'm beginning to doubt it. They approached her and I don't think she did enough digging to find out if they were true blue. For all we know, they could have been those commie Ruskies or possibly those slant eyed Chinks, maybe worse." Kilroy had spooked the hell out of Stalin during the Cold War and he still doesn't trust Russians and more recently, Chinese. Still with what the Russians have been doing to get a hold of US secrets recently and the Chinese launching cyber-attack after cyber-attack, he had valid reason to be paranoid about them.

"So what do you have for me?" I asked. "And I'm talking substantial, not just baseless paranoia."

"What do you mean baseless?" Kilroy growled. I'd say cantankerous would be the best way to describe the old spook.

"I mean what concrete information do you have for me?"

"Here is everything I have that I can give you." He handed me a large manila envelope with pictures of her, her weight and height, every vital statistic I could want including friends, and thankfully, a key to her apartment. There was also a picture of her own calling card, like the one Kilroy had used to scare the crap out of people. His had read, 'Kilroy Was Here' with a childish sketch of him peeking over a wall. For his granddaughter it read, 'Lady K Was Here.' The sketch next to it was almost identical to Kilroy's except that it had a hair ribbon on top of the head. All in all it was a fairly complete, yet at the same time vague, dossier.

"So she goes by Lady K. How appropriate," I said.

"So you're going to take the case I assume."

"For a friend and a thousand dollars a day I'll take it." I put everything from the dossier back in the envelope. "I'll call you as soon as I know something."

"Thanks Black." Kilroy shook my hand. "Do you have the time?"

I looked at my watch. "It's nine..." My voice trailed off when I looked back at Kilroy and found that he had disappeared. He really was a world class spook.

CHAPTER

I returned to my office, took a lowball glass out of my desk and poured out a couple fingers of cough medicine. After swallowing the bourbon I dumped the contents of the dossier onto my desk, spreading it out so I could see everything at once. I hoped there was something here that would give me a clue as to where she could have gone. The problem was that I had no idea where to start.

Without any solid clue about who would want to grab her, I decided to go backwards and figure out who would want her talents. The answer was simple: everyone. There were a whole host of major corporations who would be knocking down her door to buy her services for corporate espionage. However, I could probably rule out corporations because she would immediately red flag them as not being the government people they had claimed to have been. So let's go government.

NSA? FBI? CIA? ATF? Another alphabet soup entity? Any one of them would love to have her working for them, and that was just the official American entities. There were a whole host of blacked out groups that would want her. Then there were the foreign agencies like Russia's FSB or China's HUMIT; they'd love to have her. For that matter, it could have been a freelance organization. A person with the abilities of Kilroy would be perfect to spy on anyone. Of course they'd have to be completely off the grid to work with her. Area 51 was heavily classified, but that was nothing compared to how far off the books people like Kilroy and myself are. The problem was that Kilroy had reached out to his contacts and they had come up blank but I had other contacts so I'd try mine. I just needed the current code phrase for the Court of Night contacts. I looked at the clock. Almost eleven. Yvette would still be up, not that she ever slept much.

I hit the speed dial and waited for her to pick up. I didn't have to wait long. "What do you want Jason?" Her tone wasn't its usual cheerful, thank you for calling type, instead she sounded pissed. "I'm deep in the middle of something."

"I just need the current code phrase for your government agents," I told her.

"You must have a pretty big case if you need that," she said.

"What's the bill?" I asked, knowing I was going to regret it.

"I'll figure something out later. I really am pretty busy at the moment." I heard someone scream in the background. I wondered who had been stupid enough to cross the Countess this time. "Anyway it's, 'Everyone dances at night'. Now I really must go." She hung up without wishing me goodnight. Whoever had crossed her was in for a very, very painful few days. Yvette had learned to torture people from me, and she had gotten a lot of practice during the Knights' War. She could keep a victim alive for a few days if she desired. Oh well, they had probably done something to deserve it. Every once in a great while some idiot challenges the Countess's authority, and they get butchered. Well, if they're lucky they do. If they're not lucky, they get tortured to death as a warning to others.

Looking at the clock I saw that it was probably going to be too late to call anyone tonight, but that didn't mean I had to stop sleuthing. There were a lot of people up at this time of night who owed me favors or whose services could be bought pretty easily.

The first person that popped to mind was a Silicon Slave friend of mine, Hell Fire's Dame. She could scour the net for mention of Lady

K. Thankfully she was pretty much like most hackers and did most of her operating at night.

I picked up my phone and sent her a text message asking her to call me. While I waited I scanned the picture of the 'Lady K Was Here' calling card to be ready to send to her. A couple minutes later I got an answering message telling me to get ready for Skype.

I activated the program and waited for her to call, a second later her face showed up on the screen. "Mornin' Jason. To what do I owe the pleasure?"

"I find myself in need of your skills," I said. "I have a case that involves a missing person with the abilities of Kilroy."

Hell Fire's Dame looked puzzled. "I thought Kilroy was nothing more than a doodle people drew for fun."

"Oh, he's real all right. Scariest spook the Allies ever had. His granddaughter disappeared and she has the same powers."

"And what kind of powers would those be?"

Ah the ignorance of youth. "Are you familiar with Eugene the Jeep?" I asked.

"Can't say I've met him before, does he hang out at the Mystic Wolf often?"

"No, he's a character from Popeye the Sailor comics. First debuted in March of '36." Hell Fire's Dame gave me a blank look. I sighed and shook my head, man I felt old. "Never mind, before your time."

"I guess."

"Anyways, Kilroy and those like him can walk through walls, teleport, and simply appear and disappear without a trace. They can do a few other things which makes them such great spies. It also buys them more than a few enemies." To say that they had enemies was an understatement. Hitler had put a one million Reichsmark bounty on Kilroy's head; that translated to over four million US Dollars back during World War II. They had wanted him bad. "That being said, I need you to hunt down any references to the phrase 'Lady K Was Here' throughout the internet. There's a doodle that goes along with it.

I'll send you a scan of it. My guess is that it might hit on some heavily guarded government feeds."

"That sounds like some serious work, Black. I'm probably going to need help to break into those places. A lot of the computer sites for the really deep cover shit are put together by Silicon Slaves on the government payroll." Crap, Silicon Slave versus Silicon Slave battles are always a mess.

"Can you do it though?"

"I'll need Inferno's Plague to help, so this is really going to cost you."

"How much?" I was dreading the answer.

"Oh, money isn't going to be the issue. We can hack the shit out of any bank out there for everything we need."

Oh hell, what does she have in mind?

"We need a favor. We'll just have to figure it out later," she said.

I didn't like the sound of that.

"So you'll start your search now?"

"Of course, just remember, you owe us a favor."

"Trust me, I won't forget." I don't forget favors, unfortunately they have a tendency to come back and bite me in the ass.

"Here's what I have for you," I said, sending her the scanned image.

"Okay we'll get to work on this right away. This will be fun for Inferno's Plague considering how much of a conspiracy nut he is." Those two were a menace together since they had teamed up. A Silicon Slave alone was scary, two of them working together were a computer programmer's nightmare on steroids.

"Goodnight then," I said.

"Goodnight nothing, it's still early." She disconnected Skype on her side.

I looked at the clock, saw it was already midnight, decided to head home to get some sleep.

CHAPTER 4

When I woke up, it was seven in the morning and time for me to head into work. I found Shadow in the kitchen with his head on an ice cube, and groaning loudly in my head. "Hey buddy what's going on?"

I've got a hangover, that's what. He muttered at me.

"Why on earth did you tie one on last night?" Shadow wasn't much for drinking and he typically only got drunk one night a year. I looked at the calendar and realized what had caused the hangover.

"I'm sorry buddy I didn't realize that it was already that date. You want to talk about it?"

Shadow gave me a withering look. *I'll talk to you about it once you find a mate. Until then you have nothing to compare my suffering with.*

It had been over 2,000 years since his mate had died, but the anniversary of the event was still painful. I decided to leave him alone, he was going to be cranky all day now.

It took me almost thirty minutes to get to the office due to a spinout that had taken out a fire hydrant. Some people should stay home if they can't learn to drive in snow and ice. Oh well, this being Minnesota, they'll learn fast enough. Of course there is always the Darwin element to that.

When I walked into the office, I could smell the coffee. Since Jamie had brewed it, I knew it was going to be pretty good. Drinking the sludge I brew is almost as bad as the food Jamie used to make. After she took a few cooking lessons, which I had funded, her cooking had improved from "crimes against humanity," to borderline edible. Next to the coffeemaker was a fresh package of donuts. That girl had very quickly become an amazing secretary, and was in for a very large holiday bonus.

"Morning Jamie," I called into the other room, which was my personal office.

"Morning boss," she said sweetly as she walked into the outer office. She looked around. "Where's Shadow?"

"At home nursing a hangover." She looked confused for a second then shrugged. She had gotten used to the weirdness of her job very quickly. "Any calls yet?"

"Not a one. So anything new?"

"Yeah. A case showed up and it is definitely an important one. I'm going to be making a lot of calls so try not to disturb me until I let you know who is allowed to see me." Jamie knew what that meant, and there were some interesting defenses in place for her sake that would make it relatively easy for her to do that job.

"What if it's Yvette or Sarah?" Jamie knew, as did most people in the magickal realm of the Twin Cities, that those two fought over my affections constantly.

"They probably won't show up. Sarah's got a case, and last I talked to Yvette she was too busy torturing some poor bastard who had crossed her to come here." Then I thought about it for a second. "However, if Yvette does show up, let me know and I'll fit her in. Sarah is not allowed to disturb me if she shows up."

"Are you going to be borrowing any of the Countess's enforcers for this case?" Yvette often provided me with muscle when I needed it.

"Not as of this moment, no," I said. "However she did supply me with contact codes for her field agents throughout the country. If something red flags with one of them I may have to deal with her, like it or not."

"Is there anything in particular that you need me to be doing at the moment?"

I opened the drawer of my desk and found a new bottle of my favorite bourbon next to the almost finished one. As I said, great secretary. "Nothing at the moment. If something does come up, I'll let you know."

Jamie walked into my office and grabbed a couple of my old dime-store pulp detective novels from a bookcase. "In case I get bored."

"If I haven't called in an order for lunch, buzz me around one to make sure I eat."

I closed the door as soon as Jamie assured me she would. I sat down at my desk and, turning on my computer, pulled up the address book with names and numbers of all of Yvette's field agents. The list contained literally thousands of names throughout the country. There was no major city police department in the country in which she didn't have an agent or two. All federal law enforcement agencies and foreign intelligence agencies were littered with her agents of various ranks. She had generals and admirals throughout the military. She had agents who were congressional, and even presidential aides. The scariest part was that she also had agents in many major corporations. The Countess could, if she wanted to, literally flip a switch and be the true ruler of the US. She was just scary that way.

I stared at the screen and wondered who to start with. I felt it was safe to eliminate the military men, at least for now. I decided to make a call to a Werewolf in the FBI whose official job was as a tech in the department that kept an eye on field agents of other organizations. The alphabet soup that made up the US security infrastructure was paranoid of each other come budget time. Their first priority was to keep the country safe. Following hot on the heels of that was the desire to get more funding. The true job of this agent belonged to the Court of Night. He was positioned to inform on the rest of his department.

My hand was an inch from the phone when I got a text message from Hell Fire's Dame. 'BIG NEWS!!! SKYPE NOW!!!'. I knew she wouldn't text me in all caps if it wasn't important. I switched on the Skype program and sent a request for a video conference to the Silicon Slave. "Hey Hell..." Was all I got out before she cut me off.

"Whatever you're into, you're in deep," were the first words out of Hell Fire's Dame's mouth.

"What are you talking about?" I asked slowly.

"Inferno's Plague told me about that symbol that showed on Felix's website when Kill Switch Karma fucked it." My Silicon Slave seemed pretty freaked.

"Yeah, what about it?" I didn't like where this was going.

"It showed up again while we were tracking down references to Lady K. Whoever went after James is back and they've got some connection to Lady K." That was not good. That was so not good that it was scary beyond belief.

"Are you certain it's them?"

"Dead certain. You better give me a whole hell of a lot of information before I keep going. Who are these people?"

"They are known as the Crossed Bolts, the occult division of the Third Reich. These guys are true psychos. Mike Mignola got part of it right with the Hellboy stuff, but what he did was relatively tame by comparison." I needed to stamp these guys out, and I'd need to bring some serious cavalry. This was going to become a war, but right now I needed to win just this one battle.

"I'm not sure that Inferno's Plague and I are ready to get this deeply involved if this spills over," Hell Fire's Dame said. She was, understandably, scared.

"If I'm not able to start tackling these guys one at a time now, who knows what horrors they'll unleash and then you'll be involved like it or not." I needed her and Inferno's Plague's help because they had skills I didn't have. "Can you track Kill Switch Karma down so I can grab her now?"

"Give us a little bit and we'll track her down. Keep this line open."

While I waited I started a Word document and started to organize my thoughts on who would need to be called. A lot of my friends from the Knights' War were dead but there were still quite a few of us left. I had only gotten a few names down when Hell Fire's Dame popped back up on screen.

"She's in London, going by name of Amanda Tanner. Her office is in a building on Cheapside. I'll shoot you the address and map in an email. From what I can tell, the office is leased by a German shell company called Feuer-Vogol Technologies and it's been there for a while so you should be able to grab her there." That could have been better news. I've been banned from stepping foot on English soil. However...

"Thanks. I'll take her out so she won't be able to retaliate."

"Thanks." The Silicon Slave seemed genuinely scared. "Call us when you take her down because we're going to lie low for a while."

"I'll call," I said and turned off Skype.

So this Nazi agent was in England. I couldn't pick her up myself, however I had other means. There are times I really hate talking to family. I picked up my phone and tried to think of any other means to get out of calling my cousin but nothing came to mind that would be as quick.

I waited three rings before the phone picked up. "Sir David Booth speaking." Sir David freaking Booth of her Majesty's Secret Service. He had been knighted by King Henry the Eighth and was a smug git. He was also my cousin on my dad's side, at least that's what dad says. For all I know, he could really be my half-brother.

"Morning, Dave," I said just to piss him off. "How's the weather?"

"That is Sir..." There was a brief pause. "Jason is that you?"

"Wow, aren't you a sharp one," I replied sarcastically.

"I'm sure you didn't just call me to ask about the weather. So what do you want?"

"I need a favor, and it will benefit not only me but you and England as well." I had to appeal his sense of patriotism.

"What could you have that could possibly be worth all that?" Dave asked in a tone that meant I had his full attention.

"I've got a name and location of a high ranking Nazi agent in England." Hopefully that would catch is attention.

"I doubt that you know anything I don't already know." As I said, smug git.

"So you know about Amanda Tanner of Feuer-Vogol Technologies?" I asked. I hoped to trip him up.

I had the joy of being able to hear his jaw dropping. "Who are you talking about? I've never heard of anyone like that."

"She's a Silicon Slave who goes by the moniker Kill Switch Karma. I ran across her on a case awhile back and a website she'd screwed over had the sign of the crossed lightning bolts on it." I could almost hear the color drain from his face.

"Nothing showed on the radar for that. What else do you have for me on her?" This had him spooked.

"I have her address," I said. "But there's something really bad about the situation."

"We've got a member of the Crossed Bolts out there and there's worse news?" His voice would have sounded funny if the whole situation wasn't so bad.

"She, or someone close to her, has probably tricked Kilroy's granddaughter into working for her, and his granddaughter has his powers." I heard the phone drop and hit a desk or table or something.

"Are you sure she was tricked?" Dave asked once he had picked up the phone again.

"We're talking about a Kilroy here. No way she'd knowingly work for the Nazis. Also, from what the original Kilroy told me, she thought she was working for the US government." I needed his help.

"So what's the favor you need from me? I'll grab her and question her myself," Dave said sounding official about it.

"Not good enough. I need to question her myself."

"That is out of the ques..." I cut him off.

"Think of it this way—I can do things to her that you can't. Bring her to me, bound and gagged, and I'll get you everything you need to know. You can even step out of the room if you want." I have some nasty ways of breaking people that Dave could never use for two reasons. First it was against British law, but more importantly he didn't have the balls to get his hands that dirty.

"I don't like it."

"We're talking about the possible fate of Queen and Country. You're a knight damn it, I'm giving you plausible deniability if she dies. I can get fake paperwork on my side but I need her now," I growled. "Give her to me and it'll be a nail in the coffin of those genocidal maniacs."

I heard Dave sigh. "Okay I'll grab her and bring her to you."

"Thanks David. You won't regret it."

"I already do. The paperwork is going to be a mess." I heard him say before he hung up.

Now it was time to get some paperwork faked so I began looking on my list for people who could get me my paperwork. It took me awhile but I found a guy who wanted to become a vampire that fit the bill. He was in the NSA and was probably looking for a way to score points with everybody. I made a call to the switchboard of his department in Washington and got bounced around awhile. "Hello, you've reached the office of Conrad Van Dorn, I am currently out of the office. If you leave me a message, I'll get back to you." Damn it, the bastard was probably screening his calls.

"This is Jason Black, just calling to remind you that everyone dances at night," I replied to the voice mail.

I only had to wait a couple of minutes before I got a return call. "Hello Conrad," I said as soon as I saw the number show up on my caller ID.

"What can I do for the great Jason Black?" Great, a suck up. "I can get you alm..."

I cut him off. "Don't suck up. You want my help to score points with the Countess, you're going to do what I tell you to, no questions asked. Got it?"

"Of course sir." Being close friends with the Countess Blood Wolf opens so many doors it's not even funny.

"I need paperwork to bring a foreign national into the country under the radar. The woman's name is Amanda Tanner," I told him. "Here is the official reasoning. She is a professional hacker who goes by the name Kill Switch Karma. She is also known to be a member of a Nazi terrorist group."

"How are you going to get ahold of her?" Conrad sounded nervous. "This could take a while if we went the official route."

"I already have a member of MI 5 picking her up now. All I need is paperwork to get her across the ocean," I said. "I need this fast and last week. Get this done and I'll put in a good word for you with the Countess."

"Understood." Conrad hung up.

Now the only thing I could do was sit back and wait for things to turn out. I hate sitting and doing nothing but that's all I could do. Then I realized that there was something I could do.

I opened the dossier Kilroy had given me and took out the key to Lady K's apartment. Maybe there was something there that would help me track down the missing spook. It was a long shot. If she was any good, she'd have moved anything involved in her work to a more secure area, but it was possible that she had left a clue to where that may have been.

As I left the office I told Jamie to keep me in the loop if anyone important called. The list of important people was short: Kilroy, Conrad Van Dorn, Yvette, and Sir Booth were about it. Jamie was also allowed to use her better judgment for anyone else. I then wrote down the address so she could give it to Shadow when the bird decided to join me.

It took about thirty minutes to get to Lady K's apartment in a nondescript building in a nondescript neighborhood. It was the perfect place for a spy. The inside wasn't much different than the outside of the building. I decided to go through the place on a room by room sweep.

My first stop was the kitchen. She ordered carryout a lot. Her fridge was a temple to doggy bags. She seemed to have a love affair with MSG, as there were a lot of boxes of bad Chinese takeout. The leftover pizza was a little healthier, but not by much. The sink was empty and the counter was neat so she was either a clean freak, or if she had been grabbed here, the attackers didn't want to raise any suspicions. I emptied the trash can and found a small amount of the standard kitchen trash that you'd expect with a diet that came from the food in her fridge—tons of cheap chopsticks and greasy napkins. Not much in the way of significant clues, but it did start to build a clearer idea of who I was looking for than I could get from the dossier.

My second stop was the living / dining room. I turned on the TV and got MSNBC, so she was a liberal. I checked her movie collection and found a lot of historical documentaries; the topics were varied so not a lot of information there, except that she was an amateur history buff. Her book collection followed along the same lines as her DVDs. The trash can here was nearly empty.

My next stop was the bedroom. There was little of any significance in the room. By the end of the search all I had learned really was that she had eight pairs of shoes, five dresses, plus the standard little-black-dress, wore size two pants and was a Star Trek fan. I also learned that she wore a thirty-four C cup bra, not that that really meant anything. The only significant thing was that the .38 she kept in her nightstand hadn't been fired recently.

After that came the office. There I finally hit on a real clue, a couple of door keys that were in a hidden compartment in her desk. They didn't go to the apartment, and I couldn't imagine her hiding keys to a place she didn't mind people knowing about. My best guess was that they were for some other office, possibly one that held some real clues as to what she was doing. Now I just had to figure out where this other place was.

I searched all the drawers in the office and upended the trash can. An hour or so later, I found what I was looking for. It was a bill for the rent of a unit in an office building in St. Paul. That she hadn't shredded it, or better yet burned it, was sloppy on her part, but it was maybe just what I needed to save her life.

I was just about to leave the office when Shadow showed up. "Nice to see you feather brain."

Sorry it took me so long to get here Master, but I'm still feeling off, he said. *So what are we doing?*

"Get in the car and I'll bring you up to speed on the case." From there I told him in great detail where we were going.

CHAPTER

I pulled up in front of the office building identified on the bill I had found in Lady K's apartment. It was a small, almost rundown building that had definitely seen better, but never great, days. I let myself in and walked down the halls, trying out the key on every door I found until it worked in the fifth office on the second floor. When it worked I almost blew it up.

I noticed the small catch by the doorknob just in time to keep from setting off a booby trap of a series of incendiary bombs placed throughout the office. The walls were shielded to keep them from burning the entire building, but the back blast would have hurt like hell. Had I been mortal, it would have almost certainly killed me.

The front of the office was a boring collection of third hand office furniture that had been new in the seventies. The desk was split pea soup green and beat to hell. The file drawers were battered beyond belief. I walked into the back office and that was when things started adding up in some truly scary ways.

Master. We are so fucked, Shadow said in a hushed tone of thought. All I could manage was a slight nod of the head; my familiar had stated the obvious with such finality that there was nothing else to say.

Pictures from inside the Court of Night were everywhere. These pictures were not just of the outside of the main meeting hall of the Court, they were of the inside of the building. Many of the pictures showed the faces of some of the highest-ranking court members out there, including the Countess herself.

If these things added up the way they were looking, the Crossed Bolts wanted to make a move on the Court of Night, and if my guess was right, the person that Yvette had been personally torturing these last few days was Lady K. This case had truly gone so far south that it was just about to cross the pole and start moving north again. It also meant that I had to meet up with a pissed off Countess and do something that would be plain stupid. I was about to interfere with Court business and I was not a member of the Court. Yes, I had helped found the Court of Night but I was not part of it. I was an outsider. The Countess was highly protective of the court, any interference with it was a death sentence. Yvette may love me but I wasn't sure if that would offer me enough protection.

I decided that I had to get the one thing I knew for a fact would drop the Countess Blood Wolf. I had procured it when the Court of Night was founded as a safety. Yvette was a border line psychopath, a blood thirsty businesswoman. I had soon realized that I may eventually need to kill her to save the lives of a lot of people. At this time, I had no intention of doing it unless truly pressed, but I was glad I had it.

What is our next play?

"I'm not sure. I can't play my hand early and force Yvette to give me Lady K without having something to offer. What I need is Kill Switch Karma in hand to confess in front of the Countess for putting Lady K up to this."

Of course it is possible that Yvette will kill Lady K before we come up with Kill Switch Karma, Shadow said.

"And therein lies the rub," I agreed.

So?

I grabbed my cell phone out of my pocket and dialed Kilroy. When he picked up I jumped in before he could say hi. "I've got bad news."

"My granddaughter is missing. How much worse could it be?" Kilroy asked angrily.

"Court of Night and Crossed Bolts bad," I told him.

"What do you mean by that?" Kilroy sounded shaken.

"I think she was tricked by the Crossed Bolts to spy on the Court of Night."

"Wait a second ... she was tricked into spying on a blood-thirsty criminal organization, by a group of genocidal maniacs probably bent on taking over the world?" Kilroy was trying, and failing miserably, to sound calm. "Is that what you're telling me?"

"Unfortunately, yes. And there is worse news yet..." I didn't get to a chance to tell him the worse news before he cut me off.

"How could it possibly get worse?!"

"If I'm not mistaken, she was grabbed by the Countess Blood Wolf and is currently being tortured by one of the best in the business."

"Why aren't you doing something about it right now?!" Kilroy screamed at me. "You helped set up that psycho bitch, with her personal army of monsters. You need to stop her!"

"It's not that easy Kilroy, I wish it was, but it isn't. I'm not a member of the Court. I have zero standing among them. Yes, I help set it up, but the Countess runs the place with full autonomy. I couldn't stop her if I wanted to."

"You bastard. Are you saying that you're going to let my granddaughter be tortured to death?" Kilroy, was incredibly pissed, and I truthfully couldn't blame him. "I'm paying you to save her, not to sit on your thumbs and let her die."

"I have no intention of letting her die Kilroy, so don't get so worked up you have a stroke. And if you're thinking about trying to take her yourself, I should remind you that you are well over a hundred years old, out of practice, most of your buddies from the Knights' War are long dead, and the ones that are still around and in decent enough shape for any sort of fight aren't stupid enough to take on the entire Court. You are out gunned and out classed. The old guard of the Court were tough as hell. The new guys were trained by ex-special forces in combat and tactics. If we had had a thousand of these guys in forty-one, we would have waltzed over Germany and Japan in less than a year. Thankfully there is still a chance that I can save Lady K for you."

"What are you going to do? It better be good." Kilroy snarled.

"I need to stop by my office to pick up one of the most dangerous weapons I have ever had the displeasure of owning with the distinct knowledge that I may very well need to use it someday."

"What is it?"

"A bullet blessed by Aneris herself."

"What will it do?"

"It will simply unmake anything it hits once fired. It could quite possibly unmake a lot more stuff than what it hits, but I have no plan on actually firing it."

"Would you actually shoot the Countess with it?"

"If completely forced? Possibly. I'd rather bluff my way out of shooting it."

"Do whatever it takes but I want my granddaughter back."

"If the Countess hasn't killed her yet, I'll try to get her back, though I can't guarantee she'll still be in one piece." Now I had to ask a question that might cause Kilroy to have an aneurysm that I'd even dare suggest it. "What I need to know though, is what if she's knowingly working for the Crossed Bolts? Then what do you want me to do?"

"Are you kidding me? Do you have any sort of clue as to what just came out of your mouth?" I was hoping he didn't die on me. "She's a Kilroy, damn it! If she's working for those bastards knowingly, I'll put her in the ground myself!"

"Good. I'm going to be making a lot of calls. Meet me in my office and I'll get everything I need."

"You damn well better be prepared." Kilroy hung up.

The Bullet of Aneris! Tell me you're kidding me?! Shadow screamed. *I may not like the Countess too terribly much, but do you have any clue what would happen to the country if she were to die?*

"Of course I do. That's why I'm going to bluff her, and if worse comes to worst, I'll let both Kilroy and Lady K die."

Now I know you're lying. There is no way you'd do that to a client, Shadow said which of course was true. *Look, she trusts you. If you can give her something she'll talk. If nothing else, she's pragmatic. You still owe her more than a few favors; of course she owes just as many to you, so it evens out. The point is that you are too useful for her to kill you.*

"With me interfering with Court business, I'm stepping onto treacherous ground. Yvette is fiercely protective of the Court, and I'd be interfering. She's in a really pissed off mood at the moment so she may forget herself." I was not looking forward to this.

I think this will be a good day to call in sick. Shadow gave me a fake cough, and I couldn't blame him.

"You really want to miss me getting killed? I love you too." I said with an ironic grin. "However I do full get the wanting to chicken out on this."

Oh screw you. You know I'd never abandon you. Your mother made very clear that part of my mission was to keep you safe. It's just going to be hard to do that if you manage to totally piss off the Countess.

I sighed. Bird brain was right. This was going to suck, and I'm sure mother would have been screaming her head off at me if she knew what I was going to have to do. "Come on Shadow it's time to go and face the music."

CHAPTER

I walked into my office and saw Jamie cleaning up, getting ready to call it a night. "Hey boss. How is the case you're on going?" I shook my head slowly knowing she'd pick up the clue. "How bad?" Shadow jumped off my shoulder came to rest on Jamie's and started preening her hair, something he only did when he was truly upset. "That bad, huh?"

"If I survive the night I'll let you know," I said with utter finality.

"What do you mean 'if'?" I could tell Jamie was worried, and truthfully I didn't blame her.

"I'm about to do the stupidest thing I've ever done in my life, and I can see no way of getting around it." I walked over to one of the office safes and took out a large manila envelope. "Here's my updated last will and testament. If anything happens to me you're the executor, and I need you to make sure everything is carried out as written."

Jamie didn't take the envelope. "You can't be serious. You're damn near un-killable."

"If anything could get me killed, this could be it," I said simply.

After a minute or so she finally took the envelope. "Okay boss. Be careful. I really don't want to start looking for a new employer."

"Well you should get going, I'll call you as soon as I get back to the office."

"And if you don't?" She was scared and I guess I had given her good reason to be.

"I'll have someone else call you."

Jamie nodded. Shadow jumped off her shoulder and landed on his perch to give her some space. "Be careful," she said as she gave me a hug. She looked back at me again as she closed the door behind her on the way out.

You just scared the hell out of her master, Shadow said unnecessarily.

I sighed as I headed into my office. "Couldn't be helped. She needed to know where the will was. Just in case I don't survive the night."

Once in my office I opened the gun safe. In it wasn't just my collection of guns, but also some more interesting pieces of weaponry, and right now I was going to need some heavy fire power. I reached in and grabbed some blessed silver bullets and shotgun shells, and loaded the Thompson and my whippet style shotgun. I took out my sword and baited the blade with garlic oil for use on any Vampire that might get in my way. I just hoped I didn't have to use any of this stuff. The last thing I took out was my back up 1911 Wild Card. I hadn't used this gun in a long time for anything other than making sure she was still in good condition.

At about that time I felt someone looking at me from the outer office. "You know you could have knocked," I told Kilroy.

"Just wanted to remind you that I wasn't helpless," the old spook said.

"Against the Countess you're the proverbial ninety-pound weakling," I told him humorlessly. "I really should be telling you to go home and wait but you'd just follow me anyways, and maybe the Countess will listen to you about your granddaughter." I took out an empty clip for Wild Card and put one bullet, the Bullet of Aneris, in it and then slapped the clip into place.

"Are we going to talk or are we going to go to the Court?" Kilroy asked.

"Let me call ahead and maybe we can get in there without too many people, including the two of us, dying," I said.

I picked up the receiver of my desk phone and slowly dialed the Countess's number. When she answered she sounded decidedly pissed. "What do you want Jason? I'm very busy."

"Are you in the middle of torturing someone?" I asked.

"Yes, and they're being very stubborn, screaming a lot, and being most unreasonable. Now, if you don't mind, I'm going." She hung up before I could say anything.

"Well?" Kilroy asked me flatly.

"She's still alive at least." It was all I had for him in the way of good news, which wasn't much. I shut the gun safe and, shrugging my shoulders, said, "We better get over there before she kills Lady K. I just have to be very careful, and very, very lucky over the next few hours."

I led Kilroy out of the office and down to my car. On the way to the Court's meeting place, we didn't say much; there wasn't much to say. When we got there it was obvious that Kilroy hadn't known what to expect. The place had once been a posh hotel that had gone under about 30 years ago. The Court had purchased and remodeled the entire place. The top two floors had been transformed into a single, very large apartment for Yvette. The lower floors were offices and rooms for important visiting Court members. Closer to ground level were the offices that acted as the nervous system for the Court. What had been the main ballroom now acted as the courtroom. Court was only open two days a week for Court members to make their cases and do everything officially. Yvette could barely stand it that much, and after a day sitting in court she was always at the Mystic Wolf.

We parked a block away on the other side of the street and I used the car for cover to get my weapons at hand. I slipped out of my trench coat, and put on the baldric for the sword first. Then came the shoulder holster for Ace of Spades, next the whippet, which I put under my right shoulder, and Wild Card took his place in a waistline holster at my back. After I was fully armed with everything to go under the jacket, I put my trench coat back on.

Are you sure this is the best way to do this? Shadow asked.

"I need to make it known to the Countess that I mean business, and if things go south I may need to shoot my way out of there."

Your funeral and mine if you get yourself killed. Shadow didn't need to remind me that he would be a dead bird if I died. That came with the territory of being a familiar like him; as long as I was alive he'd stay alive as well.

I looked over at Kilroy who was unarmed as far as I could tell. "Do you have a gun?"

"Of course," he replied, which wasn't the answer I wanted.

"Then put it in my car. I don't want you doing something stupid and pulling it out and getting both of us killed."

"I don't th..." I cut him off.

"No, you don't think. I do the thinking right now. So stow the gun in the car and stay close." I grabbed my Thompson off the back seat and got ready for an act of pure stupidity.

"I don't like it," Kilroy grumbled as he threw his gun onto the passenger seat.

I ignored him and started walking towards the front entrance. I was going to make one hell of an impression on the Court to get Yvette's attention. I didn't plan on killing anyone, that would just be stupid, but I still needed to kick the door in.

Two Vampires stood outside the front door, and from the way they had their hands in their expensive suit coats, I knew they were packing some serious artillery. One of them stepped forward and put his hand up. "Unless you have business that involves you dying, I'd suggest you leave and return without the weapons." Polite. Stupid, but polite.

"Do you have any idea who I am?" I asked, casually resting the Thompson on my shoulder.

"It doesn't matter. You are on private property and are armed. The cops wouldn't think twice if I killed you," a Vampire said.

"Tell the Countess that Jason Black is here to see her."

"I don't care who you are; you're not coming in." The vampire must have been new to the area, or at least newly turned.

I shrugged. "So be it." I moved too fast for them to see as I rushed the first Vampire and spun him around so his back was against me. I then used him as a shield as the second Vampire pulled out a large caliber machine pistol and opened up on full auto. The Vampire I was holding jerked several times as his body soaked up the spent lead. I then snapped his neck and threw him hard against his associate as a diversion. While the still moving Vampire disentangled himself, I slammed into him and knifed an open hand into his throat. Now stunned I was able to get around him and snap his neck as well. That would keep him from pissing me off long enough to deal with the Countess without making their deaths more permanent.

I looked over at Kilroy who was simply standing there unmoving. "Well, the door's open so let's go in," I said.

Kilroy looked down at the bodies. "I forgot you could move like that."

"Normally I can't, and it took a little out of me to use that kind of magick, but it got the results we needed," I said. "Now come on. It's time to keep going."

"What about them?"

"They'll be down for a while until their necks heal, which will be in about ten minutes. I'm not going to stake them though, if that's what you're wondering. I don't want to kill them fully or the Countess would be truly pissed with me."

I have killed a couple of Yvette's enforcers in the past, and it never went well. She'd always want something from me as repayment anytime I got one of her people killed while working for me. When I killed one of them myself, things got, well, nasty. "Now come on. Let's get going."

Walking into the lobby of the Court I found out very quickly that the gunshots had been heard. From all over the plaza came a swarm of Werewolves and Vampires, many of them in tactical armor. I had enough fire power to take them down, at least I thought I did, but that wasn't part of the plan. I looked around at them and grinned smugly as I propped my Thompson on my shoulder. When dealing with the Court of Night, never show even the slightest hint of fear, especially when you're doing something as exceptionally stupid as I was doing.

I got insanely lucky though. The Werewolf to speak up first, and who seemed to be leading this whole mess, was none other than the infamous Black Hat. As usual, he was dressed like a dock worker. "What do you want Jason?" Black Hat growled.

"Evening Black Hat," I said by way of acknowledging he had spoken. I peered over his shoulder and saw his best friend, a Vampire known as The Dentist, in his crisp tuxedo looking both disinterested and annoyed at the same time. "Dentist." The Dentist nodded.

"I repeat, what do you want?"

"An audience with the Countess," I said casually.

"And if I say no?" Black Hat was calm, and in response to his actions the rest of Yvette's enforcers had relaxed as well.

"I shoot up the place, and piss off the Countess." I still had my Thompson resting on my shoulder, no reason to agitate the locals any more than I already had.

"You're kidding, right?" Black Hat laughed.

I let the Thompson drop into a two-hand grip. "Bet your life?"

The Dentist put his hand on Black Hat's shoulder and was about to say something when a couple of the younger and stupider enforcers rushed me from my eight. I heard them coming and squeezed off a burst that took them out at the knees. From then on, things went Antarctic.

I didn't have time to take notes but lead and silver were flying fast and loud, and only barely covered the sounds of the screaming. After the fur and fangs had flown there were thirty or so enforcers on the ground, an empty Thompson, a blood-soaked sword, and worst of all, my trench coat had some long, ragged tears in it.

Black Hat and the Dentist had waited until they thought I was unarmed and then Black Hat lunged at me. I reached under my trench and, grabbing the whippet, shot him in the kneecap. He didn't have time to drop when I grabbed him and pulled him tight against me, my left arm around his throat. With my right I grabbed Ace of Spades and placed it against the Werewolf's temple. "Okay Dentist, we're going to talk to the Countess or I put a silver bullet through Black Hat's temple." Black Hat snarled something but I squeezed tighter, throttling him.

The Dentist nodded. "Follow me." He headed toward the elevators.

I looked over my shoulder and saw Kilroy come out from behind a large potted plant and follow us. "Who's the old guy? I need to tell the Countess who is here to see her" the Dentist asked when he saw the old spook heading towards us.

"The one and only Kilroy," I replied, and the Dentist nodded.

"Pleased to meet you," the Dentist said to Kilroy. Ever proper, the Vampire makes it a habit of being polite with everyone, even while he is ripping their teeth out. Especially then actually. Kilroy only nodded in response.

Once the elevator brought us to the Court's interrogation room, the Dentist had us follow him down the hall and told us to wait while he announced our presence. He was gone for less than a minute when I heard Yvette start to scream my name, cursing up a storm. "Great. She's pissed," I told Kilroy.

"She's going to have your head Black," Black Hat said.

"Look, if I don't live through this, I just want to let you know that I do feel bad about shooting the place up, I really do, but it's only business. Besides it was you guys who attacked first."

"You were the one who..." I had no idea what Black Hat was going to finish saying when the doors slammed open, and there stood a Countess Blood Wolf. From the way she was dressed, I could tell that she was taking this recent round of torturing someone seriously. She looked a lot like a demented man's nightmare of a high priced dominatrix. The studs and spikes in her clothing were made from the teeth of her previous Vampiric victims, and she had a belt of human fingers hanging around her waist. I knew for a fact that the leather was cured Werewolf hide. She had made this outfit while we had been putting bodies in the ground so she could step into a power vacuum in the Lycanthropic and Vampiric societies that had taken hold in the US after World War II.

"Who the FUCK do you think you are?! Are you completely out of your FUCKING mind Black?!" The Countess was beyond enraged and I couldn't say that I could blame her any.

"Look I can expla..." Her hand wrapped around my throat, I found myself pressed high against a wall, unable to speak as she started to slowly shift into a truly nightmarish werewolf with the sound of bones breaking and skin ripping apart. I had seen her fully shift before and, to put it mildly, it is scarier than just about anything that crawled out of any Infernal pit, and it never got easier to witness. There is a reason that even Gods give her a wide berth. If you think the Werewolves from movies, with their incredible special effects, are even mildly scary, you couldn't begin to wrap your mind around the horror that is the Countess. A skeletal wolf with bluish gray skin that looked like it belonged to a corpse. Unlike most furry Werewolves she had almost no fur, as if she had the worst case of mange someone could suffer. Her eyes were burning pits that could rip your soul out if you dared look too long.

"You better be able to explain, or by the Gods, I will end you now." The threatening growl was primordial in nature with the added beauty of braking rocks. "Now why are you here?"

She loosened her grip enough to let me speak. "I came for your prisoner." I knew that would infuriate her. I let my hand drop behind my back and come to rest on the comforting steel of Wild Card.

"Now you've gone too far Black. I may love you, but this is crossing way over the line. You come to my Court and shoot it up, and now you demand my prisoner. You are interfering in Court business and no one, I repeat NO ONE, does that! I'll be sure to call Jamie and let her know what happe..." She broke off as soon as I placed Wild Card against her chest. "A gun? You..." She sniffed the air and I knew she could smell the corruption leaking off the Bullet on Aneris. "What is that?"

"The Bullet of Aneris." I returned her snarl with a cocky sneer, I must be one crazy S.O.B. to think I might survive this. "If I pull this trigger it will unmake you. Possibly everything else around here."

"You have my attention Black so make it good." Yvette let go of my neck and I dropped back to the floor.

"The girl you have is Lady K..."

"I know. The cocky bitch corrupted the Kilroy Was Here tag," Yvette said, leading me over to where Lady K was. "So who is she?"

"She's my granddaughter," Kilroy said, trying to look anything less than panicked.

"Kilroy? Well, well, well. That's how she got her moniker. So what has she been doing here other than spying on me for who knows how long?"

"She's been taking pictures of the entire court and probably knows more than that about everyone," I was saying when we got to the chamber where the Countess did her work.

When I saw Lady K, she was a mess. She had been burned, cut, water boarded, loaded up full of sodium pentothal, and that was just the beginning of her problems. Yvette had learned the trade of torture from me and I was a master at it. However, like any good and truly stubborn half-Daemon, Lady K had been able to take all of it without breaking.

Kilroy rushed over to her side and looked into her half-opened eyes. I could tell she was still healing from having been recently worked over. "What were you using at this point?"

"Sodium pentothal, along with the crushing of digits," Yvette growled. "Knowing who she is explains why she was able to stick to her story so long. Now, who is she working for? And make it good."

"As far as I've been able to dig up, she got duped into working for the Crossed Bolts, thinking that they were part of our government." I was about to elaborate when Yvette cut in.

"She had better have been duped. However, it does sound plausible to some extent. Still, I want evidence."

"What makes you say it sounds plausible? As far as further evidence, I am having my cousin, you remember him, Sir Booth of Her Majesty's Secret Service, pick up a Crossed Bolts operative to bring here."

"Well, our little, inexperienced spook here swore up and down that she was working for a small offshoot branch of the FBI. I have agents in that part of the agency so I knew very quickly that it was complete bullshit. She was still screaming that it was the truth after fifteen hours of waterboarding, and a few rounds of body work, so I'm willing to give her the benefit of the doubt. For now. What are you planning to do if she is working for the Crossed Bolts willingly?" Yvette asked as her bones cracked loudly as they reformed to human and her skin began to have the appearance of life again as she regained her teenage psycho form.

"Kilroy says he'll put her in the ground himself if she's doing that." I knew the old spook would do it too. He would hate to do it, but not because of any sense of sentimentality. The surviving Allied soldiers of the Knights' War are often short on sentiment. He would hate it because it meant he had failed to bring her up knowing what true scum Nazis are.

"So, what do we do now?" I asked.

"We're going to move this party to my apartment and have a few drinks. After that stunt you just pulled I'm going to need a few dozen Power Drivers to relax enough to forgive you. Before that I need to take care of some Court business." Yvette looked like she was going to say something more until she saw that the Dentist was on the phone. "Who's dead?" she snapped.

"Luckily for Black's sake, I'd say, no one," the Vampire replied calmly.

"Who attacked first? I'm willing to bet that it wasn't Black," Yvette growled.

"It was Jackson "the Switchblade" Rogers, Michelle Night Sky, and Pacu "the Machete" Rodriguez, who attacked first. However..." Yvette cut him off.

"I don't care about however, I want those three in my office as soon as they're well enough for me to kick the crap out of them for being so stupid without killing them," the Countess snapped. "Who was in charge down there?"

"Um it was Black Hat and myself, but..."

"No buts!" Her head snapped over to where Black Hat was flexing his mostly healed knee. "I want the two of you in my office right fucking now. I'm going to have some words with you."

"Yes Countess," the Dentist said nervously. He and Black Hat may be two of her right-hand men, but that wouldn't save them from a serious ass kicking for letting things get out of hand. He walked over to Black Hat and after a quick whisper they walked off together, both looking deservedly shaken.

She then waved for the three of us to follow her. "Come on you three. I'll get you settled before I take care of business with my underlings."

Kilroy eased a still woozy Lady K to her feet and half carried her along behind the Countess. "Can we trust her?" Kilroy whispered the question as I walked past them, but Yvette caught it.

"Yes, you can trust me," Yvette said without turning around. "As long as Black can produce a member of the Crossed Bolts who can explain the reason your granddaughter was working for them I have no reason to keep torturing her."

We followed the Countess to the elevator and took it up to her penthouse apartment. The place was tastefully decorated; no expense had been spared. The art looked like it belonged in a museum. I had been here more than a few times, and had seen her bedroom far more often than I was comfortable admitting. She led us to a lounging room and walked over to a well-stocked bar. "Can I offer you anything?" she asked, sounding more like a polite businesswoman, as opposed to the psychopath who had just spent the last couple of days torturing someone.

"Cough medicine," I replied casually, as if nothing nasty had transpired between us. Yvette took out a bottle of my favorite bourbon and poured a couple fingers of it into a lowball.

"And the two of you?" she asked the two spooks.

"We're good," Kilroy said with a seething sense of hatred in his voice.

"Hardly," Yvette replied. She took out a bottle of a viscous green ooze, poured two shots of it into a tumbler and handed it to Lady K. "Here you go. Drink it up and you'll feel right as rain in no time."

Lady K took it from her and looked at the glass as if she had just been told to drink a glass of drain cleaner. She looked to Kilroy, who in turn looked at me. When I gave him the nod of approval he told his granddaughter it was okay. After a quick swallow, the bruising, slash marks and signs of electrical burns quickly faded. "What was that?" she asked.

Yvette shrugged. "Never asked for the recipe."

For herself, Yvette pulled a container of orange juice from the mini fridge, poured a pint glass a quarter full of that, filled the rest with Everclear, and quickly downed it. The drink would have killed most people but did nothing to her. "I'll need a few more of these to help relax," she said to herself, then turned to look at us. "Now, if you don't mind, I'm going to go change. I only wear this getup on special occasions. I'm going to beat the tar out of some of my enforcers so I'm just going to change into a power suit. I'll be back in a little while. Please help yourself to anything in the bar, and if you get hungry you can order room service."

"Who are you?" Lady K asked once Yvette left.

"My name is Jason Black. I'm a private detective," I said.

"He's a friend of mine from the Knights' War," Kilroy further explained.

"The Countess Blood Wolf is an old friend of mine, so when I figured out that she was the one who had you, I knew I was probably the only one who could get your ass out of the fire," I explained. "So, the question is, why are you here?"

"I was hired by the FBI's SD section to spy on the Court of Night," she said.

"Well I hate to break it to you that you got duped," I said.

"How do you know?" she asked.

"The FBI's SD section is full of members of the Court. As soon as you told her you were working for that agency, the Countess knew it was bull. The reason she kept at you so long was to get you to break and give up who had really hired you," I said. "We're pretty certain we know who you were unwittingly working for. Once we can grab someone involved with it, we can get all of this settled," I said.

"So what happens to me now?" Lady K asked.

"You stay in one of the rooms here under guard until we get all of this sorted out," Yvette said as she walked into the room in an expensively tailored power suit. It wouldn't stain when blood got on it and she really didn't need her torture getup for what she was about to do. She was just going to slap people around for a bit. "If everything is as it should be, I will of course apologize and expect that this will be treated as water under the bridge."

"How will that make it any better?" Lady K asked.

"That's just the way it works around here," I told the young spook. "If you want to get things done you have to learn how to forgive. Just treat this whole deal as a learning experience and let it go. The Countess will forgive you so you should be willing to forgive her in return."

"That's..." Lady K seemed to be at a loss for words.

"Black," the Countess said grabbing my attention, "Please follow me."

"Okay." I knew that whatever was about to happen, I was probably going to regret it.

Once we were out of ear shot Yvette grabbed me and pulled my face down to look her dead in the eye. "You owe me a lot for shooting up the joint. At least you didn't kill anyone, but you still owe me."

This was going to suck. "What do you want?"

"A two week cruise in the tropics," she said.

I nodded. "Two weeks it is." And that is why I hate owing the Countess anything.

CHAPTER

7

While we were sitting in Yvette's apartment, I realized that I hadn't called out to Shadow to let him know where I was. "Hey Shadow," I said calling to the bird brain still sitting in the car. "I'm up in the Countess's apartment. Why don't you come up?" In the background I saw Lady K ask her grandfather what was happening, and then nod when he explained my familiar.

How long until we die? Shadow asked. *Yvette cannot be happy with you.*

"We're not going to die Shadow, though you're right. She's still in a calm down phase."

You really play fast and loose with our lives.

"Are you coming up or not?"

I'll come up. Where are you?

"I'm in the bar. I'll open a window for you."

I'll be right up. By the way, don't forget to call Jamie. It was a good thing he reminded me, I had almost forgotten.

I opened a window for him and then reached into my pocket to call Jamie. The phone rang only once when she answered. "Boss?"

"Hey sweetheart I'm going to probably be out of the office for a few days, but I'm fine."

"Thank the Gods," she said. "Anything I need to know?"

"Start going through vacation sites and look for two-week tropical cruises."

"What did you do to get the Countess asking for that as payment?" she asked.

"I shot up the Court a bit," I replied in a tone that tried to play down what I had actually done. It didn't work.

"Were you out of your Infernal mind?!" Jamie screamed. "I almost wonder if I should start looking for a new employer if you're going to keep doing something so utterly stupid!"

"Hey, I'm still in one piece." I tried to smile even though she wouldn't see it. "Besides I'm going to get you a sizable bonus for putting up with me. But if you want, and don't mind being turned, I could put in a good word for you with the Countess. Or maybe Brisbane will hire you as a bar back."

"Thank you, no, to either offer. I'll stick with you. Even if you are an idiot at times."

"Don't be so sore. Now get some sleep," I ordered.

"The thought of what the Countess could have done to you is still going to keep me up for a while."

"Just be glad you didn't see her change. You'd have had nightmares for months." I smiled, hoping that she would hear it in my voice.

"Good night boss."

"Good night sweetheart," I said and hung up.

At that moment Shadow flapped his way through the window and landed on my shoulder. *How is Jamie handling it?* he asked.

"Like a trooper who is pissed off at her C.O." I said.

I remember you having a lot of pissed off troops under your command during the Knights' War, he replied.

"True but you were my only familiar. Jamie is as loyal to me as you are." I often joked that Jamie was my second familiar.

True, and she can do the office work that I can't, and she also likes to spoil me. I love having her around.

"Well, I'll just have to keep from scaring her for a while now," I said. Shadow dipped his head in agreement.

I looked at my watch and saw that it was two in the morning when Yvette walked back into the room. She looked like she had worked off some of her frustrations on her underlings as she had changed her clothes again. I vaguely wondered how much blood there was for the cleaners to mop up. She mixed herself another massive power driver and dropped down into the overstuffed chair across from me. "There are times I almost wish I didn't have such a high tolerance to everything," she said downing the drink.

"So how did it go?" I asked.

"Everyone now knows that if you come here and ask for an audience with me just to grant it. That doesn't mean I won't keep you waiting, but at least you won't shoot up the place again." She ran a hand through her hair. "Uh ... finding good help can be so hard. There are times I almost wish I could just dump this whole mess in someone else's lap."

"Why don't you? You seem awfully young to be doing this sort of this thing," Lady K asked.

"Because someone has to keep the peace among these two groups of monsters before the battles spill out into the public light," Yvette said. "And as far as the age thing goes, thank you for saying that I look young. It's not every octogenarian who can say they still look like a teenager."

"You're how old?" Lady K sputtered.

"You really were sent in without much of a clue weren't you?" Yvette mused. "I was a Nazi experiment at mixing Lycanthropy with Vampirism to create the ultimate soldier. I was the only survivor of the experiment. Black liberated me from the lab. After the war he brought me stateside with him. With the battles between Werewolves and Vampires, most of whom had fled Eastern Europe, someone had to get things under control, so I nominated myself. There are times though I think I may have been better off just killing everybody." She sighed and closed her eyes.

Another long silence was just starting to settle upon us when my phone start ringing. The number belonged to my cousin. "Hello Dave. What can I do for you?" I asked and then switched it to speaker phone.

"Why can't you ever refer to me as Sir Booth, or at least David?" my cousin asked.

"Because I know it gets on your nerves," I replied. In the background I heard Yvette stifle a laugh. "So what are you calling about?"

"We raided the offices of Feuer-Vogol Technologies and grabbed Kill Switch Karma. I brought in a special team so we were able to take her down before she could dump everything in her computer system. That given, I still have a couple Silicon Slaves going through her systems looking for anything else that might be of use to us."

"Great. When can you get her over here?" I asked.

"Give me two days to send her over the pond. I've already seen the paperwork for the extradition dated a couple days before you called me. How did you pull that off anyways?"

"Low friends in high places who wanted to score points with their boss," I replied.

"And that boss would be you?" he asked in a skeptical tone.

"You're kidding me. Right? I have no desire to run this mad house. No I'm talking about the Countess," I replied.

"Ahhh. Well whoever you got to get the paperwork done. I've made everything good on my end to speed up the extradition on the basis of imminent terrorist attack upon an ally country," Booth said. "I'll send her to Washington and hand her over to your people."

"She won't make it much past the airport before I grab the two of you," I said.

"What do you mean?"

"With the Countess's blessing, I'm going to lead a team of her enforcers on an assault to 'liberate' Kill Switch Karma." Yvette nodded, indicating that she would go along with whatever I had in mind. "We're going to grab both of you and then she and I are going to have a pleasant little chat."

"And by pleasant chat you mean..." Sir Booth trailed off, knowing my meaning without me having to explain any further.

"Exactly, you are of course invited to sit in."

"Thank you, no. I'll see you in a couple of days," he said.

"I'll be one of the ones in a ski mask, wielding a machine gun." I said hanging up.

"So we're going to liberate a member of the Crossed Bolts?" Yvette asked with a rather evil smile. "What body part won't the cops find this time?" I laughed at the reference to the Baron, a Werewolf we had dismembered in New Orleans. In his case, the cops had never managed to find his left arm.

"I'm sure we can figure that out after I've worked her over for a while."

"Well then let's get everyone settled and I'll make the orders as to who is going to be on the assault team, and who is going to represent the US government." She picked up a house phone and called down to have rooms made up for Kilroy and Lady K as well as a guard set at Lady K's door. The guards were just in case Lady K wasn't on the level about not willingly working for the Nazis.

After Lady K and Kilroy had been escorted down to their rooms, Yvette grabbed me before I could leave. "My bedroom. Now," she growled.

"Look I should really..." I didn't get the chance to finish before I got cut off.

"I still have frustrations that I need to work off and you already owe me." She grabbed my shirt and ripped it off. "Now get into that bedroom."

I'm no match against Yvette in strength and besides I knew I would enjoy this even if I really would rather not be doing it.

CHAPTER

A convoy of unmarked, black SUVs transported Kill Switch Karma from the Washington DC airport to the CIA headquarters in Langley. We hit them with a brutal barrage of machine gun fire and smoke bombs. It was all theater for the public of course, since everyone involved were either members of the Court of Night, myself, or my cousin. The only things actually damaged were the government vehicles, which were shot to shit.

After the whole ordeal with the shootout, we hopped a private jet and were back in the Twin Cities in three hours. Between getting to DC, the 'liberation' of Kill Switch Karma, and the trip back to DC, we had been out of Minnesota for less than half a day. Now it was on to the fun stuff.

We decided to do the interrogation at my place. My interrogation room is full of stuff that unnerves even the most hard-boiled criminal. I've seen Infernal Daemons break at the mere sight of the artifacts in that room. Much of the stuff belonged hidden away from a sane person's eyes. It had come to my house by all sorts of means, many illegal, including theft from quite a few museums.

When we arrived, Yvette had two Werewolves frog march a hooded Kill Switch Karma into the interrogation room and handcuff her to a chair. After she thrashed for a few minutes, I decided to take her hood off. She looked around the room and immediately realized she was going to regret being there. I wasn't sure what her eyes first landed on. It may have been the Hanging Cage with the skeleton of its last victim still inside. Next to the cage was a table upon which were laid all sorts of hand-held implements of torture. I didn't have the time to go classic since I figured there had to be people involved in the US that needed killing before they escaped into the woodwork.

"She was saying some pretty unpleasant things about a lot of people on the flight over. I couldn't get anything useful out of her, so I'll leave it to you to get her to answer simple questions," Dave said looking vaguely annoyed at his highly unwilling traveling companion.

"Now Amanda, I've seen this man work before. I usually have to walk out at some point because I find it a tad bit, how shall I put it? Disturbing. I usually have a hard time eating for a day or two afterwards."

Before he left he whispered to me. "I don't want that bitch walking out of here alive. Do what you do best." Walking out of the room, he looked at his watch.

"It's just about time for the shipping forecast," he said. "Do you mind if I use your radio?"

"The radio doesn't pick up BBC four," I replied.

"It will when I'm done with it," Booth said with a shrug.

"It's an antique! You'd better fix it when you're done."

Booth didn't reply, he simply waved. Truthfully that little exchange had proved to be fairly unnerving to my victim. The idea that two people could have such a bland conversation when one of them was about to do some torturing usually proved to be enough to scare people into quick confessions.

"Now we are going to have a pleasant little chat," I said kindly. "Be cooperative and it won't hurt too much. Lie and well ..." I pulled back a fist and jack-hammered it into her stomach, "It quickly goes downhill."

"Do you have any idea who I am?" Amanda hissed once she regained her breath.

"Of course I do. You're Amanda Tanner, aka Kill Switch Karma, a Silicon Slave member of the Crossed Bolts. An organization that I had the pleasure of gutting back in the forties during the Knights' War," I said. "I've also been in contact with MI5 and have been looking through information they have just started funneling to the Court of Night. However, I'm the one questioning you. So the first question you really should concern yourself with is: Do you know who I am?"

"I don't care who you are," Amanda hissed. "I'll be rescued soon enough."

I smashed a fist into her face. "I highly doubt it. You see you are in the possession of me, a vigilante for hire, a psychopath named Jason Black. I have a rather nasty reputation for killing people in all sorts of interesting and unpleasant ways. It is also well known that I am close friends with the Countess Blood Wolf." I indicated the Countess who was standing in the doorway nearby. She in turn smiled sweetly and waved.

"Now, I'm fairly certain that the Crossed Bolts outside of the US don't know much about me since I have never let any of those whom I have met survive. So who knows? Maybe you'll be the first." I had the pleasure of seeing her sweat. "Now let's start talking. Who is Lady K to you?"

"I have nothing to…" the Silicon Slave said in a stupid display of bravado. I slammed a fist into her face again. Blood from her nose splattered across my shirt, which only vaguely annoyed me.

I shook out my fist and smiled. "Now, now, please be reasonable. I'm sure you don't want me to keep working you over. So who is Lady K to you?"

"I don't know who you're talking about," Kill Switch Karma hissed.

I walked over to the table and picked up a hammer and chisel. "I'm in a bit of a hurry right now, so I'm going to start off with some nasty stuff." I pulled off her shoes and placed the point of the chisel on top of a pinky toe. "Now what do the Crossed Bolts want from Lady K, and why did they hire her?" I asked, looking up into Amanda Tanner's face.

"I don't know what..." I smashed the hammer into the chisel cutting her toe clean off. She screamed in agony and I couldn't blame her. That had to have hurt.

"Now see here, I'm sure that you want the pain to end. Just answer my questions, and the pain goes away." There was no malice in my voice, in fact, my tone was almost friendly. Sounding cheerful is far more unnerving when you're torturing someone than screaming at them. "So again I ask you: Why did the Crossed Bolts hire Lady K?"

Tanner cried for a bit but was able to speak well enough once I put the chisel against her next toe. "She's good at what she does," she whimpered. "She has abilities that made her invaluable to us."

I removed the chisel from her toe and smiled. "Very good. You see how much easier it is when you cooperate? Now on to my next question. What did you want her to find out for you?"

"I don't know," Tanner said quickly.

"Mmm ... so be it," I said, and before she could say anything I cut off another one of the Silicon Slave's toes. This time her screams were louder than before. "Okay now you were going to say something else right? You were going to tell me what she was hired to find out, right?"

Tanner kept crying for a while, which was irritating, but I was willing to wait it out. "Now please hurry up and tell me, or you lose another toe. What was she supposed to find out?"

"Why should I tell you? You're just going to kill me anyway!" Well she was going to get gutsy. Bad move. I cut off two toes for that one.

"You're right, I'm probably just going to kill you, however it is up to you. Do I do it quickly or draw it out. Oh, and if you think you can hold out and keep from answering my questions just because you're dead, you should know I've gotten a lot of postmortem questions answered from Nazi scum like you. Sure, the answers get a little weird, but I do get them."

I picked up a belt sander off the table and revved it a couple times. "You'd be surprised at how painful these things are when applied to bare skin. Would you like to find out just how painful it is?"

Tanner's face went pale. "Wha ... what ... what do you want to know?"

I smiled. I was going to get civilized answers out of her, then I'd end her life quickly. "Very good of you to agree to help. It will save you a lot of pain. Now I want to know what Lady K was supposed to find out?"

"I don't know!" She screamed as the belt sander ran over her bare shin.

"Now, now, now. I want the truth. Or this happens again."

"I'm telling you. I don't know! I'm not her handler. All I know is that her handler is part of your government."

Shit. Just the kind of headache none of us needed. Someone had flipped. Question was, how many, and could we find any of them before they disappeared? Without a solid list of names, Yvette was going to turn McCarthy on the Court which meant I could very well be up to my eyes in work for the Court. Out of the corner of my eyes I could see Yvette begin to look pissed. Yep. I had a lot of work coming my way.

"Who flipped?" I asked calmly. "Lie to me and the next place the belt sander goes will be worse, and trust me, I'll know if you lie."

"I don't know!" Tanner yelped. "I was used just to track her down. I knew she existed. I just found records and let my higher ups know where they could find her." She was being honest. A pleasant smile and the threat of a more sensitive place for the belt sander was all I had needed to get her to open up to me.

"Where is her handler?"

"He's based in Minneapolis, but that's all I know about him!" She screamed in utter agony as I ran the sander on the inside of her thigh. "I swear I'm telling you the truth. That's all I know about him."

"One last question. Did Lady K know who she was working for when she was contacted?" I asked.

"Yes, of course she did. She was a spook. She checked us out before she started." That was a lie, her slipping into shock made it easy to spot.

"I warned you what would happen if you lied to me." I picked up the belt sander and ran it on her other thigh for about half a minute of screaming. "Now would you care to reassess your answer?"

"She didn't know. She wouldn't have worked for us if she had known." Tanner said as she started to slip further into shock.

"Thank you for your cooperation," I said with a pleasant smile. "Is there anything you want to add before you die?"

"Just make it quick," she said. I did. I shot her in the back of the head. She would have felt nothing.

"Why did you kill her so quickly?" Yvette asked in an annoyed tone. If there is any 'good guy' who is more blood thirsty than me it's Yvette. She tends to make examples of her enemies. No one can touch her so when she needs to make a statement, the language is a messy corpse, and a nauseated medical examiner.

"She cooperated after a bit. Plus, there was not much more she could add to the conversation. Besides we have more important things to worry about."

"Point taken. Apparently I have traitors in my ranks. I don't know how many and I don't know where they are, but once I track them down they'll all die. Slowly."

"We can worry about that later right now we have to find Lady K's handler."

"Agreed. So where do we start?"

"Simple. She said she was recruited by the FBI so we start there. If someone pulled a runner, we track them down and politely interrogate them without too much blood being spilt." If we were lucky, the handler had decided to wait around to hide the fact that he had something to hide, I just hoped he was still in the country.

"And what about this corpse?"

"Leather lamp shade?"

Yvette pulled a sour face. "Now that's gross even for me. It would never go with my drapes, and don't suggest my office, it's already cluttered."

We walked out of my interrogation room to see my cousin still listening to BBC 4, but now talking on his cellphone. "I've got good news, and bad news," he told us.

"Bad news first." I have found that it's easier to take the bad news first.

"We were only able to acquire some of the data we wanted, and unfortunately, none of it indicates who has been pulling strings over here." Shit, not what I wanted to hear. "Somehow, she managed to launch a nasty virus on her own system as soon as we breached the office door. Our Silicon Slaves are still picking through it but they say not to hold out too much hope."

"What's the good news then?"

"We were able to get names of other high ranking members throughout the world. It's possible that we can find them and get the information you need from them, but that could take a while."

"A while is not a luxury we have at the moment," Yvette said angrily. "Well thanks, Booth. I'll make sure you get back home quickly." She made a quick call and a car with British diplomatic plates arrived at my door in five minutes.

"Are those real?" I asked as Booth got into the car.

"Yes, I have people in a few embassies now."

How long until she could rule the world? I wondered.

CHAPTER 9

"Well Lady K was telling the truth," Yvette said again as we headed back towards the Court of Night's headquarters. "Drink?" she asked, indicating the incredibly well stocked mini bar in the back of the limo. The luxuries of the rich and powerful …

"Just my usual bourbon," I replied.

As the Countess poured two fingers of bourbon into a cut crystal lowball glass, she looked at me with a killer's eyes. "So what do you think we'll find when we capture K's handler?"

"Hopefully the names of any other Court members the Crossed Bolts have managed to flip. Also, it would be nice if we could confirm the names of higher up Crossed Bolts members that Booth's people got," I mused before I emptied the lowball in a single gulp. "Hit me again."

Yvette poured me another bourbon and then mixed herself a power driver. "I just hope we can catch that bastard with their pants round their ankles when we find them. I want those names. I really don't want to be forced to play Inquisition with my cour. I don't need that kind of headache. It would mean a lot of backstabbing among my people for political posturing. If I can get a hold of the names, I can make the offenders disappear quietly," she said before swallowing her own drink.

"The problem is that I have no trouble imagining people under me flipping. I can be a little..." She broke off her sentence.

"Aggressive," I finished for her. "With your past it makes sense and it's perfectly possible that your underlings would rather not have to worry about you killing them if they even came close to stepping out of line."

"Am I really that bad?"

"Sweetie, you may chronologically be in your late-eighties but you are still, emotionally at least, a teenager. You still have teenage hormones running through you, and when you start PMSing, even I don't like being around you."

"I wasn't aware I was that awful." Yvette sounded genuinely hurt by the remark.

"Look, you're not a bad person. Well, not all that bad considering what kind of job you have. The problem is that you do have a job that involves being professionally unpleasant fairly often." At this point I had to keep her in a half way decent mood. "For now, think about something more pleasant."

"Like what?"

"Like torturing Nazis to death." I suggested. "That was your favorite part of the Knights' War. You loved ripping Nazis to shreds and making a point of doing awful things with their corpses." For the rest of the trip we reminisced about what many people would consider the things of nightmares, the joys of being monsters like us. We delight in that sort of stuff.

By the time we got back to the Court, we were laughing about one time when Yvette had executed four Nazi officers by hanging them up by their hands with barbed wire, and then gutting them while they were still alive and screaming. We were an unpleasant group of soldiers on the side of the Allies. The night before though, Yvette had rescued a litter of week-old kittens and their mother from a collapsed building. We may have been monsters, but we still knew right from wrong, and letting defenseless kittens die when she could easily save them was something Yvette couldn't do. I mean there are monsters and then there are *monsters*. In fact, two descendants of those kittens still lived with Yvette.

When we got back to the Court, Yvette and I went straight to the apartment she had assigned to Lady K. The two guards were happy to be relieved and quickly found something else to do. Yvette and I walked in and found the two spooks watching something on TV. "You're free to go," Yvette said pleasantly. "I'm sorry for what happened between us, but business is business. What we need now is your help in tracking down the traitor who recruited you."

Lady K smiled a bit. "I would like that very much."

"Good. Do you have a picture of him or her?" Yvette asked. "A name would mean nothing, but a picture will do perfectly."

Lady K smiled again. "I may be new to this, but I'm not an idiot. I followed him to the Minnesota branch of the FBI and took a couple of pictures of him before I started working on the case."

"Well at least you learned something from me," Kilroy said.

"We'll have to go to my office to get the pictures, provided it hasn't been blown up."

Yvette looked at her confused. "What do you mean blown up?"

"I rigged it with incendiaries to go off in case someone tries to break in."

"There's a switch under the knob to deactivate the trap," I said. "Truthfully I barely noticed it before I opened it. Good thing for Lady K here that I did. If I hadn't she would still be getting tortured and I wouldn't have a clue as to where she was."

"Okay, then we'll head over there," Yvette said cheerfully. A picture was just what she needed to figure out who had flipped. "I hope the two of you have gotten some sleep because tonight is going to be a long one."

CHAPTER 10

When we got to the run-down building, we found a light on in her office. "Does anyone else have keys to your office?" asked.

"No. I don't know who that could be in there."

"Shadow, go take a look," I told my familiar, who had been unusually silent for the last few hours.

Sure.

Shadow jumped off my shoulder and flew up to the window. *Okay we have an issue. Whoever is in there is doing a rather through job of ransacking the place.*

"Countess, take the back entrance. Kilroy and K, you two go to the fire escape."

"Where are you going?" Kilroy asked.

"Front and into the office."

"I can make it into the office faster," Lady K protested.

"Too risky. They may know how to spot you, even if you are invisible and walking through a wall."

"Come on people, let's go," the Countess hissed.

Whatever you guys are doing make it quick master, because it looks like the guy is ready to light a match.

"Let's go. Shadow says we're running out of time." I was already opening the car door as I said it.

As soon as we were out of the car I kicked on the magick and tore off into the building. I crashed through the already open door, gun in hand. The man inside turned to look at me wide eyed and went for his gun. I shot as soon as his hand touched the gun's grip. He spun round like a top and crashed into the back room. As soon as he landed, I was on top of him. I checked the bullet hole, and got a nasty surprise when he fired six high caliber slugs into my stomach. I soaked up the lead, which hurt like hell, and smashed a fist into his apparently glass jaw.

The shots must have gotten the attention of my compatriots since I found myself in the company of the two Kilroys followed quickly by the Countess.

"You okay, Black?" Yvette asked.

"Just a minor case of lead poisoning," I joked. I then looked over at K. "Is this your handler?"

"Yeah. That's him. He told me his name was Richard Harrison."

"You know him, Countess?"

Yvette shook her head. "Can't say I do, but he may still have some connection to the Court. I have a database that has photos of every person who is connected in any way with the Court. We'll run his face through the recognition software and something should pop up quickly."

As Yvette had been talking, I had been going through the unconscious man's pockets looking for a clue. I quickly found his wallet so now I had an address, a name (which of course wasn't Richard Harrison), and his credentials with the FBI. "His name is Martin Jacohvich and apparently he really is a Fed. Either that or he's got a damn good forger."

"Do you have an address?" Yvette asked.

"According to his driver's license he lives in Apple Valley."

Yvette pulled out her cell and called Janet Thompson, who was a high-ranking member of the SD division of the FBI. She was neither a Werewolf nor a Vampire; she was still a provisional member of the Court. Yvette put the speaker phone on as soon as Janet picked up.

"Good morning Countess. What can I do for you?" Her voice was slightly slurred from having been woken up.

"Sorry for waking you up this early, but I have a question about someone in your department."

"Go ahead."

"Is Martin Jacohvich one of yours?"

"Yeah. I know the creep. He got dumped on me a few months back. Why?"

I shook my head, something sounded fishy, things weren't adding up. "His name came up somewhere and I wanted to figure out who he belonged to."

"I don't know where he came from, but as I said, he landed in my lap about four months ago."

"Sorry about disturbing you at this time of night. I'll let you go back to sleep." Yvette looked at me curiously. "What's wrong Black?"

"I'm not sure, but everything stinks in this case." I looked at our prisoner and tried to figure out the best way to get answers from him. My normal methods of interrogation were not going to be fast enough. If Janet had been flipped, I couldn't give her time to do a runner. This poor bastard may just be another errand boy for someone else.

"Yvette, have one or two of your enforcers grab Janet. I'm worried about her loyalties." Yvette nodded, pulled out her phone and started dialing. "Shadow you get in the air and keep an eye out."

You've got it master, Shadow said as he leapt into the air.

"K, Kilroy I want you two to make sure the gun shots weren't reported and lie to any cops that may show up if they were."

"You've got it, Black." Kilroy and K headed out into the hall.

I looked back at the fed and slapped him in the face a couple times. "Wake up happy!" When the slap didn't work, I jammed a thumb into the bullet hole and dug around. The guy woke up with a scream of agony. Works every time. "Have a good nap, Martin?"

"Who are you?" He asked wide eyed in fear.

"I've got two enforcers on their way to pick up Janet," Yvette said behind me. "They're bringing her to your place."

"Who the hell... Agh!!!" Martin screamed again as I dug around some more.

"We'll be asking the questions here. Now, who asked you to get in touch with Lady K?"

"I have nothing to say to you." He screamed again with another twist of my thumb in the wound.

"Do you have a death wish idiot?" This time he spit in my face. I was already in a foul mood from having been shot. I grabbed Ace of Spades and put it against his chest. "I'm giving you one last chance. Talk now and I'll let you live." Of course that was a lie. "Refuse and I get answers out of your corpse."

"Hail the Führer!" Ah fuck this. I pulled the trigger and ended him.

"Great way to complicate everything Black," Yvette said sarcastically.

I ignored her as I started invoking an Infernal spell pulling the Nazi's corrupted soul out of the nether realms and back into the corpse. "Why has thou summoned me? I have nothing to fear mortal," the corpse said as if the voice was an echo out a deep chasm.

"Oh you have plenty to fear from me," I snarled. "However, right now, according to the ancient laws, you have to truthfully answer three questions before you can leave this body."

"What do you wish to know from me?"

"Is Janet Thompson the Crossed Bolts member pulling your strings?"

"Yes."

I heard Yvette start cursing in the background but ignored her. "Who else is working with you?"

"I only know of Janet Thompson." Great. He was a disposable puppet. "What is your last question?"

"I don't have another one so you're stuck here." I sneered. "Yvette, what shall we do with this soul?"

"You cannot do this! I cannot return to death if you don't ask me a third question." The corpse's voice sounded desperate.

"He no longer feels pain right?"

"Nope."

"I'll figure something out."

"Right now I'm bringing him with us back to my place as a way to convince Ms. Thompson that it's in her best interests to talk."

"After that he's mine?"

"I suggest putting him in a wall. He'll go completely mad not being able to communicate with anything."

"Sounds fun."

We gathered up the Kilroys and had Shadow meet us in Yvette's limo, bringing along the pissed off corpse of Martin Jacohvich. "So what are we doing, Black?" Kilroy asked.

"We know who was pulling this Nazi's strings. She's being brought back to my place for questioning," I said. Yvette may be scary to look at but my room had more atmosphere, plus the corpse would look better sitting in the chair across from her.

Shortly after we arrived at my place, a large, blacked out SUV showed up with a Vampire sitting up front as chauffeur. A Werewolf and Vampire were sitting in the back with Janet between them, with a bag over her head. "Milady, we have brought your guest," the chauffeur said in a distinct British accent.

"Importing British butlers and chauffeurs now?" I asked quietly.

"Have a couple prospects for an excellent butler already lined up," she replied simply. "Well let's get this over with."

"Follow me people." I didn't recognize these particular enforcers, which wasn't surprising, but I led the way to my interrogation room. In one chair was a particularly angry corpse cursing me. I sat Janet down rather forcefully across from him. To one side of Janet, Yvette perched daintily on my desk, and behind her were the muscle that had brought Janet in. The enforcers looked slightly nauseated at their surroundings; most people didn't like being in there. Nothing pleasant, except those who came in willingly, ever crossed the threshold of this place. Any halfway decent psychic would go insane if they stepped one foot into this place. Any normal human would simply end up gibbering, and possibly blow his head off if left alone long enough.

"Good morning Ms. Thompson. I do hope we woke you early enough," I said with a cheerful smile as I pulled the bag off of her head.

"Who do you thi… Oh shit," she said upon realizing the Countess Blood Wolf was in the room with me.

"Now that we have caught your attention, we are going to play a game where I ask questions and you answer. The longer the game goes on, the more likely you end up like your lackey, Martin, over there." I pointed to the corpse. It had given up cursing me and was now cursing my captive for getting him into this mess.

Janet Thompson seemed to take a little time to soak in the whole of the nightmarish ambiance of the room. She was visibly shaken. I noticed a shadow moving around the back of the room. I decided that soon I should do a proper Infernal cleansing of the place. Either that or the disembodied cat was back again; never could get rid of the damn thing no matter how hard I tried.

"What do you want to know?" she asked, her voice at the high end of hysteria.

"The main thing I want to know is where are the rest of your people?" I said taking a seat next to Yvette, who was casually picking imaginary lint off her jacket.

"I don't know what you're talking about."

"Come, come now. As you can see, Martin here decided not to talk. I made him open up quite quickly after I put a slug in his chest. Trust me, I'll get an answer out of you one way or another. So I'll ask you again: where are the rest of your scum?"

"I'm telling you, I don't know." The woman quickly changed her tune when Yvette stood up. The look of sheer horror on her face was almost comical as Yvette's mouth elongated and twisted in unnatural ways, even the enforcers looked away. And she had yet to fully shift. "There is a building near the old Ford plant there are more of my people there."

I smiled slightly. "Thank you. That's all I needed to know. Now I'm sure Yvette will have a word with you regarding your lack of loyalty, but I'm going to ask her that she wait a little while on that. I've seen what happens when someone steps out of line, and it gets a little messy."

"But I talked!"

"That won't help you now Nazi." Yvette's voice sounded like rocks being polished in a rock tumbler. "You are going to find out what happens to Nazi officers when I get my claws on them."

At that point I heard something outside the door. There was shouting, something hit the floor, followed shortly by the sound of a car as it peeled out from in front of the house. I left Yvette and our prisoner and went out into the hall. I saw Kilroy on the floor with a black eye form. "What happened?"

"K hit me and tore out of here." He said trying to stand up.

"Fuck!"

Yvette came out and around from behind me. "What's going on?"

"I think I fucked up when I interrogated Kill Switch Karma."

"What do you mean?"

"Apparently she wasn't lying when she said Lady K was knowingly working for the Crossed Bolts. Now she's off to warn them."

"Jason! You idiot! How could you fuck up that badly!" Yvette roared.

"I guess I didn't want to believe that a Kilroy would be a Nazi. But now is not the time to be pointing fingers. We need to find that place fast."

"No fucking shit!" Yvette pulled out her cell and speed dialed a number. I don't know who she called, but she was quickly organizing a massive operation to head into the Highland Park neighborhood of St. Paul where the old Ford plant had once stood.

As Yvette organized a strike force I told Shadow to fly as fast as he could to that neighborhood and find the building that was our target. *You got it boss!* The crow disappeared from sight almost instantly as he magicked his way to his target.

"I swear I'm going to put that girl in the ground myself," Kilroy said as he stood up shakily.

"We're good to go. I have 40 plus of my best people heading that way right now," Yvette said. "Now let's get there fast."

CHAPTER

We arrived at the old plant in 10 or 15 minutes and were quickly joined by four armored personnel carriers. Where Yvette had gotten those I didn't want to know, but they hadn't been stopped on the way, which probably meant that police forces had been warned of their coming. "Shadow have you found them?"

Yes master. They're in the largest building. Two back from where you are.

"Does Shadow know where they are?" Yvette asked.

"Largest building," I said.

Yvette called her enforcers together. "Okay everyone. I want shock and awe on this. I want prisoners. We're going to do a room-to-room search. Any obvious grunt is dead, everyone else I want captured." All of her soldiers were dressed in heavy tactical gear. "Long Blade, Hatchet, Cross. I want you three scouting the path to snipe out anyone at the windows and entrances who appears to be a threat. You have 10 minutes, then we breach with recoilless rifles."

As the three scouts, all armed with the absolute latest in high power sniper rifles, headed out and disappeared into the first hazy beginning of dawn, I started getting the shakes. We were going in blind and I hated going in blind. We had no idea what the Crossed Bolts had cooked up in there. With any luck, we would be met with minor resistance. If things went truly south... I didn't want to think about how bad things could turn out.

"You look nervous Jason," Yvette said quietly enough for no one else to hear.

"Just hoping these guys are loyal."

"They are. Besides, I'm going in as well. They're going to have to be packing some serious fire power to drop me."

In the distance we heard several explosions as .50 caliber sniper rifles took out several Nazis. "Okay then, let's rock and roll."

"We're moving out!" Yvette screamed as she jumped onto an APC. I jumped onto the same one, which was fortunate. I saw the APC on our right explode into only so much shrapnel when hit by a rocket. There was another explosion on the left that set my teeth on edge as it shook the carrier. "Light those assholes up!" Yvette yelled, and quickly six recoilless rifles fired, hitting the wall with a loud explosion.

The next thing I saw just about terrified me. Swarming out of the building were at least 30 of the biggest Nazis I had ever seen. Yvette looked back at me almost worriedly as the fire fight really opened up. "What the fuck are those things?!" She yelled over the roar of machine gun fire.

"They're Hydes!" I screamed back. "They're all juiced up on the formula that turned Dr. Jekyll into Mr. Hyde!"

"Well whatever they are they are going to quickly lose their breathing privileges!" The Countess shifted quickly and charged in. I looked up and saw first hand the kind of damage being done. The Hydes were an even fight for the Countess's troops. The whole scene was a mess of spraying blood and flying body parts as it became quickly apparent to both sides that traditional firearms meant nothing. This battle would be won through sheer brute strength.

I didn't have time to watch and take notes though, I had another job. I shot past the blood fest and into the building. Inside I found more than a few scientists, and what appeared to be higher officers, trying to make a break for it. I took out Ace of Spades and started shooting people in the legs. In the case of two officers who returned fire, I put a bullet in each of their heads. By the time I had ejected my fourth mag, I was standing in a building full of cripples. From the lack of howling and screaming, things had settled down outside. I secured all of my prisoners with flex ties and headed outside.

The aftermath was gruesome. In a war you see people shot to shit. This was not that, this was body parts; arms, legs, inner organs and heads ripped apart at the jaws. I had seen some disturbing stuff over the centuries and had committed much of it, but this was unsettling even to me. Even fighting in two world wars, I had never seen anything this gruesome, and I had seen Nazi death camps.

Yvette came over to me. She was naked and dripping, covered head to toe with other people's blood. "Mind if I borrow your coat?" Her voice was calm and relaxed. "I would rather the troops not see me like this."

I handed over my trench and looked over towards the bodies. "How bad did we take it?"

"Well, my troops from the blown-up APC are alive. It's going to take them a while to fully heal, but they'll be fine. All told though, I lost 16 troops, good men and women too." She looked a bit shaken up over it. It had been a long time since she had taken a big hit on her enforcers. Truth be told, I couldn't remember a time like this. I knew she'd be crying about it tonight. She couldn't do it now, but tonight, at home, with her cats curled up on her lap, she'd let it all out.

"Well let's take a look at what was so important to guard that heavily."

"Let's," Yvette growled, I hoped she didn't shift again and shred my trench. She stalked over to where the prisoners were, grabbed one by the throat and lifted him easily, his feet dangling a few inches off the ground. "Do you know who I am?"

"You are the Countess Blood Wolf," the man choked out. "You are a monster." Stupid. Ballsy, but stupid.

"I may look like a monster and have the powers of one, but I'm not the genocidal monster that your kind worship. I've gutted more Nazis than you have ever met and if you don't cooperate, I'll run you through a wood chipper, an inch at a time."

That was my girl, she was taking out her anger on some deserving targets. "That goes for the rest of you. Cooperation saves your lives. Failure means a gruesome death. And I know some extremely unpleasant ways to kill you all, each more gruesome than the last."

While Yvette was interrogating the prisoners I took a look around the place. Deeper in the place I found a large cylinder of glass and steel. Taking a closer look, I was scared beyond belief at what I was seeing. I needed to show this to Yvette now. When I returned she was handing over the prisoners to a few of her enforcers who had shown up with a small bus designed to handle prisoners.

"Countess, grab one of the scientists and follow me," I hissed at her.

"Can't it wait Black?"

"No, it can't. You need to see this now."

"Fine. But make it quick."

I brought her to my discovery and the sight of it brought her up short. "What in the name of..." In front of us, in the glass and steel cylinder, was a clone of Yvette. It wasn't fully developed yet, but it was definitely a clone of her. "What is this thing?" she roared at her prisoner.

"It is the cure for your blight upon the world. The perfect soldier to destroy the biggest mis..." The scientist didn't get to finish as Yvette had crushed his head. I shrugged, at least she wasn't mad at me.

"We're going to take it with us. I'll figure out what to do with that thing later." She called in an order for some of her troops to come and collect the clone. She called a cleanup team from the Court to come in and collect every electronic device in the building and any paper file. They were to find everything and miss nothing. After that they were to clean up the mess in front of the building, and then burn the whole thing to the ground.

As Yvette was getting off the phone, we heard a couple of shots ring out from the direction of the Limo. Running as fast as we could, we found Lady K flat on her back as blood poured out of her chest. Over her, clutching his shoulder was Kilroy. "I failed her," Kilroy said.

"What do you mean?" Yvette asked as she looked into the driver's window and found him with his head in his lap, garlic stuffed into his neck and a stake through his heart.

"I always tried to teach her right from wrong, but apparently I didn't do a good enough job. She always felt that her abilities made her better than everyone else. I'm guessing they promised her power, more than what she would ever have if she stayed a spook like me."

I put my hand on his shoulder. "Do you want to help us find the scum that did this to her?"

"No, I have family I need to see. Chad and Foo have been waiting a long time to see me. They're the closest thing to family I have now, and I haven't seen them in years." I knew where he was going. Chad and Foo had crossed years ago; now Kilroy would be joining them. "I'm old and tired. Spy work is so completely different than it was in the old days. I don't fit in anywhere anymore."

Kilroy looked up for a while before giving me his hand to shake. "So long Black. Keep up the good fight. I may not be around anymore, but I'll keep any eye on you." He then turned to Yvette. "I didn't always approve of you, but you really are one of the good guys ... I see that now."

Both of us wished him goodbye as he walked off, seeming to fade as if he were merely fog being dispersed by the sun. We kept looking at the spot where he had been for a while. "Where do you think he's going?" Yvette asked.

"To be with the rest of his family, somewhere other than life or true death. I don't know." I didn't know a whole lot about Kilroy's family, they had all been spies, but as he had said, times had changed. People like him weren't really needed anymore. With the death of Lady K, it may be that his line would never return.

I turned around and saw that Lady K's body had vanished. "Where the hell is the body?" I yelled. She should have been dead, there was no way she could have been alive, but now she had disappeared.

"Damn it!" Yvette slammed her fist into the hood of the car, knocking the engine out of the it. "If I ever catch that scum again, I am going to figure out the worse thing I can do to kill her. Then have you summon her soul so she can go insane, trapped between worlds."

"We'll figure something out, but in the meantime, we have other problems to worry about."

"We can worry about those later. Right now, I just want to go home and rest. I need a shower, I need a good cry, and I need my kitties."

Master? Shadow started as he landed on my shoulder, *you should go home too.*

"Thanks for the concern Shadow, but I have things I need to do with Yvette. Why don't you go home? I'll be home later."

Are you sure?

"Yes go on feather head. I'll be home tomorrow."

"Thanks Jason, 1 could really use the company." Yvette leaned up against me heavily enough to cause me to brace myself while she called for another limo for pick up. She then seemed, for the first time, to realize how bloody she still was. "I'm sorry about the mess I'm making of your coat and the rest of your clothes."

"Don't worry about it. You can just replace it for me later."

"M'kay."

We waited another half hour for the limo to arrive with the cleanup crew. The chauffeur stopped in front of us and opened the door. Yvette collapsed into her seat, opened the minibar and started drinking heavily, directly from the bottles. I sat next to her and started drinking the bourbon, two fingers at a time. We rode in silence to the Court. There was nothing to say. Sixteen dead, 17 when you included the chauffeur. It was going to take a little while for Yvette to refill her ranks of muscle, but it would be soon enough. She had enough people sitting on the sidelines ready to be trained.

CHAPTER

When we arrived back at the Court we took the private elevator up to her apartment. Her cats started to run towards her but quickly jumped back at the smell of blood. "If you want to change there are clothes for you in the large guest suite. You may also want to take a shower as well."

"Thanks."

Yvette really must feel like hell. She hadn't even made a half-hearted attempt at getting me in the bath with her. When I got to the guest bathroom I simply threw my clothes on the floor, not caring where they landed. Once the shower warmed up, I slipped in and let the hot water clear away the tension in my muscles.

After nearly an hour I stepped out, dressed, and headed to the lounge. Curled up on the couch in a bathrobe, absentmindedly petting her cats, Yvette watched a children's movie. I was the only person she allowed to see her like this. The only one she allowed to see as anything more than a hard ass, or at least as a mature woman. No one else got to see the real child in her and that was how she wanted it.

"Hey kiddo," I said as I approached her. "Lilo and Stitch?"

"I wanted something funny." Her voice was tinged slightly with frustration. "I have things to think about and I'm just trying to put it off as long as possible."

I dropped into the seat next to her and she slid down so that her head was in my lap. "Anything else I can help with?"

"Only if you want to write 17 eulogies for me to read at the funerals. Along with 17 notes to next of kin. Many of those people were family men and women; now they're dead."

"I wrote enough of those during the wars. I know you've written your fair share too, but these were your people, not mine."

"I wasn't being serious."

"I know," I said stroking her hair.

"Jason, will you please stay with me tonight? I'm not looking for anything other than someone to hold me, and watch kids' movies with me."

"How can I say no to a request like that?"

"Thanks. I'll go make some popcorn," she said as she rolled off me to her feet.

She fell asleep halfway through the third movie, the two of us having eaten five bowls of popcorn. It was closing in on one in the afternoon and she was out like a rock. I picked her up gently and brought her to her bed. I was starting to slide my hands out from under her when she grabbed me and rolled me on to the bed with her. What happened next caught me off guard. Instead of trying to get sexual, she simply cried into my shoulder for at least an hour.

I woke up after a few hours, not having expected to sleep. I saw that Yvette was no longer in the bedroom. I checked the bathroom and didn't see her. There was really only one place she would probably be. I headed down to her office. Dressed in a suit, she was reviewing a text file. I was about to knock when she stopped me.

"I was wondering when you were going to wake up." There was none of the upset teenager now, she was strictly business.

"So what have you been up to?"

"I contacted Hell Fire's Dame and Inferno's Plague and hired them to go through all the electronics we seized. Right now, I'm writing the eulogies for funerals over the next three days, after that it's on to working on letters to next of kin. I've already contacted my accountant and set decent-sized settlements for each of the families affected. This is one big headache." She rubbed the bridge of her nose, and turned to look at me. "Then there are all the problems that have cropped up."

"Like what to do with the prisoners?"

"That's fairly easy enough. I'm going to try to milk them for information, both on the structure of the Crossed Bolts, as well as on their scientific research."

"You can't get information out of corpses." I reminded her.

"I'll treat them relatively well as long as they cooperate with me. If not, I'll use them each in turn to make examples of what resistance gets them."

"The clone?"

"I'll figure out what to do with it later. I'll probably encase it in lead and drop it in the Marianas Trench. I don't want to risk anything with that thing around. It's not fully formed and, according to my scientists, it isn't actually alive... yet." Her voice was ominous. "However, I can't afford the possibility of something waking it by accident.

"Still, that isn't my main worry."

"Then what is?" I was fairly sure I knew the answer, but I had to ask. "Lady K?"

"She's going to be trouble. She knows way too much about me and the rest of this place. Still she comes in second on my list. I have traitors in my pack, Jason, that is worrisome in the least. Thankfully your Silicon Slave friends will be able to help me find out who they are. Without them I'd have to start a witch hunt and that would be a massive headache. It would split loyalties and I would no longer know whom I could trust. With the help of your friends, I'll be able to make the strikes surgical and quiet. I don't need messy and message delivering. I just want these people to disappear, and I may need your help tracking some of them down."

"Just let me know when you need me. For now, I should get going. I have things I need to take care of as well." My hand was on the doorknob when she stopped me.

"Oh I was thinking on that vacation you owe me." Her voice immediately traveled from businesswoman to over excited teen. I wondered what kind of dreadful event was headed my way. "I was thinking we could do a huge Disney thing. Hit the parks for a few days, then hop a cruise ship for a week or so. Sounds like fun doesn't it?"

"Yes, Princess," I said sarcastically.

"I seriously doubt that Disney would make a kids' movie with me as a princess. It would have to be rated R for the extreme amount of bloodshed."

I laughed despite myself. "Okay. Disney it is." Who knew, maybe it would be fun.

A dark look closed over Yvette's face. "Give me three months to clean out the Court of Nazis, then it's just the two of us."

As she turned back to her computer, I let myself out of the office. After a quick search around the apartment, I tracked down my keys and called the garage for a lift back to my house. I was looking forward to a nice night's sleep.

On the ride home, I was hit by a thought train that had always been lurking at the back of my mind. Would a life with Yvette really be all that bad? Thinking back on things, I really wouldn't mind those vacations with her. Truthfully, as much as I hated to admit it, I kind of looked forward to them. Yes. I would always see her as a kid, but today? I didn't know. It was weird—me finding her watching Disney cartoons, her asking me to take her on a Disney vacation, and somehow... I couldn't explain it to myself. We were two monsters, tough to kill, who enjoyed the sight and smell of blood, yet we shared a skewed sense of compassion for those who couldn't defend themselves. I would probably never find anyone else like her.

Maybe, just maybe. I didn't know. The thought of Sarah cropped up. She wanted me in a significant other type of relationship, but I knew it would never work out. She was human, merely mortal, and would eventually die. Besides that, I could never have seriously thought of her in any romantic sense. She was also a detective, but that's where the similarities between the two of us ended. She and I were too different for there to be even a hint of a romantic relationship between us.

Yvette though? It would be interesting to say the least.

CHAPTER

How are you doing master? Shadow asked when I walked into the kitchen.

"Tired. After last night I just want to collapse and call it a day."

Yvette get frisky?

"No she was upset and wanted to watch kids' movies and cry."

We are talking about the same person right?

"Yes. She just wanted to be as close to a normal kid as possible. Which meant movies and popcorn. It was nice."

While you were out, Jamie brought something over. She said it had been delivered to the office with instructions to be opened by you as soon as possible.

"Where is Jamie then?" I would have thought she would have stuck around.

She said she was meeting someone at the Mystic Wolf and couldn't wait around all day.

"Okay. So where is the package?"

On the dining room table.

"Well then let's take a look." Shadow hopped up onto my shoulder as we walked into the dining room. On the table was an old, over-stuffed manila envelope with the name of a law firm on it. I recognized the name and knew what was in it. Back in World War II, Kilroy and I, along with five others, signed a tontine. Apparently I was the last. I had almost forgotten about it until this moment. Most of us were going to live a long time, or at least we should have, but here it was. I was the last.

www.ingramcontent.com/pod-product-compliance
Lightning Source LLC
LaVergne TN
LVHW041701060526
838201LV00043B/525